Dark Hunter's Boon

THE CHILDREN OF THE GODS
BOOK FIFTY-EIGHT

I. T. LUCAS

Dark Hunter's Boon is a work of fiction! Names, characters, places and incidents are products of the author's imagination or are used fictitiously and are not to be construed as real. Any similarity to actual persons, organizations and/or events is purely coincidental.

Copyright © 2022 by I. T. Lucas

Published by Evening Star Press

EveningStarPress.com

ISBN-13: 978-1-957139-10-4

Alena

Alena, eldest daughter of the goddess Annani, mother of thirteen, grandmother of seventeen, great-grandmother of twenty-three, and a great many times over grandmother of nearly every member of Annani's clan, sat in front of the vanity and gazed at her lover's reflection in the mirror.

It had been one of those days that would forever remain etched in her memory, and it wasn't over yet.

In the span of twelve hours, their team had been trapped under the ruins of an ancient outpost, had found a hybrid Kra-ell female who'd been hiding there for years, and after they'd returned to the hotel, Alena had finally admitted to Orion that she'd fallen in love with him and proclaimed him her mate.

Her heart was full to bursting with happiness and gratitude to the Fates for the wonderful male they'd chosen for her. They had given her a boon—a gorgeous, kind, smart male who loved her as much as she loved him.

Orion had fallen in love with her voice first, but the rest had soon followed. Somehow, hearing her pouring her suppressed emotions into that song had given him a glimpse into her soul before ever meeting her, and he'd liked what he'd seen.

As he caught her looking at him, Orion grinned and flexed his muscles. Alena smiled back and picked up the brush. She could never get enough of ogling her mate's impeccable physique, but she was supposed to get ready for dinner.

They'd made love in the shower, then on the bed, and then again in the shower, so she should be beyond satis-fied and content. But as the saying went, her appetite had just gotten sharpened by the first tasty bites, and she hungered for more.

Right now, the male she loved was giving her an eyeful as he got dressed for dinner at Kalugal and Jacki's. It was a shame to cover all that gorgeous tan skin and those beau-tiful muscles in clothing, but she had to admit that he looked quite dashing in the white button-down dress shirt and the navy-blue suit.

"Do you think I should go with the blazer or without?" Orion asked.

"We are not leaving the hotel, so you can go without, but you look so good all dressed up."

"Not nearly as good as you, gorgeous." He leaned down and kissed the top of her head. "I don't want to mess up your lipstick."

"Feel free to mess it up anytime you want." She puckered her lips.

With a groan, he lifted her off the stool and kissed the living daylights out of her.

When he let go, Alena burst out laughing. "Go wash your face. You're covered in red lipstick."

Smiling like a fiend, he turned her around to face the mirror. "I have a feeling that we are going to be late for dinner."

Her makeup was a mess.

With a sigh, Alena sat back down and pulled a tissue out of the box. "I'll just take it off."

She hardly ever bothered with makeup, but tonight was special, and not just because she and Orion were officially in love.

Alena had a feeling that the dinner at Kalugal and Jacki's presidential suite would be one of those events that would affect the future of the clan.

The Kra-ell female they'd captured and brought with them to the hotel was about to tell her story. Probably not willingly, but with Kalugal's compulsion, she wouldn't be able to refuse.

Aliya was like a trapped wild animal, and the only thing preventing her from running away the first chance she got was Kalugal's command to stay put. Hopefully, though, after showering and getting fed, she wouldn't be in such a great hurry to leave.

Aliya wasn't a prisoner, but they needed to keep her from running off just yet for her own good.

The poor woman didn't know who to trust, and she feared everyone. If she didn't allow herself time to get to know them and ran off, Aliya would spend the rest of her life alone and wouldn't get to meet the other survivors of Jade's tribe.

Before allowing her access to Emmett and Vrog, though, they needed to find out how she'd gotten from her tribe's compound near Beijing all the way to the Mosuo village on the shores of Lugo Lake. Her escape from the slaughter of her people and her journey to the remote lake in the Tibetan mountains was no doubt a fascinating tale, but what Alena was even more curious about was why Aliya had shunned society, living hidden in the tunnel system under the ruins of an ancient trading post.

The woman looked half-starved, half-wild, and she was wary of people, whether they were human or other.

A powerful female like her shouldn't have been running scared like that. Physically, Aliya was as strong as or stronger than two well-trained immortal warriors, giving Arwel and Phinas a run for their money. If not for Orion knocking her out with a rock, she might have overpowered them both and run off.

As a hybrid Kra-ell, Aliya could also thrall, and combined with her physical strength, she could have used her gifts to live like a queen. Instead, she'd chosen to live like a pauper.

Why?

Was it grief?

After Aliya's human mother had died, the girl had probably fallen into despair. Depression and anger often contributed to self-destructive behaviors, and in some cases, even suicide. For immortals, ending their own life required such extreme measures that it was nearly impossible, and thankfully, none of Annani's clan had ever gone that far, but over the years there had been some members who'd recklessly endangered their lives in the hopes of ending their emotional misery.

In Aliya's case, her emotional pain might have manifested in withdrawal from society and self-inflicted austerity.

Every motherly instinct she had was telling Alena to take the girl under her protective wing. But Aliya was a grown woman, and it was her choice whether to accept Alena's help or refuse it.

Orion

When all the smeared lipstick was gone, Alena pivoted on the vanity stool to face Orion. "I feel bad about leaving Ovidu and Oridu in their hotel room once again."

"They don't need to eat, do they?"

Alena grimaced. "They eat garbage."

"Really?"

"Did you see *Back to the Future II*?"

"Are you referencing Mr. Fusion? The Home Energy Reactor?"

She nodded. "When I saw that movie, I thought about the Odus. You don't need a garbage disposal with one of them around."

"That would be a very expensive garbage disposal." Orion looped his tie and tied the knot. "I'm surprised that Kian hasn't had one of them reverse-engineered.

Imagine a cyborg butler in every house." He chuckled. "The brand name should be Mr. Turbo Clean—the recycling superstar."

He thought it was a very clever name, but Alena didn't seem impressed.

She sighed. "We know how that would end. We should heed the warning of history and not repeat the same mistakes our ancestors made. The Odus were created to be servants, but they were easily converted into killing machines. It got so bad that they were decommissioned and the technology to make them was banned."

"People will always find ways to use things as weapons, but that doesn't mean that new technologies shouldn't be developed just because they have the potential to destroy as well as to build. Computer chips are used in missiles as well as in medical devices." He smiled. "I wish I was more technologically savvy so I could give you better examples, but my point is that with proper safeguards, the amazing technology that created the Odus could revolutionize the way people live and work."

Alena pulled out a calf-long sweater from the closet and shrugged it on. "I get what you're saying. What's interesting is that Syssi's vision linked the Kra-ell with the Odus. Back then, we didn't know that the Kra-ell were real, and we thought that Syssi's vision was influenced by the virtual reality story she'd created for the Perfect Match studios. As it turns out, it was the other way around. Her precognition created the imagery for what she believed was her own creation."

"That's interesting." Orion pushed the door open. "How were the Kra-ell connected to the Odus?"

As Alena stepped out onto the hallway, Ovidu opened the door and dipped his head. "Good evening, mistress. Should I escort you and Master Orion?"

It was unnecessary, but that was what Kian wanted. "We are just going to the third floor. You can escort us there and return to your room."

"Yes, mistress."

She turned back to Orion. "In her vision, Syssi saw a dark alien world, with skies that had a reddish hue and very strong winds. The vision happened in a spaceport, where Odus were being loaded into shuttles by handlers who she described as looking like the Kra-ell. They were tall, slim, and dark-haired, and the only female among all the male handlers was the one running the show. The most interesting detail about her was that she had fangs."

"Did the females in Syssi's imagined world also have them?" Orion looped his arm around Alena's waist as they took the stairs to the third floor.

"They did. Except for the location, everything about her Krall adventure was eerily similar to the Kra-ell."

He would have loved to see the created world, but he wasn't sure about getting hooked up to a virtual reality contraption. Perhaps there was a way to see it as a movie? Then again, going on an adventure with Alena that wasn't actually dangerous could be fun. After their earlier excitement in the tunnels, he wanted to play it

8

safe, and there was nothing safer than enjoying an interesting experience from the comfort of an easy chair.

"Where did Syssi place the Krall?"

"Greenland. The story was that they landed there a thousand years ago, and their spaceship got trapped under the ice. One day, a massive earthquake shattered the ice, the Krall woke up from their stasis, and then took over the entire Arctic Circle."

"Sounds like a great story." Orion cast her a sidelong glance. "You've piqued my curiosity. Would you like to go on a Krall adventure with me?"

She laughed. "There are so many wonderful scenarios we can pick from, why go to freezing Greenland and encounter nasty, bloodthirsty Krall?"

"That's a valid point. Were the Krall bloodthirsty in Syssi's vision as well?"

"She only said that everyone's eyes were glowing, which led her to believe that it wasn't just nighttime over there, but that it was a dark world. It might have been just her impression, though, because the atmosphere in the vision was so somber. The Kra-ell were sending the Odus out to space, and Syssi believed that they were getting rid of them."

Orion stopped in front of the presidential suite's double doors. "So let me get it straight. In Syssi's vision, the Kra-ell were in charge of decommissioning the Odus?"

"Or sending them to war. The problem with Syssi's visions is that they show her just snippets, and she doesn't know if what she sees is in the past or the future, or where it's happening or why. That leaves a lot of room for interpretation, or misinterpretation. For all we know, the Kra-ell might have been saving the Odus and sending them somewhere safe, or they might have hidden them on some distant moon to be used in future warfare, or it could have been none of the above. If the vision was true, though, which I believe it was, then it clearly connects the Kra-ell to the gods. We know that the Odus were created on the gods' home planet, and if the Kra-ell were handling them, they either shared that planet with the gods or were close neighbors."

As Orion knocked on the door, his head was swimming with the implications. The clan already suspected that the gods and the Kra-ell had a shared ancestry and that they came from the same corner of the universe, but the vision of them being involved with the Odus opened up a whole new can of worms.

Shamash, Kalugal's personal assistant, opened the door. "Good evening. Please, come in."

Ovidu bowed. "Should you require my services, please call for me."

"Thank you." Alena dismissed him.

Kalugal and Jacki's suite was about five times the size of Orion and Alena's hotel room. It had a living room, a dining room, a kitchenette, a bathroom, and a separate bedroom suite.

The dining room was probably designed to host board meetings because the table could comfortably seat the eleven people in their party and Aliya with room to spare. If needed, they could easily squeeze in four additional guests.

Everyone was already there, and two waiters were waiting by their carts to start serving the meal.

Alena glanced at her watch. "I didn't realize that we were late. My apologies."

"You're just in time," Jacki said. "Aliya insisted on saving the seat next to her for you."

When Orion shifted his eyes in the direction Jacki waved her hand, he was taken aback. The female looked like a different person.

With her skin and hair washed clean, her beauty shone through, but her attitude hadn't improved. She looked agitated, and he had a good idea why.

Even from where he was standing, which was at least twenty feet away from her, he could hear her stomach grumbling.

Aliya was hungry and waiting impatiently for the meal to start.

Hadn't Kalugal fed her?

If she'd been placed in Orion's care, that would have been the first thing he would have done. Perhaps the Odus could be moved to another room so they could invite Aliya to stay with him and Alena. The two of them would take much better care of her than Kalugal and Jacki seemed to be doing. Kian wouldn't be happy about that, though. The Odus were there to protect Alena and therefore needed to stay close to her.

"We'd better sit down quickly." He took Alena's elbow and led her to their seats. "Everyone is hungry." He cast a quick smile at Aliya, but she didn't return it.

Alena

⚬⚬⚬

Alena's heart went out to the young woman devouring food as if she'd gone hungry for days, which she probably had. Even Jin's animosity toward Aliya subsided as she watched her pile yet another serving on her plate and then eat it as fast as was possible in polite company.

Aliya was trying to measure her pace, but she couldn't hide the slight tremor of her hands as she reached for the platters. Casting quick looks around, she checked if anyone else wanted to finish what was left over, and when she was satisfied that there were no other takers, she scooped every last morsel onto her plate.

"I don't know what happened to the portion sizes," Kalugal complained loudly. "They are entirely inadequate." He grabbed the phone and called to order more food to be delivered.

Alena could have kissed him for it. The portions were just as generous as they had been the night before, but with all of them pretending to be full so Aliya could eat her fill, Kalugal had wisely decided to order more.

It had been incredibly sweet of him to do so in a way that allowed her to save face.

Once all the platters were empty, including the additional dishes Kalugal had ordered, the waiters cleared the table and served tea, coffee, and dessert.

Aliya looked catatonic from food overdose, but she still had to make good on her promise to tell them her story.

"Would you like some tea?" Kalugal asked her. "It will help wash the food down so you can tell us what we've been waiting patiently to hear."

"Thank you." She straightened in her chair. "I would love some tea."

He lifted the teapot and actually got to his feet to pour tea into her cup instead of passing it to Alena. "Are you ready to tell us your story?"

Aliya hesitated. "I don't know who you are and if I can trust you, but I know that you can force me to talk like you forced me to help you and to come here. I'm at your sorrow."

"The correct phrase is at my mercy." Kalugal pulled out his phone. "Would talking to Vrog assuage your fears?"

She shrugged. "He could be a traitor. Maybe it was him who betrayed us to our enemies and brought the killers to slaughter our people."

With a sigh, Kalugal put the phone back in his pocket. "I would much prefer it if you told us your story without being forced. But you are a very suspicious young lady, and you leave me no choice. Tell me everything that you remember about the attack, Aliya. Tell me how you managed to escape when all the other Kra-ell and hybrids were either killed or taken. I also want you to tell us what has happened to you since then and why you've been living alone in the ruins."

Alena could see the defiance in Aliya's eyes, and for a long moment, the young woman kept her lips tightly pressed together, trying to fight the compulsion. It was a valiant effort and proof of a strong will, but Kalugal was a powerful compeller, and Aliya wasn't immune.

She stood no chance against him.

"I was eight years old," she spat and lifted her hands to press her palms to her temples. "I still looked human. That's how I managed to escape."

"Go on," Kalugal prompted.

Letting out a groan that sounded like a growl, Aliya surrendered to the compulsion. "When the bad Kra-ell attacked, they let the humans go. They hypnotically coerced them to forget where they lived and put lies in their heads."

"We call it thralling," Kalugal said. "To thrall means to enslave through enchantment. We can do more to humans than just hypnotically coerce them to forget things. We can also plant fake memories in their minds."

"I know that." Aliya glared at him. "That can also be called hypnotic coercion, but thralling is shorter, so I'll use that."

"Thank you." Kalugal gave her a reassuring smile. "So, what kind of lies did they plant in the humans' heads?"

"My mother believed that she'd been in a work camp for all those years, and she didn't remember who my father was because the bad people told the humans to forget about the Kra-ell. But I was a hybrid, and their thralling didn't work on me. I knew who I was, and I remembered everything, including what I learned from Jade and the other pureblooded females." She looked down at the dessert on her plate but didn't touch it. "I was so scared, and I kept asking my mother what happened to my father, but she didn't know who I was talking about. My father was a pureblooded Kra-ell, but he wasn't as bad as the others. When no one was looking, he was kind to my mother and me. He brought us little gifts from time to time, and he gave me money for my birthdays."

Alena wondered if Aliya's father was also Vrog's. She hadn't had a chance to talk to Vrog when they'd been boarding the planes, but she'd heard that he'd spoken with affection about his pureblooded father. There hadn't been many pureblooded Kra-ell in the compound, and most had been described as either cruel or indifferent to humans and hybrids alike. What were the chances that there had been two kind males in that small group?

Was it possible that most of them had been decent males, but given their societal rules they had to keep up the pretense?

Alena knew all about social expectations and how they affected one's behavior. Not that it was a bad thing, at least not as a rule. Usually, people behaved better when they knew others were watching. In small, close-knit communities, spousal and child abuse were rare, and so were theft and vandalism. People wanted to be judged positively by others.

"Did your mother have family here?" Jacki asked. "Is that why she brought you to the lake?"

Aliya shook her head. "I knew about the Mosuo people, and I told my mother that we would be safe here. It was far away from where we lived before, and the people here respected women. We were alone, and I'd heard stories about human men mistreating females, so I was scared for my mother and a little for myself too. My mother was too terrified to think, but she didn't remember why she was so scared, so she listened to me. We had very little money. The humans in the compound didn't get paid. But I had never spent the money my father gave me for my birthdays because I never left the compound, so it was all still there, and my mother used it to buy train tickets for us. Back then, there wasn't even a paved road leading to the lake, and the train could get us only part of the way. We walked a lot, and we asked kind farmers to give us rides, and finally, we arrived at the Mosuo village. One of the matriarchs took pity on us and let us join her household in exchange for my mother's work. My mother was a hard worker, and she could sew clothes, a skill that was badly needed at the time. The tourism to the lake was growing, and the villagers were looking for more ways to make money off the tourists. They made traditional outfits for sale, but they sewed them by hand. My mother knew how to operate a sewing machine."

"How did you know about the Mosuo?" Orion asked.

"From Jade." Aliya smiled. "I was a rare female hybrid, so unlike the boys who were treated just slightly better than the human children, Jade was nice to me. She liked to keep me around when I was done with my schoolwork and my chores. I was a quiet little girl, and sometimes she forgot that I was there when she talked with the other females, or maybe she thought that I couldn't understand Kra-ell well enough to follow what they were talking about. But I was always good with languages, and if she had bothered to actually talk to me, she would have known that I spoke fluent Kra-ell. One day, she was talking with Kagra about how they were betrayed, and their ship was broken on purpose."

"You mean sabotaged," Orion offered.

"Yes, thank you. Sometimes I don't know the correct words in English."

"Your English is excellent," Jin said. "How did you learn to speak it so well?"

Aliya shrugged. "I have a good ear, and I learned from shows on television, songs on the radio, and from the tourists."

"Television?" Jacki arched a brow. "Did the lake area have reception back then?"

Aliya shook her head. "We had television in the Kra-ell compound. I didn't need as much sleep as the humans, so I snuck out at night and went to the common room to watch TV."

"I didn't know they had English-speaking films on Chinese television," Carol said.

"It was mostly American movies on video cassettes. I think Jade brought them with her from her trips to the US."

That was a piece of information they hadn't heard yet. "Did Jade and the other purebloods leave the compound often?" Alena asked.

"Jade traveled a lot, and she usually took one or two males with her."

"That's interesting," Kalugal said. "But let's get back to what you heard Jade say about the ship's sabotage."

Aliya

~~~~

A liya lifted the teacup and took a small sip to moisten her dry throat. It was difficult to talk about the past, but it was also liberating.

She'd had no one to tell her story to, not even her mother while she had still been alive. Sometimes, she wasn't sure that any of it had really happened and that it hadn't been a dream, or rather a nightmare.

She'd wished it hadn't been true and that she was just a little odd-looking human girl, but she had the fangs and red glowing eyes to prove that she wasn't human and that what had happened in the compound had been real. She belonged to an alien race of people whose customs and beliefs had influenced the Mosuo people, and who'd slaughtered each other for no good reason.

Why had those other Kra-ell attacked her tribe? They couldn't have retaliated for some wrongdoing committed by Jade or the other tribe members because no one had even known that they existed. The attack had been unprovoked, and to this day, Aliya still wondered why.

Then again, the purebloods must have known about the others because they must have arrived on the same ship that had been sabotaged, but perhaps they hadn't known who had survived. Maybe they'd evacuated the ships in small vessels that were like the escape pods she'd seen in science fiction movies, and those vessels had landed in different parts of the world.

Perhaps it had been a territorial thing?

Now that she was older and understood a little more about how the world worked, she knew all about eliminating competition for resources. Even in the wild, one kind of predator killed another's cubs to ensure their own cubs' survival.

Except, even that couldn't explain the attack. Earth was a big place, so big that the two Kra-ell groups had been oblivious to each other's existence until something or someone had betrayed Aliya's tribe to those other murderous Kra-ell.

"Whenever you're ready," Kalugal said gently.

"It was a long time ago, and I don't remember all the details." She looked at him. "Sometimes I think that I imagined it all, but the proof is right here." She pointed to her fangs. "And if that's real, so is the rest of it."

He nodded, his eyes soft and full of understanding. "You were just a little girl, and you suffered a horrible trauma. It's okay if you confuse some details. Just tell us what you remember, and we will try to piece it together to make sense of it."

That would be helpful.

Perhaps these people could finally fill in the missing pieces for her.

"I heard Jade say something about a scouting crew who were supposed to arrive first and prepare things for her. She told Kagra that she suspected the scouts had sabotaged their ship, so their landing was delayed by thousands of years. I thought that I must have misunderstood because the Kra-ell couldn't live that long. But I knew the Kra-ell word for thousands, and that was what she said. Then I thought that maybe the ship was like a huge village and that the Kra-ell who boarded the ship were not the ones who landed on Earth, but their grandchildren or even great-grandchildren did."

"They could have traveled in stasis," Arwel said. "We don't know anything about their interstellar travel technology, but if it obeys the same laws of physics we are familiar with, then the only way to traverse the enormous distances of space is in stasis, which is a sort of very long hibernation."

That made sense. If the Kra-ell had the technology to travel through space, they probably also had the technology to put themselves to sleep for thousands of years.

"What must have happened was that the scouting team woke up first," Kalugal said. "Their pods were probably programmed to open ahead of the others, and when they did, they decided to give themselves a longer head start on the others and reprogrammed their fellow travelers' pods to stay closed for much longer."

"You are jumping to conclusions," Arwel said. "It might have been a malfunction. If the scouting team had nefarious intentions, they would have killed the others instead of reprogramming their pods."

"Killing with no provocation is an affront to the Mother," Aliya said. "But it didn't stop the killers who attacked my tribe, so maybe they were heretics."

"Or they might have perceived something as a provocation," Kalugal said. "You don't know what Jade did on these frequent trips abroad."

"True, but she never mentioned any other Kra-ell except for that scouting team, and she said that the joke was on them because Earth females were not compatible. They couldn't produce long-lived children for them, so they died out long before Jade and her people woke up."

Jade's exact words had been that the children born to Kra-ell fathers and human mothers were inferior and defective, that they were a diluted breed who couldn't have long-lived children of their own, but she didn't want to repeat those offensive remarks that had made her feel like a failure all those years ago.

When Arwel looked at her with his piercing blue eyes, there was so much compassion in them that she suspected he knew what she'd said only in her head. Was he a mind reader?

"Did Jade think that the scouting team influenced the Mosuo social structure?" he asked.

Relieved at the change of subject, Aliya had no problem answering that. "Jade knew about the Mosuo, visited their villages, and even brought back souvenirs, or what I thought were souvenirs. I think she found some artifacts that caught her interest. She said it was obvious that the scouting crew had lived in the area and influenced the Mosuo society."

"I wonder whether the Kra-ell were put in stasis with venom or with technology." Lokan turned to Kalugal. "If it was done with venom, they would have been skeletal when they landed. But if they were on life support in some sort of pods, they would have probably awakened just fine. Did our father tell you anything about how the gods first arrived on Earth? Or maybe our mother mentioned something?"

Gods? Had she heard him right? Could gods have more than one meaning in English?

Kalugal shook his head. "Frankly, I don't remember either of them mentioning that, but I always assumed that the gods were asleep during the long journey to Earth, so maybe one of them said something to me when I was very young, and it sank into my subconscious. But it's also possible that I was influenced by science fiction movies."

"Does god mean like God Almighty, or does it have another meaning in English?" Aliya asked.

Alena smiled. "Our ancestors weren't deities. They were a divergent species of humanoids, probably from the same place as yours, but they were so advanced compared to humans and had such power over them that humans believed they were gods. Naturally, our ancestors reinforced those beliefs and created a whole mythology around a kernel of truth, aggrandizing everything they did, including their sexual shenanigans. Other mythologies copied from the first one, and that's how most of the world came to believe that they were gods. There is much more to the story, but let's save it for later, or you will never get to finish yours. What happened after you and your mother arrived at the Mosuo village?"

Aliya would have loved to hear more about the ancestors of these immortals, but if she insisted, Kalugal would just force her to go back to her story, and she hated how that felt. She'd rather keep talking and avoid it.

"The people were kind to us, and for a while, things were good. But then I matured, and my fangs started showing when I got excited or agitated, and I became so tall that I was the tallest person in the village. Most of the time, I managed to hide the fangs, never smiling and keeping my head down. But I couldn't hide my height, and people made fun of me, calling me a freak. And then my mother died when I was fifteen, and things got really bad."

"In what way?" Kalugal asked.

"The humans started to fear me. When I got angry, which happened a lot, my eyes turned red, and my fangs elongated. Some people noticed, and I heard them whispering behind my back that I must be possessed by a demon. I didn't want to wait and see what they planned to do about it. And since I knew that I couldn't thrall the entire village to forget me, I didn't feel safe to stay. I gathered my things, left in the middle of the night in a borrowed canoe, and rowed all the way to the ruins. I knew that I could survive there on my own. By then, I'd already been hunting for several years, and I was familiar with the area."

Orion

〜

"How long have you been living in those ruins?" Orion asked.

"Since I was sixteen. About fourteen years."

Orion should have added up the years and realized that Aliya must be in her thirties. Her compound had been sacked over twenty-two years ago, and she hadn't been a baby when it happened. But she seemed so young and vulnerable that her answer had taken him by surprise. Aliya might be a thirty-year-old female, but to Orion, she seemed like a young woman who had suffered loneliness for far too long and needed people who would take her in and give her a home.

Casting a quick glance at Alena, he saw the same sentiment reflected in her eyes. Could they become Aliya's foster family?

He and Alena were old enough to be not only Aliya's parents, but her many times great-grandparents. Alena had told him that she would love to have a hundred children if she could, and he knew her heart was big enough to love them all, but would her motherly instincts extend to a grown woman?

Aliya might be chronologically and biologically all grown up, but emotionally she was still a scared little girl, and although she was smart and learned fast, her education level was most likely elementary.

"You remind me of Wonder," Alena said.

Jin snorted. "They are both tall and freakishly strong, but we know that Wonder is not Kra-ell."

Alena waved a hand. "Of course she's not, and that was not what I meant. They are both strong, and they were both isolated, although not in the same way. Wonder was frozen in stasis for thousands of years, and when she woke up, it was to a new world. She needed to learn everything about it and get her education up to modern standards." She turned to Aliya. "What was the last grade you attended in school?"

"Ninth grade," she said proudly. "I'm not ignorant."

"I know that you're not, and given how good your English is just from watching movies and talking to tourists, you are a fast learner. But the world has changed a lot in the last fourteen years, no doubt more so in the West than here. What I'm saying is that if you want to re-enter society, you have a lot of catching up to do."

Aliya's cheeks darkened with embarrassment. "I know about modern things, I just don't have them because I couldn't buy them."

"I bet," Carol said. "What would you like to have?"

"I would like to have a cell phone and learn how to use it. I don't have anyone to call, but I've seen people playing games and watching movies on their phones. I even saw a woman reading a book on it."

"The wonders of technology," Alena said. "We do love it."

Kalugal shifted in his chair, his frown indicating his impatience. "If you are done discussing the wonders of cell phones, I would like to know whether there is anything in that tunnel system that indicates a Kra-ell presence. Did you find any writing, artifacts, anything that didn't look human in origin?"

Aliya pursed her lips. "I've seen weird writing in one place. It was faded, and only a few lines remained, but it looked like letters, not just scratches."

"Can you read Kra-ell?" Carol asked.

Aliya shook her head. "I was supposed to start learning after my thirteenth birthday. Until then, we only learned what our mothers could teach us. The Kra-ell didn't even acknowledge the hybrid children until they reached puberty and started showing fangs. But hybrid females were so rare that I got special treatment. I was allowed to hang around the purebloaded females, and that's how I learned the spoken language. But I've never gotten to see what written Kra-ell looks like."

Orion realized that having been allowed to hang around Jade was a source of pride for Aliya. She'd mentioned it several times, and each time she had, her shoulders had gotten a little squarer.

"Tomorrow, I want you to show me those markings," Kalugal said. "It might be worthwhile to start excavation in the underground."

When Aliya frowned, Jacki leaned forward. "What's the matter? You don't want us digging around in there?"

"It's my home." Aliya glared at her. "Or it was until you came and took it away from me. Now I have nowhere to go and no place to live."

"You can come back home with us," Alena said. "You've been alone for an awfully long time. You must have been so terribly lonely, and I suspect that you went hungry on occasion, and that you were cold and probably bored. I can't imagine living in such isolation. I'm surprised that you didn't lose your mind."

Aliya snorted. "Maybe I did."

Aliya

Alena had nailed it.

There had been many times Aliya felt like she was going insane. Often, she talked to herself or sang just to hear a voice, any voice. She hated the quiet of the tunnels, and when the archeological crew had arrived, she'd been equal parts worried about having her home discovered and glad for something to alleviate her loneliness, even though she'd never interacted with them.

They'd been oblivious to her presence even when she'd been so close that she could smell their breath.

Aliya had no television to entertain her, no books to read. Her only source of entertainment was an old transistor radio that didn't work in the ruins, not topside nor underground, and it needed batteries, which she had to steal when the old ones died out. So basically, she had nothing to keep her busy other than hunting for food.

It was difficult to subsist just on blood, and since she didn't want to kill the animals that she drank from, she only took a few sips from each, let them go, and hunted for the next. That alone filled most of her days.

When the loneliness became too much, she ventured into the village during the evening hours when it was getting dark, but the streets were still full of tourists. With the way she looked, going unnoticed was nearly impossible. Usually, she tied a scarf around the lower part of her face, hunched her shoulders, and tried to stick to the shadows, and yet many times she'd been forced to hypnotically coerce people to forget that they'd seen her. It wasn't a problem when she needed to do it to one or two people at a time, but more than that was difficult. It drained her of energy, sometimes so severely that she'd lacked the strength to get back to her tunnels and had to either spend a few hours resting or find a source of blood to replenish her energy. But since hunting also required strength, she usually found a shadowy resting spot under a tree or behind some bushes.

"Where is your home?" she asked Alena.

"In California. Do you know where that is?"

Aliya shrugged. "Somewhere in America."

"Correct. It's on the West Coast of the United States. We have a secret village where only immortals live. You will not have to hide from people there, you'll have friends, and you will no longer be alone."

That sounded too good to be true, which meant that there was a catch. Did they need her for breeding? Or maybe they wanted to experiment on her?

Jade had warned Aliya and the other hybrids that if the humans discovered them, they would be locked in a lab and cut up like rats. Jade had put the fear of the Mother in them, and she hadn't been wrong. Aliya had learned in school about the atrocities the Japanese committed against the Chinese people during the big war. If humans could be so horrible to each other, Aliya could only imagine what they would do to an alien freak like her.

"Why are you inviting me to your secret village? What's in it for you?"

Looking offended, Alena leaned away. "I'm not inviting you because I have anything to gain by it. I'm doing it for you out of kindness." She let out a breath as if to calm herself, and a moment later her eyes softened. "You and your mother were taken in by the Mosuo, so you've experienced kindness from strangers before. You shouldn't be so suspicious when someone wants to help you."

"They needed my mother's skill with the sewing machine. She worked very hard to earn our stay."

"The phrase is to earn your keep," Kalugal corrected. "Alena has a kind soul, and that's why she's inviting you to come home with her, but I'm not sure she should, or even if she has the authority to extend such an invitation to you. You need to prove yourself valuable first." He crossed his arms over his chest. "Alena's brother is in charge of the village, and although he's a fair male, he's not as kind-hearted as his sister. He might refuse you entry to his community."

Aliya shifted her eyes to Alena. "Is that true?"

"I'm afraid so. I can put in a good word on your behalf, but Kian would want proof that you can be trusted and that you are willing to contribute to the community. Since you were not born into the clan, you will have to earn your keep."

It seemed like they needed workers, which made sense. If they were a secret community of immortals, and they didn't have humans to serve them, they would be very glad for a servant girl that was strong and could work long hours.

Hard work had never scared Aliya, but she didn't want to be treated like a slave. She didn't mind cleaning their houses and tending to their gardens, but she wanted to get paid for her work and to be treated with respect.

"How much would I get paid?"

Alena chuckled. "Before we negotiate your pay, we need to discuss what kind of work you'd be doing for the clan."

"I can do many things. I can clean, I can tend to crops and animals, and I can carry heavy things. I can cook a little, but that would be a waste of my abilities. My biggest assets are my strength and endurance. I could probably clean twenty houses in one day."

Alena

❦

Once again, Kalugal had impressed Alena. His move to use reverse psychology on Aliya had been brilliant. By making her acceptance conditional on her actions, he was taking away the invitation and making her work for it.

Aliya was suspicious of their motives, and she couldn't accept that they were offering her a place in the village out of kindness. She also didn't like getting something for nothing or feeling obligated to anyone. Kalugal had put the offer in terms she could understand and accept without feeling like she was being trapped or given charity.

That was why Alena had played along and hadn't corrected him even though what he'd told Aliya hadn't been entirely true.

Theoretically, Kian could refuse, and Alena would have to respect his decision, but she knew he wouldn't. Under his gruff exterior, Kian was just as soft-hearted as she was, especially when it came to a lonely female with no people to call her own.

Heck, if he'd invited Emmett and Vrog to live in the village, there was no chance he would turn Aliya away.

"Twenty houses, eh?" Kalugal sounded amused. "I have a pretty big house. I think it should count as five." He turned to Jacki. "What do you think?"

"I think that Aliya's unique attributes would be wasted on menial labor and should be better utilized. There is nothing wrong with a cleaning job, of course, and if that's what she wants to do, she would have plenty of clients in the village who would be willing to pay handsomely for her services, but I think Guardians are paid even better."

Were Jacki and Kalugal playing good cop, bad cop? Or did Jacki seriously think that Kian would allow Aliya to join the Guardian force?

Alena doubted that. Eleanor, who'd already proven that she was capable and loyal, and who had a niece and a nephew in the village, still hadn't been officially accepted into the training program. Aliya would most likely have to prove herself over an even longer period of time. She was Kra-ell, and she had no one in the village she cared for and was protective of. She would also have to go through several tests before she could start training.

Kalugal's eyes were full of amusement as he took it from there. "As I said before, Aliya needs to prove herself deserving of a spot in the village, and then further prove herself to be considered for the Guardian force."

"What are Guardians?" Aliya asked. "Are they defenders of the village?"

"That's part of the job," Arwel said. "We also wage war against human trafficking."

Aliya looked confused. "Why would you wage war against transportation? Isn't it necessary for shipping goods and transporting people to where they need to go?"

Alena wondered whether it was just the language barrier or was Aliya ignorant of what was going on in the world around her.

Probably both.

In some ways she was like a child, innocent, vulnerable. And yet in others, she was remarkably strong. Aliya had been through hell, losing her place in the world twice, and somehow, she had not only survived but had clung to her principles and hadn't used her abilities to harm people or animals.

That was quite admirable, and Alena was sure Kian would recognize the diamond in the rough that Aliya was.

"Trafficking is a misleading term," Jin said. "It means capturing humans, mainly women, and forcing them into sex slavery."

Aliya gaped at her. "That's terrible. Why is it called trafficking?"

"They use the term because the bad guys capture young women and girls and transport them from one place to another illegally." Jin leaned forward. "But that's like calling murder a misuse of weaponry or some other stupid term that makes a horrific crime sound more palatable to delicate ears."

Aliya pursed her lips. "Is this an American thing? Or do they call it trafficking all over the world?"

"I don't know." Jin leaned back and crossed her arms over her chest. "It doesn't matter what they call it—the flesh market, sex slavery, ruining of lives—it needs to be stopped. I was considering joining the force myself, but my mate, who is a Head Guardian, wouldn't hear of it." She turned a baleful look at Arwel.

He shrugged. "If you really wanted to, you could have filled out an application like everyone else, and I wouldn't have stopped you. You decided that you prefer to run a business with your sister, so don't make me into the bad guy here."

"You're not bad. You're just stubborn and chauvinistic."

"Children." Carol lifted her hand. "This is not about you. This is about Aliya, and I think she'd make a great Guardian." She smiled at the girl. "I trained for a while, but then I met Lokan and my priorities changed. Also, I didn't have the patience to train for years on end. But you most likely wouldn't have to. With your strength and speed, you could probably graduate in months instead of decades."

"It's not just about physical ability," Arwel said. "There is a lot involved in being a professional Guardian—weapons training, strategizing, fighting techniques, negotiation tactics, and so on."

As Arwel listed the things Guardians were supposed to know, Aliya's excited expression turned into a frown. "I don't know if I want to be a Guardian. You said that you wage war against traffickers, but how is that war waged? Do you use machine guns and grenades? Because I don't know how to use them, and I don't think I want to learn that."

Leaning over, Alena patted Aliya's hand. "The Guardians learn how to use those weapons, but that's not how they fight trafficking. They find the places where the victims are held, rescue them, and leave the scum that exploited them to the human police. The clan has a rehabilitation center for the victims, where they get medical and psychological help. They can also learn a trade, so when they are ready, they can re-enter society and live independently."

"That sounds like a very honorable occupation." Aliya regarded Arwel with respect in her eyes. "Mother bless you for what you are doing for these poor women and girls. I would love to help, but with the way I look, I might scare them." She shifted her eyes to Alena. "When people see a woman like you, they think you're an angel. When they see me, they think I'm a demon."

Aliya

"That's nonsense," Alena said. "You are very pretty, and no one will think that you are a demon."

Aliya arched a brow. "Did you really look at me? What else could they think?"

"I have fangs too," Jin said. "I cover them up with attitude."

"Your fangs are tiny in comparison to mine, but fangs are not my only problem." Aliya let her eyes flash red. "When I'm calm, I can control my eyes and my fangs, but when I'm excited, I can't."

"That's what sunglasses are for," Carol said. "And the rest can be done with the right clothes. Vlad, who is also one-quarter Kra-ell like Jin, is very tall and very thin, has one eye that's green and the other blue, and his fangs used to elongate with the slightest provocation. He adopted a Goth style, and everyone assumed that he was wearing contact lenses to change his eye color and prosthetic fangs. You could do the same thing."

"Goth? What's that?"

"I'll show you." Jin pulled out her phone, typed something on the screen, and then handed it to Aliya.

The girl in the picture had her brows and nose pierced, her eyes lined with heavy black makeup, and her fingernails painted black with purple splotches. Her hair was also black, but the tips were painted blood red. She wore black clothes with rips and buckles all over and boots that added at least six centimeters to her height.

But underneath it all, the girl was just a human in a costume. If Aliya did all that, she would look even weirder than she looked now.

"I don't think that can help me." She handed Jin her phone back.

"I'm tired." Jacki yawned. "It's been a long day for all of us. Can we continue this talk tomorrow?"

"Of course, my love." Kalugal put his arm around his mate's shoulders and kissed the top of her head.

"Where am I going to sleep?" Aliya asked.

With all the excitement, she'd forgotten that her plan had been to escape once her belly was full. She was supposed to pretend that she was excited by their offer, not actually consider it.

"Right here on the couch," Kalugal said. "I want you where I can keep an eye on you."

Aliya crossed her arms over her chest and glared at him. "So I'm a prisoner after all?"

"No, you are a guest, and I'm keeping you here for your own good. We are offering you a better life, a chance to reach your full potential, but you are skittish, mistrustful, and impulsive, and you might decide to run before we can convince you that you can trust us."

He sounded so sincere, but she couldn't trust him. He was too charming, too smooth, and men like him were players and manipulators. Even she knew that.

"Do I have to sleep here? Can't I get my own room?"

Jin snorted. "For someone who's lived in a cave for fourteen years, a couch in the living room of the presidential suite should seem like a luxury to be delighted about. Demanding your own room is kind of obnoxious and could only mean that you're plotting something, and that something is probably an escape."

The woman had a point. "I'm not demanding anything. But you keep telling me that I'm a guest, not a prisoner, so shouldn't I get a room of my own?"

"You can sleep in mine," Phinas offered. "There are two beds, and I only need one."

The mated males seemed safe, but Phinas didn't have a mate. "I'm not spending the night with a bachelor."

"Why not?" Jin asked. "As a half Kra-ell who grew up watching the purebloooded females command a harem of males, you shouldn't be concerned with human propriety rules. Besides, Phinas is quite a catch. He's handsome and he's Kalugal's right-hand man. But if you don't want him, you have nothing to fear because he's not going to try anything, and even if he did, you could overpower him with ease. You are so damn strong that you have nothing to worry about. No male can over-power you unless he holds a knife to your throat, a gun to your temple, or slips drugs into your drink."

"That's not true. Kalugal and Orion can force me to do whatever they want. They are both mated, so I'm not worried that they would take sexual advantage of me, but they could command me to have sex with Phinas or one of the other bachelors."

"Why would they do that?" Alena asked.

Aliya shrugged. "As a favor to the unmated males or for their own amusement."

"They would never do that," Alena said. "Orion and Kalugal are good people and honorable males."

The truth was that Aliya didn't fear any of them would want sex from her, but she needed an excuse to be left alone so she could escape. "You saying that they are honorable doesn't mean that it's true."

"You are so full of it," Jin said. "You grew up in a Kra-ell compound and then among the Mosuo. You shouldn't have any of the human hang-ups about sex."

"I don't." Yes, she did.

Despite being half Kra-ell, and despite growing up in the Mosuo village, Aliya was still a virgin at thirty.

When her flowering time had come, none of the boys indicated that they were interested in her inviting them to her flowering room. She'd been too tall, too skinny, too flat-chested, and too weird.

But those had all been excuses. The truth was that all the boys feared her, and for a good reason.

"Perhaps you'd be more comfortable sleeping with the Odus," Alena suggested.

Aliya looked around the table. By now, she knew everyone's name, but perhaps Odu was a surname?

"Do you mean Carol and Lokan or Jin and Arwel?"

Alena

После a moment of confusion, Alena chuckled. "Odu is not anyone's last name or nickname. You didn't meet the Odus yet. They are my butlers." When Aliya tilted her head, Alena added, "They are my servants."

Aliya seemed even more baffled. Looking at Kalugal and Jacki and then back at Alena, she shook her head. "I thought that he was the rich one, and he only has an assistant. Are you a princess or something?"

How to answer that?

Her companions would expect her to say that she was, but although her mother was a queen in every conceivable way, Alena never thought of herself as royalty.

Annani had been born to the gods' leading couple and had been groomed to one day take over rulership. The gods had been destroyed, her throne along with them, but she was still a powerful goddess, the head of their clan, and the ultimate drama queen.

Perhaps her mother's supercharged grandness was why Alena had always underplayed her importance and insisted that she shouldn't be treated any differently than any other clan member. Sari and Kian led their respective arms of the clan, so they deserved some deference, but they never referred to themselves as prince or princess either. Only Amanda, who took after their mother in the drama department, was the one nicknamed princess.

"Although my mother, who is the head of our clan, acts like a queen, she doesn't refer to herself as one." As a goddess, Annani probably considered being called a queen a step down in status. "Therefore, neither my siblings nor I are treated as royalty either. One of the Odus has always been my servant and protector, and for this trip, my mother loaned me one of hers, so I will be doubly protected."

Aliya regarded her with suspicion in her dark eyes. "So they are not your servants. They are your bodyguards."

"In a way, they are, but that's not their primary function. Their job is to take care of me the way a servant would."

Aliya's suspicious expression only deepened. "But if their job is also to protect you, why weren't they with you in the ruins? And where are they now?"

"They are in their room."

Explaining to Aliya why the Odus had been left behind required a backstory that Alena preferred not to get into at the moment.

"I was wondering about that as well," Jacki said. "Kian made such a big deal about wanting you protected, and yet you leave your Odus in the hotel room. Why didn't you bring them along on our boat trip or to the excavation site?"

It seemed like the backstory would have to be told after all.

Alena sighed. "Since Okidu's accident, I'm hesitant about getting them anywhere near water. I don't want them to accidentally reboot before we know the consequences of Okidu and Onidu's new protocol's emergence."

"I get it," Jacki said. "But it defies the purpose of them being here. The Odus are supposed to protect you, but since we are near a lake, there is water everywhere, and they are no good to you in their hotel room."

Alena nodded. "I should have thought it through before bringing them along." She smiled at Arwel. "Kian wanted me to take Guardians instead, and I insisted that the Odus would suffice. I'm glad that he sent you anyway. There is no substitute for having a Head Guardian as my protector."

Arwel's upper lip curled in a grimace. "I didn't do such a great job of it, and if we'd had the Odus with us in the ruins, I would have been much less worried when we found ourselves trapped. From now on, I would prefer if they tagged along. There is no reason to fear that they will accidentally drown."

Kalugal cleared his throat. "I disagree. I was told that the Odus are very heavy. If even one of them joined us on the lake, the canoe's center of gravity might have been disturbed, and if the Odu made the wrong move, he could've tipped the boat over." He wrapped his arm around Jacki's shoulders. "I would have been really upset if my wife got dunked in the lake's cold water."

"Yeah," Jacki confirmed. "I would have been pissed as hell. I might be immortal, and getting submerged in cold water won't kill me, but Junior is still human and fragile." She gave Alena an amused look. "Unlike you, the cold bothers me very much."

Pretending to be upset, Alena huffed and crossed her arms over her chest. "It appears that none of you will let me live down that silly performance."

"Silly?" Orion lifted a brow. "That performance made me fall in love with you. It was the most important performance of our lives."

"Oh," Carol sighed. "That's so romantic. Jacki told me about your rendition of "Let It Go," and she said it was one of the best ones she'd ever heard. I would love to hear you sing it."

"Not tonight."

"Why not?"

"Because the entire hotel will hear me, and we are not supposed to draw attention to ourselves. Remind me when we visit the ruins again, and I'll sing it for you in the tunnels. On one condition, though. You will sing with me."

Carol extended her hand to Alena. "You've got yourself a deal. We can sing a duet. You'll be the snow queen, and I'll be the little sister."

That sounded like fun, but then Alena remembered all the taunting she'd heard over the years and reconsidered. "On second thought, that might not be a good idea. The walls might topple and bury us alive. I was told that my singing could have outdone the horns of Jericho."

As her friends and family laughed, Alena noticed that Aliya remained somber, or maybe just pensive.

"What's wrong, Aliya?"

"I'm confused," the girl said. "If these Odus are so big and fat that it's dangerous to let them sit in the canoe, then they can't be very good bodyguards."

Alena had hoped that talking about her singing would lighten Aliya's mood, but it seemed that the girl's mind was stuck on the previous subject of conversation.

"The Odus are neither big nor fat," Arwel said. "In fact, they look like average middle-aged men. The reason that they are so heavy is that they are part people and part machine, and the parts that are machine are very heavy."

"Were they injured in a war?" Aliya asked. "Did they get low-quality replacement arms or legs?" She cast Alena an accusing look. "The replacements are not supposed to be heavy, and you are rich enough to get your servants the best."

Alena had a feeling that no roundabout explanation would satisfy Aliya. She already knew about the clan, so telling her the truth about the Odus was probably okay.

"They weren't injured," Alena said. "The Odus were never human or immortal. They were not born. They were built, and they are very sophisticated machines." She hated calling the Odus that, but she doubted Aliya would know what a cyborg was. Besides, that wasn't a good description of the Odus either.

Even prior to Okidu and Onidu's reboot, Alena had always thought of them as a different kind of people, an emergent species that couldn't reproduce biologically but that could potentially manufacture their offspring. Was that why Okidu had given Kian the blueprints to their design?

It was a scary idea. Okidu didn't seem capable of being the mastermind behind a future cyborg revolution, but whoever had programmed him might be.

Perhaps the family needed to meet again and discuss Okidu's gift some more. So far, William hadn't managed to decipher the instructions, but he was in the process of assembling a team of bioinformaticians to help him with the genetic code part. If the family decided that it was too risky, they should shut down that project before the clan committed large resources to it.

"Machines?" Aliya tilted her head again. "What do you mean?"

"They look and act human," Alena continued, "but they have a computer for a brain and a mechanical pump for a heart. They also don't need to sleep, so even though I got them a hotel room, they don't use the beds, and you can sleep on one. They are not going to bother you because they are neither male nor female. They don't have sexual organs, they are not aggressive, and they are programmed to be polite, accommodating, and helpful."

Aliya didn't look nearly as flabbergasted on hearing about the technological wonder of the Odus as Alena had expected.

"You don't seem surprised."

Carol snorted. "The poor girl's reached the overload stage. That's all. She's become numb."

"No," Aliya shook her head. "It's just that I must have heard about robot servants before." She rubbed her temple. "I'm not sure, though. Maybe I just saw a movie about cyborgs."

Alena chuckled. "I didn't use the word cyborg to describe the Odus because I didn't think you'd know what that meant. Jade must have brought back a sci-fi movie from one of her trips."

Kalugal leaned over the table, his eyes more curious than Alena had seen them throughout the evening. "Did Jade or any of the other purebloods mention the Odus?"

"I don't remember. It's just that the idea of servants who don't need sleep and are stronger and better than human servants in every way doesn't sound new to me."

Aliya

"I wouldn't say that they are better than humans," Alena said. "The Odus have a very limited capacity for decision making." She hesitated for a moment. "We don't really understand their technology, but we suspect that they were deliberately limited by their creators. Still, I doubt that even at their full capacity, they could match human creativity, ingenuity, and problem-solving capabilities."

What Aliya understood from Alena's description was that the Odus were simple creatures that would be easy to fool. Escaping them shouldn't be as difficult as escaping these descendants of gods who called themselves immortals. Except, for that to work, she shouldn't appear too eager to sleep in the cyborgs' room, or the sly Kalugal would guess her intentions.

She would use his own tactics against him.

The male thought that she'd bought his bait and switch maneuver, making her think that Alena's invitation was conditional on her brother's approval and on Aliya's willingness to work.

At first, she hadn't realized that Kalugal had been playing her, and perhaps she wouldn't have caught on to it if Alena was a better actress. But the woman had been so obvious that it had been funny to watch.

The truth was that Alena's bad acting made Aliya like her even more. The woman wasn't fake or smooth like Kalugal, which made her more trustworthy, but Aliya wasn't stupid enough to think that she could trust Alena implicitly.

"Can you take me to meet them?" she asked. "From your description, they sound harmless, but since they are your bodyguards, they can't be that simple. Besides, even though you said that they are neither male nor female, you refer to them as male. I would like to judge for myself if I'll be comfortable sleeping in their room."

Aliya wasn't a great actress either, and learning from Alena's mistakes, she'd chosen to stick as close to the truth as she could. Since she'd meant every word, no one could detect a lie she hadn't voiced.

Nevertheless, Kalugal regarded her with that annoying smirk of his. "Before you get any ideas in your head, you should know that they are incredibly strong, much stronger than even you. If Alena tells them to keep you from leaving the room, they will stop you. And since they don't need to sleep, they will watch you constantly. Even if you manage to overcome my compulsion not to leave the hotel without my permission, escaping the Odus would be even less likely than escaping any of us."

Crap, was she that transparent?

"Who said I was planning to escape?"

He chuckled. "It's written all over your face. You wouldn't make a good spy, Aliya."

She grimaced. "With the way I look, being a spy would be the worst career choice for me."

"So true." Carol pushed away from the table and rose to her feet. "I'll accompany you to the Odus and tell you all about being a spy on the way." She fluffed her pretty blond curls as she waited for Aliya to follow. "No one ever suspects the little curvy blond. The more harmless you look, the better spy you make." She threaded her arm through Aliya's. "And you, my dear, look the opposite of harmless."

"I know. I look scary to humans."

As Alena got up, Orion started to rise, but she put a hand on his shoulder. "You should stay. I'm just going downstairs with Aliya and Carol to the Odus' room and then back up here. I'm supposed to call one of the Odus to escort me, but that would ruin the element of surprise. Welgost can do that."

"It would be my pleasure." The warrior got up.

Orion looked disappointed, and Aliya wondered why. Was it because he wanted to be with his mate every minute of the day?

The males of this long-lived species were overly attached to their females. At first, it seemed pleasant, and Aliya had wondered what it would be like to have a single male so devoted to her, but after watching them some more, she'd decided that it was too much. She wouldn't like so much constant attention.

It would feel suffocating.

"I'm curious to see their reaction to you, and yours to them," Carol said as they walked out of Kalugal's suite.

"Why?"

"You look very Kra-ell. I wonder if they will recognize you as one."

"Did they recognize the other hybrids living in your village?"

"I don't know." Carol glanced at Alena. "Do you?"

"No one mentioned it, so I assume that they didn't react any differently to Emmett and Vrog than to other newcomers."

"Okay, then." Carol tightened her hold on Aliya's arm. "Let me tell you about my pre-matehood days." As they took the stairs down to the hotel's second floor, Carol amused Alena and Aliya with an anecdote from her past as an escort to a powerful man. The few minutes it took to get to the Odus' room weren't long enough to get into more details, and Aliya was dying to learn more about Carol's adventures. Carol was a gifted storyteller, and listening to her was better than watching television. Aliya hadn't had the pleasure of doing that in years.

When Alena knocked on the door, it opened almost instantly, and a short, stockily built male smiled and bowed. "Mistress Alena, what a pleasure it is to be graced by your presence. How can Oridu and I be of service?"

"I have a new friend I would like you to meet." She entered the room and motioned for Aliya and Carol to follow. "This is Aliya, and she belongs to the same people as Emmett and Vrog. She is half-human and half-Kra-ell."

The Odu looked so human that Aliya suspected Alena and the others had been messing with her, but when she got closer and sniffed him, she knew they had told her the truth.

Under the normal smell of flesh, she could scent much more metal than should be in any living thing's body. It wasn't any of the metals she was familiar with either. She hadn't smelled anything like that before.

"Hello, Mistress Aliya," the Odu smiled a fake-looking smile and bowed. "I am Ovidu."

His twin, whose name was Oridu, did the same. "Is there anything we can do to serve you?"

"I just wanted to meet you, but thank you for offering." Aliya scrambled for something to say to get herself out of having to spend the night with the cyborgs.

They were creepy, and she would rather spend the night on Kalugal and Jacki's couch than alone with them.

"Well?" Alena arched a brow. "Now that you've met the Odus, are you comfortable sleeping in their room?"

"Are you sure that they don't need the beds?" Aliya looked around the small hotel room. There was one chair but no couch. "I don't want to make one of them spend the night sitting on a chair."

"I do not mind, mistress," Ovidu said. "Oridu and I will watch television all night long. We want to learn the local customs."

Perhaps she could use that as an excuse. "I wouldn't want to spoil their plans. I also want to watch some television, but probably not the same programs as the Odus. Do you think Kalugal and Jacki would mind if I watched in their living room? I'll keep the volume down."

Thankfully, Alena got the hint. "You can ask, and if they don't want to be bothered by the noise, I can give you a pair of headphones."

Arwel

A s the door closed behind Aliya, Kalugal turned to Arwel. "What does your empathy tell you about her?"

"Aliya is very guarded, and she's projecting even fewer emotions than most immortals, and I don't know whether it's because of her Kra-ell upbringing, her life experiences, or her natural disposition."

Orion chuckled. "You don't need to be an empath to know that she's looking for ways to escape. She's like a trapped animal, only much smarter and more cunning."

"She needs new clothing," Jin said. "If we take her shopping, she might warm to us."

Kalugal waved a dismissive hand. "She'll just use the opportunity to split."

"You'll compel her to stay with us." Jin crossed her arms over her chest. "In fact, I think she will feel more relaxed if only the girls go with her. I don't know any woman who doesn't enjoy clothes shopping with her girlfriends. Even a half Kra-ell hard-ass like Aliya wants to look nice."

Kalugal shook his head. "The nearest town with department stores that carry the kind of clothing you want to get her is about two hours' drive away, and I doubt you'll find anything for a female that's over six feet tall even there."

"I'm sure we will find something. At the very least, she needs underwear and shoes. She walked out of here barefoot, if you didn't notice. I don't have any new underwear to give her, and wearing someone else's panties even after they've been laundered is gross, so I didn't give her any, and I bet she's gone commando."

Phinas groaned. "I could have done without that image."

Jacki's eyes widened. "Do you find her attractive?"

"Why wouldn't I? She's pretty, and I like her personality. She's a smart and proud female."

"Aliya looks very alien," Jacki said. "I really can't understand how the pureblooded Kra-ell managed to pass for humans. I'm glad that immortals look for the most part human, and I can't imagine being attracted to someone so alien-looking."

"Doesn't bother me," Phinas said. "I find Aliya rather interesting."

"What about her super-strength and her aggressiveness?" Jin asked. "Isn't that a turn-off for a macho guy like you?"

He gave her an amused look. "Who said that I'm macho? Maybe I enjoy aggressive women?"

"You don't," Jin said with surprising conviction. "You're just messing with us."

"How do you know that?" Phinas asked.

"I just do." Jin uncrossed her arms. "Aliya is not for you."

Arwel wasn't sure about that at all. Despite being a former Doomer, Phinas was a fine male, and he sure as hell was attracted to Aliya. Furthermore, Arwel had noticed her stealing covert looks at the guy. She wasn't indifferent to him either.

"I'll send Shamash to get Aliya new clothes." Kalugal took Jacki's hand. "Can you make a list of what she needs?"

"She needs everything." Jacki sighed. "And Jin is right. We should take her shopping instead. It will build trust and friendship between us."

"Not everyone is like you, my love." He lifted her hand and kissed the back of it. "Aliya will see right through it. Besides, she's intensely proud and doesn't like handouts. She needs to earn her new clothing, and she can do that by guiding us through the tunnels."

Arwel nodded. "Kalugal is right. Aliya would hate to get a new wardrobe as charity. She will be much happier if she has to work for it."

"I can offer her money as compensation for taking over her home." Kalugal ran a hand over his goatee. "Frankly,

I feel a little guilty about that, and paying her is the least I can do."

"You're such a sweetheart." Jacki kissed his cheek. "But I don't know what you're expecting to find there. Unless Aliya was lying, the only thing she's ever found in there was illegible scribbles on the wall that might or might not be Kra-ell symbols. And given that she's had fourteen years to explore, that's probably all you're going to find."

"Perhaps." Kalugal lifted her hand and kissed it again. "But maybe my talented wife could put her hand on the writing and get a vision about its origins."

Jacki eyed him from under lowered lashes. "I thought that you didn't want me to have visions while I was pregnant."

"I changed my mind. After you got the vision of Aliya as a young girl, you were more than fine. You were excited, and there was a spark in your eyes. I realized that your visions don't harm you and might actually benefit you."

"Thank the merciful Fates." She gave him a relieved smile. "I didn't want to worry you before, but now that your approach has changed and you've become more reasonable, I can tell you that my visions don't ask for my permission or yours to appear. I was lucky not to get any before today, but that doesn't mean that my luck will hold throughout my pregnancy."

"I know that, which was why I didn't want to take you to Egypt. I was afraid that everything you touched there would bring up visions. I didn't expect to find many artifacts at this site because it has been excavated several times before, so I assumed there was less of a chance of you touching something that would evoke a vision. Besides, you don't speak Chinese."

"I don't speak Arabic either."

As Kalugal scrambled to say something to explain what had probably been a gut feeling, Arwel came to his rescue. "We should call Vrog and tell him about Aliya. He will be happy to hear that one of the hybrid females managed to escape."

Jin snorted. "I wouldn't be surprised if Vrog convinces Mey and Yamanu to leave the echoes alone and take him to her. Aliya is an even rarer find than a Dormant."

Vrog

"We should call Arwel." Yamanu put his coffee cup down. "We need to tell him about the echoes of the Kra-ell purebloods that Mey saw."

Vrog reached for the carafe and refilled the Guardian's cup. "We should. They called us with what they'd found, we should offer them the same courtesy."

"They had a picture of what looked like the Kra-ell goddess," Mey said. "We have nothing. I didn't learn anything from those echoes except what the pureblooded females looked like. I couldn't understand anything they said. Vrog and I have made some progress with my Kra-ell, so maybe the next time I listen to that echo, I'll understand what they were fighting about, but I doubt I will figure it all out in one go. I would probably have to listen to them many times, try to memorize what they say, and repeat it to Vrog to translate."

"Nevertheless, we need to call Arwel," Yamanu said. "Let's do it right now."

As the Guardian pulled out his phone, Vrog's began ringing, and as he picked it up and glanced at the caller ID, he had to smile. "Speak of the devil." He answered and activated the speaker function. "Hello, Arwel. I know that you're an empath, but I didn't know that you are powerful enough to feel us talking about calling you from so many miles away."

"Do you have news for us?" Arwel asked.

"We've debated whether the echoes Mey saw and heard were newsworthy. She doesn't think so, but I agree with Yamanu that they are. I'll let her tell you about it."

Shaking her head, Mey let out a breath. "I saw two Kra-ell purebloaded females fighting, but they were talking too fast for me to understand what they were fighting about. They looked very alien and were incredibly strong and vicious. Pretty, in a weird way though, like porcelain dolls that had been stretched out. They were both well over six feet tall and very thin."

"That description matches what we found here," Arwel said. "Aliya had trouble blending in because she looked too alien."

Vrog's heart started pounding against his ribcage. None of the Kra-ell females he remembered had been called Aliya. Had the other group found a hybrid among the Mosuo? A live female, or a story of one?

"Who's Aliya?" he asked.

"I'm surprised that you don't recognize her name. She's a hybrid female who escaped the compound as a child. She still looked human when the attack happened, and the invading Kra-ell let her go with her human mother."

Vrog's throat dried out in an instant. "Does she know what happened there?"

"She knows more than you do, but she was just eight at the time, so I don't know how reliable her memories are. The one thing I'm sure of, though, is that your people were massacred by a different Kra-ell tribe. Aliya refers to them as the bad Kra-ell."

Given the girl's age at the time of the attack, he should have known her at least by name. Perhaps Aliya was her Chinese name, and she had another one in the Kra-ell language?

"Can you ask her what her Kra-ell name is?"

"She's not here at the moment. Alena and Carol took her to meet the Odus."

"Why?"

"She's skittish as hell, stubborn, suspicious, and strong of body and mind. We are afraid that she'll manage to overcome Kalugal's compulsion to stay and run away. For her own good, we need to keep her with us."

His gut clenching with worry, Vrog asked, "Did you have to hurt her while apprehending her?"

Arwel chuckled. "We did our best not to harm her, but she didn't extend us the same courtesy. If not for Orion, she might have overpowered both Phinas and me, two well-trained and experienced warriors. Aliya is incredibly strong."

Pride swelled in Vrog's chest. "Did Orion compel her to stop fighting?"

"He knocked her out with a rock."

"Why would he do that?" Vrog asked.

"In the heat of the pursuit, he forgot that he was a compeller."

How could anyone forget their ability? Once they got to Lugu Lake, Vrog would have a talk with Orion and give him a piece of his mind.

"Is she okay?" Mey asked.

"She's fine. The moment she woke up, she started fighting again, but this time around, Orion remembered that he's a compeller and used his ability to subdue her."

"How did you find her?" Mey asked. "Did she live with the Mosuo?"

"She did, but she had to leave once her Kra-ell features became too dominant."

As Arwel told them the rest of the story of how Aliya had trapped them in the tunnels underneath the ruins, and what it had taken to catch her, Vrog found himself infatuated with the female even before he'd laid eyes on her.

Aliya was everything a Kra-ell female should be and then some. Smart, resourceful, cunning, strong, and she even followed the Mother's code of conduct, which was most admirable. As a hybrid who'd lived among humans for most of her life, that was unexpected.

"Does she remember me?" he asked when Arwel was done.

"She remembered your name."

"Does she want to see me?"

"I'm sure she does, but when we offered to call you as proof that we didn't mean her harm, she refused. As I said, she's very suspicious of everyone, and she thinks that you might have betrayed the tribe to those bad Kra-ell."

The baseless accusation felt like a kick to Vrog's gut. "Why would she think that?"

"Because you were away, and you survived," Arwel said.

68

Vrog

"I need to see her." Vrog turned to Morris. "Can you fly us out to Lugu Lake tomorrow?"

"What about the echoes?" May asked. "I'm not done with them."

"There is no rush," Arwel said. "Aliya is not going anywhere anytime soon. Kalugal wants her to take us down to the tunnels and show us what she found there, which isn't much, but maybe she just didn't know where to look."

Vrog didn't want to wait for Mey to hear the echoes again. They weren't going anywhere, and she could come back to them at any time. The same wasn't true of Aliya.

"What did she find?" Yamanu asked.

"Some markings that might be in the Kra-ell language. She can speak it, but she doesn't read or write it or even know what it looks like."

Vrog perked up. "Then you need me there. I can read and write it."

"I know what it looks like," Jin said. "And we can take pictures and send them to you, but not right away. Our phones don't work in the ruins. There is some weird interference in the soil that blocks transmission. Kalugal was told that it's caused by copper deposits, but he plans on bringing in a geologist to check."

Vrog couldn't care less about the copper in the soil, the interference, or even traces of Kra-ell habitation. All he cared about was the hybrid female who was probably scared and needed someone to reassure her and take care of her.

If she would let him, he was the perfect choice for the job of her guide and protector. He could invite her to live in the staff quarters at the school, and he could supplement her education himself. He wouldn't expect anything in return either. He would be thrilled just to have her around.

The question was what the clan wanted to do, or rather Kian, who called the shots even though it wasn't his place.

They had no right to Aliya. No one had. She should be offered the choice to either join them, or come live with him at the school, or live on her own.

Hopefully, Kian would take the moral high ground and give her those choices instead of forcing her to live in the village. If he didn't, there was little Vrog could do other than argue on her behalf.

"After you are done exploring the tunnels, what are you planning to do with Aliya?" he asked.

"We want to take her with us to the village," Kalugal's wife said. "The poor girl lived alone in those tunnels for fourteen years. You should've seen her when we found her. She looked like a homeless wild woman. After she'd showered and put on the clothes Jin lent her, Aliya looked like a different person."

"I think she should come live with me in the school. I can tutor her, so she at least has a high-school education."

"Don't take this the wrong way, Vrog," Kalugal said. "But Aliya is not like the Kra-ell females you knew. She's a prude, and she doesn't want to be left alone with bachelors, and that's when she knows none of us can overpower her. With you, she will feel defenseless. Besides, she needs people to hang out with, and she can't do it in your school. She would either have to hide in her room or thrall everyone she meets. She looks too alien."

"I'm sure there is a solution for that. Jade used to travel all over the world, using commercial airlines."

"Jade was a powerful thraller," Kalugal said. "She could probably effect a continuous thrall that worked like my shroud. Aliya is not nearly as powerful, and her solution is to hide and go out only at night when she absolutely has to. That's no way to live."

Vrog realized that Kalugal and the rest of his team had already decided Aliya's future, and he would have to fight for her right to choose after all.

"First of all, the decision should be Aliya's. Her case is no different than mine, and Kian offered me the choice to either join the clan or not."

"Her case is not the same," Arwel said. "You have a son in the village that you want to protect, while she doesn't have ties to anyone. Therefore, letting her come and go as she pleases is not an option. Secondly, you can pass for a human with ease, while she would need to resort to extreme measures to hide her otherness. For Aliya, the village is the safest and the best place."

With Arwel and Kalugal voicing the same conviction, Kian would no doubt accept their opinion and force the decision on Aliya. She had no one to advocate for her except for Vrog.

"What is she going to do in your village? Work in the café? Are they even hiring?"

"They always need more help," Jin said. "But we have a better idea for her. With her incredible strength and her smarts, she could fly through the Guardian training program. Guardians are very well paid, and they are well respected, which seems to matter a lot to Aliya."

"Of course it does. She's a proud Kra-ell female."

"You could join her in the village," Jacki suggested. "I know that the school means a lot to you, but you can take a sabbatical, and visit from time to time to make sure that everything runs smoothly."

Obviously, Jacki had guessed why he was fighting them over the decision to take Aliya to the village. It wasn't all about her right to choose her future, it was also about her possible future with him.

Alena

"Do that again." Aliya clapped her hands with a child's glee.

"Certainly, mistress." Oridu dipped his head, or rather her head.

Aliya was fascinated by the Odus' ability to morph their features from male to female and back, and right now, Oridu was a female.

Thankfully, Ovidu and Oridu hadn't become sentient yet, or they would have been put off by Aliya's demands to perform.

"This is amazing." Aliya giggled. "They would make the perfect spies or thieves. They can go in looking like guys, go out looking like women, and then change again. I wish I could do that." Her happy expression turned serious again. "I heard that many people in the West have surgeries to change their faces." She turned to Carol. "Do you think that would help me?"

Carol shook her head. "You could have your fangs surgically removed and regular teeth implanted instead, but you need them to feed. So unless you're willing to eat an animal's flesh instead of drinking its blood, or if you don't mind drinking it from a cup, you shouldn't get rid of your fangs. You could wear contact lenses, though. Do your eyes glow when they turn red?"

Aliya nodded.

"Then contact lenses aren't going to help, but sunglasses should do the job. And if anyone asks why you're wearing them when it's dark, you can say that you have some rare eye disorder that makes them sensitive to even the dimmest of lights."

Alena didn't think that would do the trick. Aliya could hide the fangs, and she could hide her eyes, but she was going to attract attention because of her height, and once people took a second look, they would notice the other subtle differences that marked her as not human.

"We should get back." Alena rose to her feet. "Are you sure that you prefer to sleep on Jacki and Kalugal's couch? Here you can have a comfortable bed."

"I'm sure." Aliya stood up and walked up to Oridu. "Thank you for showing me your changing features." She patted his shoulder as if he were human.

Smiling, he inclined his head. "You are most welcome, mistress."

"Thank you too." She offered her hand to Ovidu.

"It was my pleasure, mistress." He shook her hand.

"Well, goodnight." Aliya opened the door and walked out to the hallway.

When they reached the stairs, she let out a breath. "At first, I thought that the Odus were creepy, but I like them now. They seem eager to please."

"They are amusing," Welgost said from behind them.

"You need to remember that those are not real emotions," Alena said. "They are programmed to act that way. But I have to admit that I also sometimes forget that they are not real. In fact, I'm very attached to Ovidu. He has been my nanny, my bodyguard, and my butler since the day I was born. I can't imagine life without him."

Aliya sighed. "I wish I had an Odu. Life wouldn't be so lonely if I had a robot who could talk back to me. I wouldn't have even minded that he was a machine and that his emotions were fake."

Wrapping her arm around Aliya's slim waist, Carol leaned her head against the girl's bicep. "Come to the village, Aliya. You'll never be lonely again. You might even find a nice immortal male to love who will love you back."

Aliya stopped mid stairs. "What about Vrog and Emmett? Do they have immortal mates?"

"Vrog doesn't," Alena said. "And from what I hear, he's a decent male. His son, the one who dresses like a Goth, is one of the nicest people I know, and he didn't inherit all that goodness just from his mother. Stella is a good person, but she gets moody, and when she does, she's not very pleasant."

Aliya stopped again. "How come Vrog is not mated to the mother of his son? I thought that your kind had exclusive relationships with just one person."

"We do, but Stella and Vrog are not each other's fated mates. Vlad was the result of a hookup, and Stella found her match twenty-one years after her son was born."

"So she's mated," Aliya said.

Carol chuckled. "Yes, Vrog is up for grabs. Are you interested?"

A blush colored the girl's hollow cheeks. "I don't know. I look like a Kra-ell female, and I'm as strong as one, but I don't want to live like they do."

"And how's that?" Alena asked.

"Similar to how the Mosuo live, but without the love. The Mosuo are human and they are capable of feeling love. So even though they practice what they call walking marriages, and the men don't move in with their lovers, most stay loyal to one partner throughout their lives, and they love their mates. I don't think Jade and the other purebled females were capable of love, not for the males in their harem and maybe not even for their children."

Alena shook her head. "I'm sure that the Kra-ell love their children. It's just that their culture reveres strength, and to show affection is considered a weakness. The Kra-ell can't be too different from humans and from the gods or they wouldn't be able to produce offspring with one another. Loving our children is hardwired into our genes. It takes a long time for a human or humanoid child to become independent, and without the feelings of love, the parents wouldn't commit the energy and resources needed to raise their children."

"It's necessary for the propagation of the species," Carol added. "Love is the greatest motivator and the strongest chain. We live for those we love."

"So who do I live for?" Aliya asked.

Carol smiled. "For those you are going to love in the future."

Alena thought of Aliya's restraint, of her preferring to go hungry and cold rather than using her powers to take what she needed from others. "Even though you had to leave, you still loved the people you grew up with. If you didn't, you wouldn't have hesitated to enslave them to your will."

Aliya shook her head. "I don't love them. I just follow the Mother's way."

Alena nodded. "Maybe love is too strong of a word. But you care about them. If they were attacked or if some natural disaster struck and you could've helped, I know that you would have done so even if it wasn't the Mother's way. You care for these people."

"They were kind to my mother and me when we had no one else to turn to. It would be dishonorable of me not to repay them in their time of need, but that doesn't mean that I care about them."

Orion

~~~

Orion listened to his companions' discussion over Aliya's future but decided to stay out of it.

On the one hand, he agreed with Vrog that Aliya shouldn't be forced to do anything she didn't want to. But he also agreed with Kalugal that she didn't have enough information to make an informed decision.

Obviously, she would be better off in the village, but did they have the right to force it on her even if it was for her own good?

Not too long ago, he'd been in a similar situation. If the clan hadn't captured him and held him until he learned more about them, he would have bolted as well. The difference was that he'd had Geraldine and Cassandra to vouch for the clan, and their experience and successful assimilation had helped shape his opinion and attitude toward these immortals.

There was one more difference, though.

He was the descendant of gods, same as them, while Aliya was the descendant of the Kra-ell. Did it matter that they weren't exactly the same?

It shouldn't.

The fact that the Kra-ell were long-lived and not immortal wasn't as important as both species needing to hide their existence from humans. However, there was a hitch in his idyllic vision of peaceful coexistence. Hybrid Kra-ell males could have immortal children with clan females, but hybrid Kra-ell females could not have long-lived children with clan males.

Could two hybrid Kra-ell have a long-lived child?

"How long are you going to stay at the lake?" Vrog asked.

"The plan was to stay two weeks, but I don't think we will have enough to do for that long. We might shorten the trip to a total of one week." When Lokan shook his head, Kalugal continued, "My brother seems to want to stay longer, so we might do so as well." He turned to Jacki. "What say you, my love?"

"I'm not ready to go home yet."

"You heard the boss. We are not going back yet."

"Good." Vrog sounded relieved. "That means that Mey can spend a few more days listening to echoes, and once she's done, we will join you there. I really think that you need me there to convince Aliya she has nothing to fear from you or anyone in the village."

Orion nodded. "I agree with Vrog. If I hadn't had Geraldine and Cassandra to vouch for the clan, it would have been much more difficult for me to trust what Kian and Onegus were telling me."

"You still need to check with Kian," Jacki told Kalugal. "What if he doesn't want her there?"

Kalugal smirked. "I know my cousin. He's a big softie, and there is no way he would turn away a stray like her."

As the door opened and Alena walked in with Aliya and Carol, they all fell silent.

Except for Vrog. "Hello? Where did everybody go?"

"We are still here," Jin said. "Say hello to Vrog, Aliya."

The girl swallowed. "Hello."

"*Ni hao*, Aliya. I'm so glad that you survived the attack and weren't taken, and I'm going to join you at the lake in a few days. I would have come right away, but there are some things we need to finish over here before we can leave."

"Who are we?" Aliya seemed to get over her initial shock of hearing that Vrog was on the line.

Orion wondered why they hadn't done a video call. Vrog and Aliya were no doubt curious about each other.

"Mey, who is Jin's sister, has a special talent that she utilizes here in the school, and she's the reason I can't leave immediately. Her mate Yamanu and two Guardians are here to keep her safe, and we also have the pilot who flew us over."

"What's her talent? And why are you in a school?"

"I'll tell you later," Arwel said. "If you want to continue your conversation with Vrog in private, you can take my phone to the bedroom."

She shook her head. "We can talk when he gets here."

Orion had a feeling that she didn't want to talk to Vrog just yet. Maybe she needed time to prepare.

"Before we hang up, I just want to ask you one question, if I may."

Aliya frowned at the phone. "What's your question?"

"What is your Kra-ell name?"

"Kajey."

"That's what I thought. I remembered that the compound had two hybrid girls that matched your age more or less, but neither was named Aliya."

"I prefer Aliya. That's the name my mother gave me."

"Of course. I will not mention your Kra-ell name again."

She shrugged. "You can mention it all you want, just don't call me Kajey because I probably won't respond."

"Your English is very good. Where did you learn to speak it?"

Aliya shifted her weight to her other leg and eyed the half-eaten platter of desserts. "Can we talk about it when you get here?"

"Of course. Goodnight, Aliya."

"Goodnight, Vrog."

When Arwel terminated the call, Aliya let out a breath. "Vrog and I are both hybrid Kra-ell, but that doesn't mean that we have to be friends." She walked over to the table and sat on Jacki's other side. "I don't know him."

Kalugal pushed the platter toward her. "You don't know him yet, but you will in a few days. He's a good guy, and I have a feeling that you're going to like him. But if you don't, that's not a big deal. I'm sure we can find you another male to entertain yourself with."

"I don't need you to find anyone for me. I can do that myself."

"Naturally." He gave her a smile. "I meant we as in the entire clan. You can choose any of the unattached males."

Phinas, who hadn't said a word during the entire talk with Vrog, straightened in his chair and grinned at Aliya, but she pretended not to notice.

"How did it go with the Odus?" Jin asked.

"I had so much fun." Aliya's smile was genuine. "They showed me how they morph their faces and their bodies from male to female and back."

"So are you going to spend the night with them?" Jacki asked hesitantly.

"No. I decided to accept the offer to sleep on your couch. I want to watch television, but I don't want to disturb your sleep. Alena said that if the noise bothers you, she can lend me a pair of headphones."

"I'll give you a pair." Jacki turned to her mate. "What about our plans for tomorrow? Can we go shopping?"

He let out a dramatic sigh. "How can I refuse you anything? We are all going to Lijiang tomorrow." He smiled at Aliya. "My wife and the other ladies are adamant about taking you shopping. I know that you are proud and that you like to work for the things you have, so I'm going to offer you a deal."

She narrowed her eyes at him. "What kind of a deal?"

"I will consider whatever you buy tomorrow as compensation for your lost home. I feel responsible, and I want to make it up to you, so go wild and buy an entire store if you want. After that, I'll pay you for guiding us through the tunnels and helping us find clues about the ancient Kra-ell that might have used the outpost and the tunnel system underneath it. You can spend that money any way you like."

"What if I want to spend it on a train ticket to Beijing? Are you going to let me?"

Kalugal shook his head. "If after you visit the village, you decide that you don't want to live there, I will buy you a plane ticket to wherever you want to go. But before I do that, I will have to compel you to forget ever meeting us."

She cast a sidelong glance at Alena. "Can I trust his promise?"

Alena nodded. "You have my word that what Kalugal offered you will be done."

Onegus

negus stood on the path in front of their house and watched Cassandra walk down the steps of their front porch, looking splendid in a loose yellow silk blouse, tailored black slacks, and a pair of low-heeled black pumps.

The gold necklace he'd gotten her for this month's anniversary was draped around her long neck, and the bracelets he'd gotten her for the previous one dangled around her slender wrist. He was already planning next month's gift, another gold chain that was slightly longer and had more delicate links. The two necklaces would look great together.

"What are you smiling about?" She threaded her arm through his.

"I love seeing you wearing the jewelry I get you."

She lifted her other arm and jingled the five delicate gold bracelets. "You have impeccable taste."

"Obviously." He leaned to kiss the corner of her mouth. "I mated you."

"That's right." She grinned.

He loved that Cassandra wasn't modest and knew her own worth. Heck, he loved everything about her.

"I hope Vivian didn't prepare dinner," Cassandra said as they neared Magnus and Vivian's home. "I'll feel really awkward if she did. We didn't bring anything."

"I'm sure Magnus would have told me if she did. They know the reason for our visit is not social."

When Onegus had told Magnus that they might need Parker to use his talent for a private matter, he'd had no problem with that, but he'd said that Vivian had to approve, and that's why they were heading to their house. Vivian wanted to know why they needed Parker and what would be required of him.

As they walked up to the door and Onegus knocked, Parker opened the way. "Hi."

"Hello." Cassandra offered him her hand. "I hear great things about you, young man."

"Thank you." He shook it. "So, what's the mission?"

Onegus chuckled. "Patience, Parker. We need to discuss it with your mother first."

"Can I be there? Because Magnus didn't know whether I should stick around or not."

That was a good question.

Explaining to Vivian why Darlene should leave Leo was a somewhat touchy subject, but nothing a boy Parker's age would be surprised by. Kids these days knew a lot more than they had even a few decades ago, and they were not naive.

"It's up to your mother."

"Don't keep them at the door, Parker." Vivian walked over and smiled apologetically. "Please, come in. I have tea and coffee ready, and Ella baked muffins."

"Is she here?" Cassandra asked.

"She just dropped them off. On Sundays, Ella helps Julian in the halfway house. She organizes social activities for the girls." Vivian motioned for them to take a seat on the couch. "Usually, Yamanu is there on Sundays as well, but he's in China with Mey, and the girls are going to be upset about missing out on their karaoke night again. It's just not the same without him."

Cassandra arched a brow. "I didn't know Yamanu could sing."

"He sings beautifully," Magnus said.

"Can I pour you some coffee?" Vivian lifted the carafe.

"Thank you." Cassandra held up her cup. "I assume that you know why we are here."

Onegus stifled a chuckle. If he were there alone, he would have probably kept the chitchat going for another half an hour or so before getting to the reason for the visit, but his mate didn't like to beat around the bush.

"Onegus said that you need Parker to compel your sister. I need to know more about your plans and what exactly Parker's job will be before I allow him to go on his first mission." Vivian cast her son a smile. "He's so excited, and I hope I won't have to say no."

"I see no reason why you would." Cassandra put the cup down. "We told Darlene about her potential to become immortal, but she couldn't make up her mind on the spot and asked for more time. Naturally, we couldn't let her walk away with the knowledge, and we had to thrall her to forget everything we told her about immortals and gods, etc. The problem is that she can't give it more thought if she doesn't remember anything. So before thralling her, we explained why we needed to do that, and that the next time we would bring a compeller along, so when we release her memories, she would have time to decide what she wanted to do but wouldn't be able to reveal our secrets. Darlene agreed, but since all the adult compellers are currently absent, we need Parker."

"What's the rush?" Vivian asked. "The adult compellers are on other missions at the moment, but they are coming back soon, and if you need it done even sooner for some reason, why not ask one of them to compel your sister through a video call? If Parker can do that, I'm sure the more experienced compellers can do it remotely as well."

Cassandra nodded. "I can explain. My sister is forty-nine years old, which would make her the oldest Dormant to attempt transition. I want her to do it while Annani is in the village and can give her a blessing. The problem is that Darlene needs to leave her worthless husband and then find a nice immortal male to induce her. Those things take time, and I'm afraid that the Clan Mother will leave before those objectives are achieved."

"I understand." Vivian lifted a plate of muffins and offered it to Onegus and Cassandra. "But what about asking one of the adults to do it over the phone?"

"Timing," Onegus said. "This is a private matter, and I can't demand Kalugal or Lokan get up in the middle of the night to compel Cassandra's sister. Eleanor is extremely busy trying to achieve several objectives in West Virginia, and I don't want to bother her with it either. Besides, I think it's a good opportunity for Parker to flex his compulsion muscles on a mission that is not critical." He smiled at the kid. "This mission is very important to my family, and I wouldn't have asked for your help if I didn't think you were up to it."

"I can do that easily, I think." Parker grimaced. "Other than Lisa, I don't have anyone to practice on, so I don't have many opportunities to test my skills."

"Will Parker need to be there when you talk to Darlene?" Vivian asked. "Or can it be done over a video call?"

"I want to be there," Parker said. "I want to test my ability on Cassandra's sister before they release her memories. If I can't compel her for some reason, they would have to thrall her to forget again, and that's not good for her." He rubbed his hands over his knees. "I also want to see and feel how she reacts. How am I going to get better if I don't get to practice on people? And since

I'm not allowed to compel anyone without their permission, and I can only compel humans, my only test subject is Lisa, and by now, I can't tell if I'm really compelling her or if it's a placebo effect."

Poor Lisa.

Perhaps they needed to relax the rules a little so Parker could practice. Onegus needed to come up with a non-harmful and consensual way for the kid to practice on humans. Perhaps Amanda could take Parker to her lab and have him test his ability on student volunteers? She could say that he was a natural hypnotist.

Except, Amanda was on maternity leave because she was nearing her due date and could barely move.

Vivian let out a breath. "Okay. I agree, but it has to be after school hours or on the weekend, and I want all of you to be mindful of Parker's age when you discuss with Darlene whatever you need to discuss with her."

"Of course." Cassandra gave her a thankful smile. "We are going to treat Parker to a nice lunch or dinner, and we are going to pay him for his services."

Magnus shook his head. "No need to pay him. He wants to do it."

Parker cast his father an incredulous look. "So what? If they offer to pay me, I won't say no. You enjoy being a Guardian. Does that mean you should work for free?"

Magnus chuckled. "You've got a point. How much are you going to charge for your compulsion services?"

Parker's bravado was replaced with awkward indecision. "Whatever they are offering."

"Would a hundred bucks do?" Onegus pulled out his wallet.

Parker's eyes sparkled. "Yes, sir."

Lisa

er phone clutched in her hand and her foot tapping on the carpet, Lisa sat on the living room couch and waited to hear from Parker whether his mother had agreed to let him go on his first mission as a compeller. She was so excited for him. He'd been practicing on her for months, but both of them had started to doubt that it still worked.

She was so used to his little tests that she automatically did what he commanded whether he imbued his voice with compulsion or not.

Parker needed other test subjects, people who didn't know what he was doing. It didn't need to be anything major, and it could be supervised by Magnus to ensure that Parker wasn't abusing his ability, but unless they let him practice, how was he going to get good at it?

In the kitchen, her mother was whistling to the tune of the music playing on her earphones and swaying her hips to the beat. It was good to see her so happy, probably happier than Lisa had ever seen her, and she wanted to be happy for her, but instead she was consumed by worry, guilt, and dread.

Perhaps she shouldn't have encouraged her mother to attempt transition?

Lisa had practically arranged for Ronja and Merlin to have the house all to themselves so they would finally take the next step and stop torturing themselves, pretending to be just friends.

Given her mother's satisfied smile as of late, things were going well with Merlin, and it wasn't only about inducing Ronja's transition. They were bonding, and it was great, provided that the transition went well, and her mother survived it.

Annani was in the village, which was why Lisa had given her mother and Merlin the final push to go for it. As long as the goddess was nearby, Ronja's odds of successful transition were much better, and Annani was only going to stay until Amanda delivered her baby, or perhaps a week or two after.

But what if her mother didn't make it even with the goddess's help?

Lisa would never forgive herself.

"Dinner is almost ready." Ronja walked into the living room, her headphones draped around her neck like a necklace. "Do you want to invite Parker to join us?"

"I'm waiting for a call from him." Lisa put her phone on the couch beside her. "Onegus and Cassandra went over to his house to discuss him using his compulsion ability on Cassandra's sister. Vivian is not too happy about it, but Parker really wants to do it. He's had no one to practice on except for me, and by now, I can't tell if his compulsion is really working on me or if it's a placebo effect."

"He can practice on me." Her mother smiled. "I offered, and I'm still human."

The vise on Lisa's heart tightened. "Not for long." Her chin wobbled.

"Oh, sweetie." Her mother sat down beside her and wrapped an arm around her shoulders. "Don't worry. Everything is going to be okay, and we are going to spend eternity together."

The tears she'd been holding back overflowed their container and started spilling from the corners of her eyes. "I can't help it, and I feel so guilty for pushing you to do it."

"You didn't push me, sweetie." Ronja tightened her arm around her and kissed her temple. "And Merlin didn't push me either. It was entirely my decision, and I don't regret it. Fear shouldn't stop us from going after what we want."

Chuckling, Lisa wiped her eyes with her fingers. "Does that mean I can go bungee jumping with Parker?"

"Not going to happen, my dear. Not even after you turn immortal. Even immortals can't survive getting their bodies smashed to pieces."

Lisa laughed. "Just checking. What about parachuting? With an instructor?"

"I might allow it after I check the instructor's credentials. I'm not encouraging you to be fearless. A healthy dose of fear will keep you from taking reckless risks, like bungee jumping. But if you are really passionate about it and want to try it, make sure you find the best in the field to instruct you and help you do it safely."

"Is that why you chose a doctor as your inducer?" Lisa teased.

Her mother smiled indulgently. "I chose Merlin because he's everything I ever wanted in a life partner. He's brilliant, kind, funny, and he needs me."

He did. Without Ronja, Merlin was hopelessly disorganized, which affected more than just the state of his house. His research could move on much faster if he didn't keep misplacing notes or forgetting to buy ingredients or starting a new experiment and forgetting about the five already in progress.

"And he's also a hunk." Lisa winked.

"That too." Ronja frowned and looked down at her lap. "Your phone is vibrating under my bottom." She pulled it out and handed it to Lisa.

"It's Parker." She read the message. "He's coming over with Scarlet. Is it okay if he comes in with her?"

Her mother loved dogs, but Scarlet shed hair all over.

"Sure." She rose to her feet. "You're in charge of vacuuming after her."

"I'm always in charge of vacuuming." Lisa pushed to her feet and walked to open the door. "How did it go?"

Grinning, Parker walked up the stairs to the front porch. "I got my first paid mission."

"Congratulations. But why would they pay you for it?" Lisa thwarted Scarlet's attempts to lick her face and motioned for him to bring the dog inside. "None of the other compellers get paid for their services."

Parker shrugged. "They offered, and I never say no to money."

"Are you excited?"

He nodded. "I'm also a little scared. What if it doesn't work? I've only had you to practice on."

Her mother walked over to Parker and pulled him in for a hug. "Congratulations on your first official compulsion job."

"Thank you."

"You can practice on me anytime you want," she offered.

"Thank you for that too. I'm going to take you up on your offer. Can I practice on you today? Cassandra said that she would try to arrange a lunch meeting with Darlene next weekend. But if Darlene's husband leaves on one of his business trips, she might schedule the meeting for a weekday, and it might even be tomorrow."

Alena

It had been a long day, and Alena was tired, but the evening dragged on. Kalugal kept ordering more desserts for Aliya, who seemed to have a bottomless pit for a stomach. Carol was on a roll, telling them anecdotes from her new life in China and her old one in the village when she'd still worked in the café and collected all the gossip. Phinas kept flirting with Aliya, who could no longer pretend that she didn't notice but had no idea how to respond.

Alena was starting to think that the girl had never experienced male attention before, which suggested that she was still a virgin. For a hybrid Kra-ell female, that was probably a source of embarrassment.

As soon as there was a lull in the conversation, Alena asked, "When are we leaving for our shopping trip tomorrow morning?"

"Not too early," Jacki said. "I'm so tired that I could sleep for twelve hours straight."

"The city is nearly two hours away," Jin reminded her. "We can't start our day too late, or we will not have enough time for all the shopping we need to do. I suggest that we meet for breakfast in the hotel lobby at eight and be on our way by nine."

"I'll order breakfast to the suite," Kalugal said. "Aliya will be more comfortable here."

Jacki waved a hand in dismissal. "You can shroud her."

"What's shrouding?" Aliya asked.

"I can make the humans see whatever I want them to see, or I can just make them not notice you."

Aliya's eyes widened. "Can you teach me to do that?"

"I don't think it's something that can be taught. I was born with the ability."

"If she can thrall, she can shroud," Jin said. "She won't be able to do it as well as you do, but if she can shroud herself even partially, it would be a game-changer for her."

"Can you thrall?" Alena asked Jin.

"I'm practicing, but I'm not very good. It's like learning a new language as an adult compared to learning it as a child. It's much more difficult, takes longer, and is never as good."

Alena didn't want to point out that most immortals never lost that ability and could learn new languages with a child's ease. Jin already felt different enough with her fangs and venom glands. She didn't need another reminder that she wasn't like other immortals.

"I'm curious to see the selection in Chinese clothing stores," Alena said to change the subject. "I wonder if they export all the good stuff they make or leave some for their own market."

"The Chinese fashionistas love European labels," Carol said. "They appreciate quality and are willing to pay for it. Things have been changing over the last decade or so, though, and there are several domestic luxury brands that have become nearly as coveted as the European ones and are in high demand." She regarded Aliya with a critical eye. "I think that for you we should look for American brands. Typically, they design clothing for taller women than the Europeans and the Chinese brands do. On average, the Chinese ladies are more like me than like you and Jin."

"What about midrange market?" Jin asked. "Can we find the local equivalent of Zara or H&M? I think Aliya would love their designs. They are trendy and inexpensive. Both Mey and I found stuff in those stores that fit us."

"You can search online. Can you read Chinese?"

"Nope. I can speak a little bit, and I understand simple language if spoken slowly. What about you? Did you manage to learn it during the time you were here?"

Carol hadn't been in China all that long, but like most immortals, she learned languages fast.

"I understand almost everything, and I can speak it pretty well, but learning to read and write is going slower."

Alena wondered if Carol was being truthful or if she was exaggerating her difficulties to help Jin save face.

Stifling a yawn, Carol patted Lokan's arm. "If we want to start bright and early tomorrow morning, we'd better go to sleep soon. I need a good rest after today's adventures." She pushed to her feet.

"I'm tired as well," Alena admitted.

It had been such an incredibly long day that the trip into the tunnels seemed like something that had happened days ago, not just a few hours.

Their immortal bodies could tolerate a lot of stress, physical and emotional, but even they needed time to recuperate.

Orion got up and offered Alena a hand. "Big thanks to Jacki and Kalugal for hosting us, and I wish you all goodnight."

"I should get a pair of pajamas for Aliya." Jin pushed to her feet.

"Thank you for your generosity." Aliya bowed her head. "Since Kalugal said I can buy whatever I want tomorrow as compensation for losing my home, I will purchase replacements for all the items you gave me."

Jin chuckled. "Kalugal already promised to reimburse me, so it's all good, Aliya. Don't worry about it. We are going to have oodles of fun tomorrow and spend obscene amounts of Kalugal's money."

As Aliya cast Kalugal a worried glance, he smiled at her. "Don't worry. My wife and I are financially blessed, and we can afford whatever you and Jin spend, and I mean whatever. Don't feel shy about spending a fortune. The caveat is that you will have to do it all tomorrow. The deal is good for only one day."

"There is really no limit? What if I spend a million yuan?"

"No problem. In fact, I dare you to spend a million yuan in one day without donating any portion of it or buying things for the Mosuo village. Everything you get has to be just for you."

"That's impossible," Aliya murmured.

Jacki snorted. "It's easier than you think. Just go into the first jewelry store you see and buy yourself a diamond necklace. You can use up the budget in one swoop."

"That's not fair." Kalugal pretended to be angry at his wife. "She was supposed to figure it out on her own."

Aliya shook her head. "I'm not going to buy diamonds or anything stupid like that. I'm going to buy an apartment. You took away my home, so it's only fair that you buy me a new one."

"Oh, boy." Kalugal sighed dramatically. "You're way smarter than I gave you credit for."

Orion

"**A**re you tired?" Orion asked Alena as they left Jacki and Kalugal's suite.

Alena was supposed to have one of the Odus escort them back, but she hadn't called them, and he hadn't reminded her. If there was any danger lurking in the corridors of the luxury hotel, he was more than capable of protecting Alena. He could freeze anyone with a verbal command.

"I am a little tired. Why? What do you have in mind?"

"I wondered if you were up for a walk, but apparently, you're not."

She leaned her head on his shoulder. "A walk along the lakeshore in the moonlight sounds lovely."

"Are you sure? We can go on a walk tomorrow."

"I'm sure. I just need to grab my coat from our room. This sweater is not enough for how cold it is outside."

"I'll get the puffer jacket you got me as well." He kissed the top of her head. "Did I thank you already for making sure I don't freeze out here?"

She'd gotten him everything he needed for the trip and had even packed his suitcase. So far, every item he'd tried fit perfectly and was of the highest quality.

"Yes, you did. It's a shame that jacket is ruined, though. It was such a nice one."

"It's not ruined. I'm sure I can have the tears mended."

She canted her head. "Don't be silly. No one mends clothes these days. We live in the disposable era. Disposable dishes, disposable clothing, and even disposable lovers."

"Ain't that the truth." He opened the door to their hotel room. "As immortals, we had no choice but to engage in fleeting encounters, but it never felt right. We are meant to be monogamous, to cleave to one person for the rest of our lives."

"I don't know about that." Alena reached into the closet for her coat. "According to my mother, the gods were very promiscuous, and having multiple partners was the norm rather than the exception."

He shrugged on his torn jacket. "Really? From what I've seen so far, everyone who's mated is devoted to his or her partner. Did I miss something?"

"You didn't." Alena followed him out the door. "We have the Fates and the addiction to thank for that. True-love mates can't stray."

Addiction? He must have misunderstood, but as he was about to ask what Alena had meant, the door to the Odus' room opened and Ovidu stepped out.

"Should I escort you and Master Orion, mistress?"

She cast Orion an apologetic glance. "Kian would have a meltdown if I don't take one of them along."

"I don't mind. As long as he keeps his distance, he can trail behind us."

When Alena repeated the instructions, Ovidu bowed. "I shall do as Mistress pleases."

When they were outside, Orion asked, "What did you mean by addiction?"

"Didn't I tell you about that?"

"I would have remembered if you did. What is it about?"

"When an immortal couple is exclusive, the female becomes addicted to the male's venom, and her scent changes in a way that keeps him addicted to her and repulses other immortal males. The same was true for the gods, which was why they mixed it up on purpose. Those who weren't true-love mates didn't want to be tied to their partners, and the way to avoid it was to have many different ones."

He chuckled. "So the mythology got that right as well."

"It did."

"Are we addicted to each other?" He pushed the lobby door open.

"I don't know. Would it bother you if we were?"

"No." Orion wrapped his arm around Alena's shoulders. "There are worse fates than being addicted to the woman I love."

"Same here. I feel so incredibly blessed to have found you, and I don't mind one bit being addicted to you."

"Do you want to have a child with me?" he blurted out.

She lifted a pair of wistful eyes to him. "More than anything, but it's up to the Fates."

"What about the fertility doctor? Can he help us conceive?"

"We can try, that's for sure. But isn't it too early to be talking about children? How long have we known each other?"

"Nine days, eternity, who cares? I know you, and you know me, and we both know that we want to spend the rest of our immortal lives together. I don't know if it happens so quickly for other immortal couples, and I don't really care. I know that we were always meant to be together."

Alena's smile was radiant as she stopped and turned to face him. "I love you." She wound her arms around his neck. "It never gets old to say that."

"You are my world." He kissed her softly. "Any more doubts?"

"None. I was just making sure that you didn't have any." Her expression turned serious. "I've never been in love before, but you have. Are you over the guilt of allowing yourself to love again?"

"I am. Miriam never wanted me to stay alone, and she would have liked you."

"There might be a way to find out." Alena started walking again.

"Find out what?"

"Whether Miriam approves."

Orion's steps faltered. "How?"

"You've met Nathalie, Syssi's brother's wife. Her talent is talking to ghosts. If Miriam wants to send you a message, she could use Nathalie as a conduit."

Orion's throat dried out in an instant. "You mean like a séance?"

He was embarrassed to admit it, but he'd sought psychics' help to communicate with Miriam's spirit. After she'd died, he'd been desperate to get proof that her spirit lived on, that it wasn't the end, and that she was okay in whatever realm the spirits lived in.

But none of them could tell him the things only Miriam would know, and he'd given up hope. Deep down, he still believed that the end of physical life wasn't the real end, but without proof, he couldn't be sure.

"Nathalie doesn't do séances, and she doesn't summon spirits. In fact, she does her best to shield her mind against them. Only the most tenacious of ghosts get past her blockades, but if Miriam cared about you as much as you cared about her, she would want to communicate a message to you and tell you to live your life."

Alena

rion looked pained. "Are you sure Nathalie actually speaks to spirits?"

"She does, and she's proven it conclusively." Alena sighed. "I know how you feel. On the one hand, it's such a tremendous relief to know that your loved ones are not forever lost, and that there is more to existence than this physical realm. But on the other hand, you start to wonder why those you lost and miss didn't find a way to tell you that they were okay, that they've gone on in another form. When my brother Lilen was killed, both my mother and I were devastated. Kian was as well, but he kept it bottled inside. I prayed for a sign, a dream, anything that his spirit was still with us in some form, but he didn't come. Not for me, and not for my mother."

"How do you reconcile it? Why do some get visited by their loved ones? Are they more sensitive? More open?"

After Nathalie had given Amanda the message from Mark, Alena had spent many hours trying to understand that, hating herself for being angry at Lilen for not giving her a sign. Eventually, she'd resigned herself to accept that Lilen had moved on quickly because he hadn't left behind any major issues that needed to be resolved.

"It's not easy to gain access to a channel, which is how Nathalie describes what she is. The spirit that took residence in her mind for many years told her that she's like a beacon to those who need to communicate with the living. They were clamoring for access to her, driving her nuts until that one spirit took control and blocked the others. Later, when she learned to do it herself, he moved on. But Nathalie is not our only proof. David, Sari's mate, saw his own previous incarnation during his transition, and his deceased twin brother visited him. What he learned during that visit he couldn't have learned in any other way, and that is another proof of the soul's continuation."

As Orion's natural curiosity took over, his pinched expression relaxed a little. "What did David learn?"

The more she told him, the more at ease he became. "So if Miriam is reincarnated, she is not able to communicate with me. She can only do that between reincarnations."

"David thinks that the soul might remember its prior lives in dreams, so perhaps it can also find a way to communicate with loved ones while dreaming during those other lives, but we have no proof of that."

"I hope Miriam is happy." The corners of Orion's lips lifted in a small smile. "And I hope that she has many children during her subsequent reincarnations. Now that

I know it was probably my fault that she never conceived, I feel so guilty. She loved children."

Alena's heart ached for him, and it ached for Miriam too.

"I had children but no mate to love, and Miriam had a mate but no children." Alena threaded her arm through Orion's and leaned her head on his shoulder. "According to David, reincarnations often happen within the same family, which is a little creepy in my opinion. Imagine if we had a daughter who is Miriam's reincarnation. If you knew that for sure, how would it make you feel?"

"Weird," he admitted. "Less so if we have a son. I assume that souls are genderless. Am I right?"

"David and his brother kept reincarnating as males because of what they needed to improve, which were their overly masculine traits. They were too aggressive, too competitive, and not empathetic enough to others. David seems to have fixed all those character flaws, but since he turned immortal, he's done with the cycles."

For a long moment, they walked in silence, with Orion once again frowning. "Isn't aggression a hormonal thing? I'm not a scientist, but I keep reading that nature is as important as nurture, if not more so. If David and his brother were aggressive males, they might have suffered from excessive testosterone, and behavior modification might not have been possible."

Alena was glad of the change of subject. Talking about Miriam had been upsetting to Orion, and she shouldn't have started it. It was his prerogative to talk about his first love, and when he did, Alena would listen, but she wouldn't bring it up again.

"Testosterone is not inherently bad, and neither are aggression and competitiveness if they are harnessed and used for good. Regrettably, humanoid societies cannot survive if all of their members are gentle poets. Testosterone made the men of David's family strong fighters and defenders of their clan. The undesirable side effect was that it also made them jerks and shortened their lifespans. They needed to learn to harness it and not let it ruin their lives or the lives of those they loved. Another good example is immortal males, who are even more aggressive by nature than humans. The males of our clan who choose a career as Guardians use their aggressiveness to protect and fight for those who have no one else to fight for them. The Doomers, who are genetically the same, use their abilities to conquer and subdue. Or used to. Now they operate drug and prostitution rings while their leader raises the next generation of smart warriors."

Orion shook his head. "How incredible is it that both his sons joined your clan? I guess Lokan and Kalugal are proof that neither nature nor nurture can stand in the way of strong will and a sharp mind. They seem like good men."

Lokan hadn't officially crossed over yet, but he was mated to Carol, which made him a clan member nonetheless.

"Both Lokan and Kalugal have their own agendas, and I don't know if they are purely good." She smiled. "They have a mix of genes, some good, and some not so much. It might be argued that they inherited some of Areana's goodness, and that her genes softened their father's. Navuh is an incredibly powerful and smart immortal, and his sons inherited that from him. His line also suffers from insanity, and that might be in their genes as well."

Orion snorted. "So we are back to nature trumping nurture and free will?"

Alena cast him an amused sidelong glance. "I have lived for over two thousand years, and I've had a lot of time to observe and learn, and the only answer I have is that it's different for each individual. For some, nature is the strongest factor shaping their characters, for others, it is nurture, and for a select few, it's their powerful will."

Aliya

Aliya lay on the couch in the hotel suite's living room with the television on, the lights off, and a set of earphones hugging her ears. She luxuriated in the softness of the pajamas Jin had brought for her, the pillows and blankets the hotel's housekeeping had sent up, and the tray of sweets Kalugal had ordered for her.

Perhaps being their prisoner wasn't so bad.

She was clean, her belly was full, and she was more comfortable than she'd ever been. Was freedom worth giving up all of that?

Hell, no.

If the Kra-ell religion included the concept of a devil, she would have sold her soul to him to keep living like that.

But the Mother didn't need a devil to counterbalance her. She wasn't a benevolent entity who needed a bad guy to do her dirty work. Like nature itself, the Mother was both creator and destroyer, gracious and terrible, nurturing and punishing.

The Kra-ell who displeased her suffered the consequences in this life and in future reincarnations.

Aliya wished she knew more about the Mother's teachings. In difficult times, talking to the goddess and asking her for help had been comforting, but she was well aware that her knowledge was lacking.

What Aliya had learned about the Kra-ell religion was what she'd overheard Jade preach. As the leader of their community, Jade was the Mother's physical representation and was to be revered and honored almost to the same degree as the goddess.

Now that Aliya was older and had more experience, she suspected that not everything Jade had said was true.

When Jade told the males that those who pleased the Mother greatly were rewarded in the next life with a female of their own, one that they wouldn't have to share with others, it might have been a lie to make them obedient. The harder they worked, the more they sacrificed, the more merit points they earned for the next life.

Jade had told them that they should be grateful for the opportunity to serve her, and that the harsh treatment they'd been getting was for their own good. After all, she was doing them a favor, so they could earn the ultimate reward in the next life.

Had it all been a lie?

Did those who were grateful for the Mother's bounty, those who served her with courage and honor, truly earn a reward?

Aliya had followed what she knew of the Mother's teachings to the best of her abilities. Was her capture by these people a reward?

Was Vrog?

Except, the rewards were supposed to be reaped in the next life, not this one.

What would the Mother want her to do?

Stay, or run?

Aliya probably couldn't run even if she wanted to. Kalugal had reinforced his compulsion before retiring for the night. He commanded her not to leave the suite, specifically telling her not to open the front door or the doors leading to the balcony either.

She could still use the small window in the bathroom and jump down the three stories. The jump wouldn't kill her, but she might break a leg or an arm, and that would take much longer to heal than a flesh wound.

Should she try the suite's front door anyway? Maybe compulsion faded over time? Many hours had passed since Kalugal had commanded her to stay away from the doors. Perhaps she could will herself to refuse?

Taking the earphones off, Aliya listened to the sounds coming from Jacki and Kalugal's bedroom.

They were still awake. She heard them whisper but couldn't understand what they were saying. Whatever it was must have been funny because Jacki giggled, and then Kalugal whispered something, and Jacki moaned.

Grimacing, Aliya put the headphones back on.

After living in a Mosuo household, she was no stranger to the sounds of sex, but it was different hearing Jacki and Kalugal's sounds of passion.

They loved each other, and Aliya was jealous.

She wanted that for herself, and she hated being a thirty-year-old virgin. It was embarrassing even for a human, and tenfold more embarrassing for a Kra-ell.

Even though Vrog was a potential candidate for helping her get rid of her virginity, she would be too embarrassed to admit to him that she'd never had sex. He would think that there was something wrong with her, and he would be correct.

Perhaps she was better off choosing one of the immortals. Phinas was a decent fighter, good-looking, and he kept flirting with her. So far, she'd ignored his light-hearted teasing, mainly because she didn't know how to respond, but maybe tomorrow during their shopping spree, she would indicate her interest.

These immortals didn't live by Kra-ell rules, so she didn't need to be the one to issue an invitation. If she appeared interested, and the male was interested too, he would initiate. She wouldn't have to embarrass herself by having her invitation declined.

Ugh. It was better to stay celibate than deal with all that stupid relationship crap. The Kra-ell were smart to take that out of their culture and make it the males' duty to serve the females. It was an affront to the Goddess to refuse an invitation, and a great offense to the female for which she was entitled to demand retribution.

Not that it had ever happened in Jade's compound. All the males had been eager to please.

If Aliya were still living with her tribe, she would have lost her damn virginity the moment her female urges had started to emerge at fifteen.

Not daring to take the headphones off again, she threw the blanket aside, lowered her feet to the floor, and tiptoed to the front door. That was as far as she made it. She couldn't even reach for the handle. Her arm just refused to move.

More relieved than disappointed, Aliya tiptoed back to the couch and lay down.

Kian

As the phone ringing interrupted Kian's Sunday ritual of late breakfast and newspaper scan, he was tempted to let it go to voicemail, but naturally he didn't.

Everyone knew not to bother him on Sundays unless it was either an emergency or important news that couldn't wait. His bet was on one of the teams from China. It was after midnight over there, so it was probably Arwel reporting at the end of the day.

With a sigh, Kian lifted the device off its charging station, checked the caller ID, and accepted the call. "Hello, Arwel. Is everyone alive?"

"Funny you should ask. We ran into a bit of trouble earlier today. Everyone is okay, and no one got hurt, well other than Phinas and me, but we are fine now."

As Arwel continued his report, Kian was glad that he'd started with the preamble about everyone being safe.

After hearing that Alena had been trapped underground, Kian's temper had flared, his venom glands had swelled, and his fangs had punched out.

"Why the hell did she leave the Odus behind? They could have gotten you out right away."

Tomorrow, he would have words with his sister. The Odus were there to protect her, not to stay behind in the hotel.

"True, but Alena didn't want them anywhere near the water, and with three compellers and three warriors at her side, even I couldn't argue with that logic. Besides, if the Odus got us out, we might have never discovered the female." As Arwel continued telling him about the hybrid Kra-ell who'd been hiding in the tunnels under the ruins for the past fourteen years, Kian's anger subsided.

That was a major breakthrough in the investigation, much better than he'd ever hoped for.

"That's one hell of a discovery. You were supposed to find clues about the Kra-ell. Instead, you catch a female who survived the attack. Does she remember what happened?"

"Aliya was only eight years old, and she lived with her mother in the human quarters. She didn't see much, but she confirmed what Vrog had deduced and what Mey had seen and heard in the echoes. The compound was attacked, an unknown Kra-ell male thralled the humans to forget that they ever lived among aliens and told them to leave. Aliya was presumed human, and that's how she got away."

"How could they have thralled away years of memories? That's impossible."

"That occurred to me as well, but their thralling is different than ours. It's a combination of thralling and compulsion, and evidently, it's very effective on humans."

"It would seem so." Kian tucked the newspaper under his arm, took his coffee mug, and headed out to his backyard. "Where is the hybrid now?"

"She's sleeping on Kalugal's couch in his suite. He wanted to keep an eye on her."

"If he compelled her not to run, he could have gotten her a room of her own. I'm sure that his decision to make her sleep on his couch wasn't influenced by monetary concerns. He can afford to rent out the entire hotel."

"Aliya is strong-willed. I assumed that he was afraid of her being able to throw off his compulsion."

Kian chuckled. "I'm amazed at how strong she is. I knew that Vrog, Emmett, and even Vlad were very strong, but she's a female, and she fought off two well-trained warriors."

"Don't forget that we were trying not to hurt her, but I have to admit that I was surprised by her strength. She moved that boulder on her own, a rock that seven immortal males had barely managed to budge. She used a cleverly constructed pulley system, but still. She'd also built effective traps with the most basic materials she found. The girl is smart, resourceful, strong, and fast. She would make an excellent Guardian."

Kian put the newspaper down on the side table and sat on his favorite lounger. "Aren't you getting carried away?"

"I'm thinking long-term. Aliya has nowhere to go, and we can't just leave her here. Those tunnels were her home, and now they are compromised. We need to bring her back with us to the village, and after she proves herself in one way or another, we might allow her to join the training program. You allowed Eleanor to join, and she's much less trustworthy than Aliya, or at least that's my impression. I've never been too fond of Eleanor, but she grew on me."

"We know nothing about the girl. We knew a lot about Eleanor, and she has family in the village that even an opportunistic woman like her wants to protect. Aliya has no one."

"What we knew about Eleanor was nothing good. Aliya lives by a strict, self-imposed code of honor. She could've thralled the villagers to provide her with everything she needed, but she refused to resort to stealing and went hungry and cold instead. Can you imagine Eleanor doing that?"

Kian chuckled. "Eleanor wouldn't have hesitated to steal and coerce to get everything she needed, and she wouldn't have felt an ounce of remorse for taking from those who barely had enough to feed their families."

"Precisely. I think that bringing Aliya to the village is the right thing to do, but I need your consent."

"Does she want to come?"

"She doesn't know what she wants. Right now, she's scared of us and doesn't trust us, but hopefully that will change in the next few days."

"Would you vouch for her?"

"I would, and I'm saying that after knowing her only a few hours. The girl impressed me."

Arwel wasn't easily impressed, and he was an empath. If he felt so strongly about Aliya, Kian had no reason to doubt his judgment.

"You have my consent to bring her, but you'll be in charge of keeping an eye on her."

"I have no problem with that."

Mey

"Here we go again," Mey said as Vrog punched in the code and opened the door to the storage building. "Wish me luck." She tucked the yoga mat he'd brought for her under her arm. "And thank you again for the mat. It was very thoughtful of you."

"You're welcome, and good luck." Vrog gave her a tight smile. "I hope today you get your answers, so we can be done here."

"I hope so too." She waved goodbye to Yamanu, crossed the threshold, and closed the door behind her.

Ever since hearing the news about the female hybrid the other team had found at the ruins, Vrog had been in a bad mood. Usually the guy was polite and soft-spoken, but today he'd seemed irritated, which was completely understandable.

In his shoes, she would have been eager to leave as well. For all intents and purposes, Vrog and Aliya were each other's only option. If Mey were a lone immortal with no others of her kind and suddenly one more was found, she would also be impatient to meet that person.

After spreading the yoga mat on the floor, she sat down and crossed her legs in the lotus position, but even though her eyes were closed and her breathing was even, the calm state that opened her mind to the echoes eluded her.

Thoughts of Vrog and Aliya and their possible future in the village stirred up excitement in her, and that wasn't conducive to the feeling of calm Mey needed to enter the meditative state. Instead of trying to banish them, she let her mind wander.

Late last night, Jin had sent her a picture that she'd snapped of Aliya when the girl hadn't been looking. She looked nearly as alien as the pureblooded females in the echoes and was just as beautiful. From what Jin had told her, she was also as aggressive.

Jin thought that Aliya could take the fast track to becoming a Guardian, but was that what Aliya wanted to do with her life?

Were her goals and aspiration aligned with the clan? Probably not.

Maybe she wanted to marry Vrog and have a bunch of babies with him?

Nah, Mey was projecting her own wishes onto a female who probably was as alien by nature as she was in appearance. Hopefully, she wasn't a cruel bitch like the pure-blooded Kra-ell females who'd gotten rid of babies fathered by hybrid males and human females, or dormant females in the case of her and Jin's mother.

Was their birth mother still alive? Should they try to find her?

Mey wished Eva would resume her detective activities so she could hire her to search for their mother. Once they were back in the village, she planned on talking to her about it. Perhaps Sharon could do that? Since Ethan's birth, Sharon had taken Eva's place as the lead investigator of their firm, and she had probably gained enough experience by now to do the job with remote guidance from her boss.

Once the random thoughts had run their course, Mey's mind finally quieted enough to allow the echoes in. This time around, she was ready for the two long ghostly forms as they entered the building and closed the door behind them.

Focusing on their expressions, she noted that their dark eyes were already emitting a faint red glow, their fangs were slightly elongated, and their high foreheads were creased.

It was obvious that they'd come to the storage room to have a private fight. When they started arguing, Mey understood every third or fifth word, but it was enough to make some sense of what they were arguing about.

"You ——— go. The tribe is——big——. I —-ready —-."

Mey filled in the blanks, and the gist of it was, "You need to let me—or us— go. The tribe is too big. I am ready and able—or ripe."

The other one bared her fangs and hissed several words of which Mey understood only a handful, but combined with the tone, it went something like, "You are not the one making the decisions here. I'll decide when you are ready."

The shorter female bared her fangs as well, and her rapid response was nearly unintelligible, but Mey guessed it went something like, "It's your sacred obligation to help me form my own tribe. That's what the Mother commands. You are not letting me do that because you are a greedy pakta."

Mey made a note to ask Vrog what pakta meant, but she had no doubt that it was a very offensive Kra-ell word because that was when the taller female, who was most likely Jade, backhanded the other one and sent her flying into the storage shelving.

The rest of what was hissed and shouted during the vicious fighting was probably more Kra-ell cuss words, but this time Mey endured it to the end.

Exhausted and bloodied, the females sat on the floor and leaned their backs against the wall.

Jade's expression lost some of its harshness as she wrapped her arm around the other female's shoulders and mussed her hair with her other hand. When she spoke, her tone was softer, and her words were measured, allowing Mey to understand most of it and translate it in her head.

"This is not our home," Jade said. "You are too young and vulnerable to split up and lead your own tribe among the humans. We are alone in this world, and there is strength in numbers. We need to stay together."

"What about the other Kra-ell?"

"We don't know if any survived, and if they did, they might not be our friends."

"The tribe is too big. The males are not happy to be shared between all of us. Maybe we can split up but stay together. Let each female choose her males instead of us sharing them all."

Jade shook her head. "We can't. We need to make as many children as we can, and you know just as well as I do that a larger pool of males increases the chances of pregnancy."

"It feels wrong."

"I know. But we have no choice."

Alena

The ride to Lijiang took nearly three hours instead of two. They had to stop several times and let Aliya out of the limousine to walk about for a few minutes until her nausea subsided.

Her excuse was that she hadn't traveled by car in sixteen years, and it didn't agree with her stomach, but Alena had a feeling that it had more to do with anxiety about going to the city than the ride in the limo. She'd been fine the first hour of the drive but had grown progressively more nervous as they neared Lijiang.

"Don't worry. Kalugal is going to shroud you, and everyone looking at you will see an average-looking Chinese woman."

"Can he shroud my height?"

Kalugal turned around to look at her. "I can make you invisible if that's what you want, but that might make trying on clothing difficult."

"Just make me shorter and more normal looking. I don't care about anything else."

Alena patted her thigh. "There is a lot to do in Lijiang other than shopping. We can visit the Dayan Old Town. It's one of the four best-preserved ancient cities in China, and it's listed as a UNESCO world heritage site."

"What is UNESCO?" Aliya asked.

"It's the United Nations Educational, Scientific, and Cultural Organization," Alena said. "The Great Wall of China is also one of its heritage sites, so Lijiang is in good company. It has bars, restaurants, cafés, and shops where tourists can experience the Naxi culture. The old city also has 354 bridges spanning over waterwheel-driven canals that are full of goldfish, and it even has a palace."

"How are we going to see all that and go shopping in one day?" Jin asked. "We will need to come back here some other day. It sounds too good to miss out on."

"I have to admit that I didn't expect China to be so beautiful," Alena said. "When I pulled information about Lijiang, I was surprised that I had never heard about it before."

"We can even see a festival." Jin lifted her head from the screen. "This Wednesday is the San Duo festival. The Naxi are gathering to celebrate San Duo, a warrior who is the incarnation of the Jade Dragon Snow Mountain. According to legend, he's the protector of the Naxi people. They sing and dance and ask for his blessing.

Should be fun to watch." She tapped Kalugal's shoulder. "Can we go?"

"You and Arwel can go, and if Alena and Orion want to join you, that's fine with me, but I'm more interested in the Mosuo than the Naxi, and I want to keep looking for clues in the ruins."

"I'm sure Aliya wants to attend the festival as well."

Aliya didn't look sure at all. "I can't go. Not without Kalugal shrouding me."

"I can shroud you as well," Alena offered. "But I really don't see the need. After you get new clothing and a pair of sunglasses, you should be fine."

"I don't want to waste today on sightseeing. I have a million-yuan budget to spend, and that will take all day."

So that was the problem.

Alena chuckled. "You shouldn't take Kalugal too literally. He said that you can spend up to a million. He didn't say that you have to."

"I know. But since I have all that money to spend, I want to buy a place to live."

Kalugal turned to look at her again. "Need I remind you that you are coming with us to the US?"

She pinned him with a hard look. "I remember every-thing you said to me. You told me that if I'm not happy in the immortals' village, you will buy me a plane ticket to anywhere I want to go. If I buy an apartment now, I will have a place to live when I come back here."

"Didn't you want to move to Beijing?" Jin asked.

"I changed my mind." Aliya cast a quick glance at Jin's phone. "Does it say there how many people live in Lijiang?"

"Let me check on *Wikipedia*." Jin scrolled through the page. "About a million and three hundred thousand." She lifted her head and smiled at Aliya. "That's considered a small city in China."

"It's big enough for me to hide in," Aliya said. "But it's not so big that I can't get out of the city and hunt in the wild."

"Speaking of hunting," Arwel said. "I need to stop by the jet and load up on more weapons. When we go into the tunnels again, I want to have explosives, flares, and walkie-talkies. I'm not getting caught with my pants down again."

"Walkie-talkies will be useless there," Kalugal said. "Whatever is causing the interference will also interfere with radio waves. But the flares are a good idea."

"I have a better one," Jin said. "I can tether one of you and stay outside while the rest of you go in. I will be your walkie-talkie."

Aliya looked confused. "What are you talking about?"

Jin opened her mouth to explain, but Arwel interrupted. "Unless Alena agrees to stay out of the tunnels as well, I will have to follow her, and I'm not leaving you alone topside, unprotected. We go or stay together."

If looks could kill, Arwel would be dead, or at least painfully wounded.

"You are so full of it, Arwel," Jin bristled. "You are loading up on weapons and explosives, and yet you would send the rest of the team unprotected if Alena decides to stay with me?"

He glared back at her. "My job here is to protect Alena. I can give the flares and explosives to Phinas and Welgost. I'm sure they know how to use them."

Kalugal cleared his throat. "You forgot one important thing, Arwel. We came here on my jet, and I don't have explosives on board. All I have are flares, handguns, and more knives."

Arwel looked embarrassed. "I didn't forget. I assumed that you carried the same standard equipment as we do, but what you have will do."

Alena had a feeling that Kalugal had nailed it, and that Arwel had forgotten that they hadn't arrived on a clan jet.

"So, what will it be?" Jin turned to Alena. "Do you want to stay with me so the team can communicate with the outside world? We can stay in the hotel and get massages, manicures, and pedicures." She looked at Jacki. "You can join us too."

Jacki shook her head. "I need to be in the tunnels in case they discover something that will trigger a vision. We can do all that on Thursday, and then Aliya can join us." She smiled at the girl. "We can have a girls-only fun day."

Alena chuckled. "We wanted this to be a girls' day out, but the guys wouldn't hear of it. I doubt they would let us out of their sights even to go to the spa."

Not only that, but she also had to take the Odus along because Kian had called and had given her an earful about leaving them behind. He'd eventually conceded that taking them to the ruins wasn't an option because they couldn't cross the rickety rope bridge without falling into the water, and they couldn't fit through some of the narrower tunnels. She'd just omitted to mention that the water was only waist deep and they could walk through. Kian was being ridiculous. With three powerful compellers and three fighters to keep her safe, the Odus weren't necessary, and she planned to leave them in the limousine when their group went shopping and sightseeing.

"I can arrange for the masseuses and manicurists to come to our suite." Kalugal said. "You can commandeer the bedroom."

"No way," Jin said. "If you're so concerned with our safety, you can join us at the spa."

Aliya had remained silent throughout their discussion, but as soon as there was a lull, she repeated her question from before. "What does it mean to tether someone? And why can only Jin do that?"

"That's my special talent," Jin said. "If I touch someone with the intention of tethering them, I can attach a string of my consciousness to theirs and see what they see and hear what they hear until I sever the tether. I used to keep tabs on my sister that way."

Aliya looked horrified. "Is that why you loaned me your clothes? Did you attach a tether to them?"

Jin laughed. "That's not how it works, and I have no reason to attach a tether to you because you don't have anyone to talk to but us. What would I listen to?"

Vrog

V rog unfolded a cardboard box and then changed his mind and tossed it aside.

The ledgers were too valuable to be transported in cardboard boxes. He needed containers that were sturdy and watertight. Perhaps he could load his entire safe onto the plane?

It was heavy as hell, but since they were traveling by private jet, that shouldn't be a problem. He needed to ask Morris, though. The pilot was out with Yamanu and the two Guardians, sitting outside of the storage building where Mey was listening to echoes and playing the stone game with them. The four were bored out of their mind and would probably be much happier in Lugu Lake.

That place was a tourist attraction, and there was a lot to see besides the archeological site and the tunnels running under it.

They could get busy sightseeing, while he got busy wooing Aliya.

Just thinking about her made him hard, and that was without the benefit of seeing what she looked like.

It didn't matter.

He would have liked Aliya to be pretty, but that wasn't the attribute he thought of as most important.

Would she be as cruel as the other Kra-ell females? Or did her human half make her mellower the same way his human half made him?

His dream female would be fierce but not cruel, assertive but not dominant, and most importantly, capable of falling in love with him.

What were the chances of Aliya checking off all those boxes?

Probably slim, and he shouldn't build her up in his mind and then get disappointed by the reality of her.

The problem was that he couldn't help it.

The only love Vrog had ever felt was for his human mother and for his son. How would it feel to love his own female?

Incredible.

If they could have a long-lived child together, all of his wishes would come true. But if they didn't, that was okay. He already had an immortal son, but for her, he would like to have another.

"Get a hold of yourself, Vrog," he murmured as he pushed the ledgers back into the safe and locked the door.

Pushing to his feet, he straightened his collar and adjusted his tie. On his way out, he stopped in Doctor Wang's office. "I'm going out of town in a day or two, so if there are any matters you need to discuss with me, please come to my office later today."

The principal's eyes widened. "Are Mr. and Mrs. Williams done with their investigation already?"

"I believe so."

"Did they make up their minds about buying the school?"

Vrog shrugged. "If they did, they haven't informed me of their decision." He gave the principal a smile before turning on his heel and heading down the stairs.

He'd decided to return to the United States even before they'd found Aliya, and now that they were planning to take her with them to live in the village, he was most likely going to stay much longer than he'd initially planned.

That reminded him of the virtual adventure he was supposed to go on upon his return. Should he still do that now that he had his sights on Aliya?

The female who he'd matched with was waiting for him, and declining to participate after he'd already agreed was akin to a breach of contract and dishonorable.

He would go on the adventure if Aliya showed no interest in him, which was very probable. When he still lived with the other Kra-ell, none of the females had found him attractive enough to invite him to their beds. He wasn't as strong as the pureblooded males, and his mixed genes couldn't produce a pureblooded child, which made him useless to Jade and the other females.

As he walked out of the administrative building, he was surprised to see Mey and her entourage heading his way.

"Did you learn anything new today?" he asked.

"I did." She glanced around the campus. "Perhaps we should discuss what I learned in your quarters."

Classes were in session, so there was no one on the center lawn or anywhere within earshot, but Mey was right to be cautious. "Certainly. I can offer you coffee or tea and we can discuss your plans for acquiring the school."

In case anyone was covertly listening to their exchange, that was what they expected to hear.

"The spirits seem to be resting peacefully," Mey said. "There are still several areas of the school which I haven't covered yet, but I can complete my spiritual investigation in a day or two."

"Can you do that any faster?" He started walking toward the staff quarters. "We have that urgent matter to attend to, and I would like to expedite things if possible."

"I know that you would, but I'd rather be done with my investigation in one shot, so I don't have to come back here again."

"Are you having such an awful time in the school? You shouldn't consider purchasing it if you do."

Yamanu clapped his back. "We are having a great time, but we miss our friends and family, and I miss my own custom-built bed." He winked at Vrog. "A guy my size is not comfortable on a standard bed."

"You forgot to mention Junior," Vrog whispered.

That had been their initial cover story, and they'd stuck to it. Mey and Yamanu had a son who they wanted to teach about his mother's heritage.

"I miss my son," Mey said loudly. "Perhaps sending him to school abroad wasn't such a great idea."

"We can buy a house nearby," Yamanu said. "So we can visit him every day."

Mey chuckled. "He would hate that. Besides, unless we can convince all of our friends and relatives to move to China with us, I don't think I could stand being away from them for so long."

"We will fly back and forth." Yamanu wrapped his arm around his wife's shoulders.

Vrog wasn't sure whether the two were indeed married or if it was part of their cover story. They were mated, though, and given what Vrog had learned from Vlad and

Wendy, being mated was more binding than being married.

Supposedly, the immortals' mated bond was stronger than any official document proclaiming a couple husband and wife.

The Kra-ell had neither. No official ceremony, no bond, and no love.

But perhaps things could be different between him and Aliya. They could start a new tradition. Would the Clan Mother agree to marry them?

Damn, he was letting himself get carried away again.

Aliya might not want him, or he might not want her. The fact that they were each other's only hybrid Kra-ell option didn't mean that they would end up together.

Aliya

I have no reason to attach a tether to you because you don't have anyone to talk to but us.

That sentence kept replaying in Aliya's mind on a never-ending loop. It succinctly described her pathetic existence, and it made her stupid plans of returning to China seem even more pathetic.

These people were offering her a lifeline, and unless they were really evil and were planning on selling her to the bad Kra-ell for breeding, she was willing to do whatever they asked of her in return.

"Have you ever seen an airport?" Kalugal asked as the limousine was let through a gate into the private section of the airport.

"I've seen airplanes flying through the sky, but I've never seen one up close."

Kalugal smirked. "You are in for a treat. The first plane you're going to see is my luxurious private jet."

Was that a trap?

Were they luring her into the airplane and planning on flying away with her?

If they didn't have three males who could compel her to follow their orders, that would have been a viable suspicion, but with those powers, they didn't need to trick her into doing anything. They could just tell her what to do and she would have to obey.

"Kalugal likes everything on a grand scale." Carol threaded her arm through Aliya's. "I'm dying to see his jet."

"Haven't you seen it already?"

The petite blond shook her head, her pretty curls bouncing around her beautiful face. "Lokan and I flew separately. This is kind of a family reunion." She sighed. "I haven't seen Jacki and Kalugal in months. I hope to make it back home in time for their baby's arrival. I'm going to be an aunt for the first time."

"That's nice." Aliya said what she thought was expected of her.

Carol looked proud and excited as if she was giving birth to the baby, not Jacki.

Thinking of how the pureblooded females had regarded each other's pregnancies, Aliya couldn't remember whether they'd been happy when another female conceived. They had been very competitive, and since conceiving was the ultimate prize, it didn't make sense for them to be happy about a pregnancy that wasn't theirs.

As Carol led her up the stairs into the airplane, Aliya didn't know what to expect, but she sure hadn't expected the inside of it to look like a fancy living room.

"Come." Carol tugged her by the hand toward one of the armchairs. "Sit down."

"Why?"

"The seats recline and turn into beds. I want to show you."

"Okay." Hesitantly, Aliya lowered herself into the seat. "What do I do now?"

"Do you see the metal plate with a picture of a chair on it and arrows? Press the arrow in the direction you want that part of the seat to go. If you want just the back or just the leg part, press the corresponding arrows. If you want to turn the seat into a bed, press the symbol that looks like one."

That was simple enough even for her to understand. Aliya pressed the bed symbol and the entire seat started slowly moving until it was fully reclined. "This is great for short people." She sat up and looked for the button to return the seat to its position.

"You are absolutely right," Kalugal said. "I need to order custom seats that fit Guardian-sized people."

"Is there a special size a Guardian needs to be?"

Chuckling, Carol shook her head. "I was training to become a Guardian, and I'm tiny. But the truth is that other than me, all the other Guardians are on the taller side."

Come to think of it, everyone in their group aside from Carol and Jacki was rather tall, and Jacki wasn't short by human standards. She was average.

"Tell me more about the other immortals in your village. Are they all as tall and good-looking as these?"

"We are the descendants of gods, so obviously everyone is good-looking, but heights vary. The Clan Mother herself is so tiny that she's even shorter than me, but she's the most powerful being on the planet." Carol cast a sidelong glance at Orion, who was sitting with Alena across from them and engaging in covert amorous activities.

The jealous beast inside Aliya started to awaken, but Carol distracted her, whispering into her ear, "We recently discovered that another god had survived, Orion's father, but we don't know how powerful he is. Most likely, he's not as powerful as Annani. She's a force of nature even compared to other gods."

"What happened to them? I mean to the other gods?"

Carol patted her arm. "I'll tell you on the way to the city."

"I'm done." Arwel emerged from the front of the jet with a bulging duffel bag slung over his shoulder. "As soon as Shamash and Phinas are done loading up as well, we can go."

Vrog

When the coffee had finished brewing, Vrog poured it into the new mugs he'd had brought to his apartment and handed them out to his guests.

During the several days since the team's arrival at his school, he'd equipped his apartment with additional chairs, a small fridge, mugs, teacups, spoons, napkins, and a modest supply of snacks.

Vrog had never hosted people before, but he was discovering that he enjoyed it. He'd also enjoyed his stay with Vlad and Wendy. The breakfasts and dinners they'd shared, hanging out with Wendy in the café during the day, meeting up with Margaret, Bowen, Stella, and even Richard.

It was nice to have friends and family who knew who and what he was, people who he didn't need to pretend to be human with, people to talk to about things outside of school business.

"Good coffee." Yamanu put his mug down. "Where did you get it? It's much better than what you served us the first day."

"I ordered it online." Vrog sat on one of the straight-back chairs. "I'm getting better at entertaining guests."

"You're a gracious and generous host," Mey said. "So, do you want to hear what I learned today?"

"I can't wait."

Hopefully it was good enough to end her investigation, so they could get out of there.

"Jade and the other female were fighting because the other one wanted to leave with part of the tribe and start one of her own." Mey added sugar to her coffee and stirred it in. "By the way. What does pakta mean?"

"I'm not sure what the literal meaning is, but it's considered a great offense to call a female pakta. It's the equivalent of calling a woman bitch in English. I assume that pakta is a female animal from the Kra-ell home that is not held in high regard."

Mey pursed her lips. "I have no idea why humans chose male and female dogs as derogatory terms. I happen to love dogs. If I had to choose, I would have chosen rats or spiders as insults." She made a face. "You are such a greedy tarantula," she gave it a try.

"Nah, that doesn't pack a punch," Yamanu said.

"You're such a greedy rat," Mey tried again.

Yamanu nodded. "That's much better. A greedy snake sounds good as well."

Mey smiled. "Anyway, pakta was what the other female called Jade, and that's how the brawling started. This time, though, I managed to stay in the zone to the end of the echo, and I saw their reconciliation. They acted like bros reconciling after letting off some steam in a fist fight. Jade told the other one that she didn't want her to leave because it wasn't safe. They were alone among humans, and there was strength in numbers."

"The other one was probably Kagra," Vrog supplied. "If the tribe ever split, she would have led the offshoot. So that's nothing new. But I didn't know that they had been fighting over that. They'd always shown a unified front as if there were no discord between them."

"Toward the end of the echo, it became clear that they cared about each other, or perhaps that Jade cared about Kagra. I'm not sure Kagra cared about Jade, though." Mey took a sip of her coffee before putting the mug down. "When Kagra asked Jade about the other Kra-ell, Jade said that she didn't know whether anyone else survived, but if they had, they might not be friendly."

Jay got up to refill his mug. "Did either of them mention the supposed betrayal of the scouting crew that Aliya remembered Jade talking about with Kagra?"

"No, and that's why I want to go back again tomorrow and wait for another echo to play. We might learn more about that."

Vrog groaned. "You might have to listen to endless hours of echoes and still not stumble upon anything relating to the scouting crew. The only echoes you have access to are those that were imbued with strong emotions. What are the chances of Jade or any of the others getting emotionally upset while talking about that particular subject?"

"If I were betrayed by my own people, I would be upset," Yamanu said. "Even decades later, I would get angry every time the subject was brought up."

"Me too," Mey said. "Besides, that was not what we were looking for in the first place. Stumbling upon that fight was just a bonus. What we are really after are echoes left by the attackers or the attacked that will shed light on who they were, how they found your tribe, and why they killed all the males."

"The last one is not hard to guess," Alfie said. "They were after the females. In the old days, when one human tribe conquered another, they slaughtered the males and took the females. It's a tale as old as time."

As everyone nodded in agreement, Vrog's stomach twisted. To them, it was a sad event they'd heard about. To him, it was an open wound that refused to heal. It had been his family that had been murdered.

As his fangs started to elongate, he bent his head and took several sips from the coffee until the sensation passed.

"On another subject." He turned to Morris. "Can we load two medium-sized safes onto the plane? They are about four hundred pounds each."

"No problem," the pilot said. "What do you have in them, gold?"

"To me, it is. I originally thought to put the ledgers Kian asked me for in cardboard boxes, but I realized that they are too valuable to risk transporting in such unsafe packaging. It would be best to take them with the safes I keep them in."

"We can do that," Morris said.

"Good. That's one problem solved." Vrog turned to Mey. "The other one is how long are you planning on staying here? I'd rather leave as soon as I can. I'm eager to get to Aliya. She's all alone and she must be scared. Having me there will make her feel safer." Or so he hoped.

"I can take you," Morris said. "The others can stay here."

"That's a hard no." Yamanu crossed his massive arms over his chest. "We leave together."

"The Kra-ell quarters were burned to the ground." Vrog looked Mey in the eyes. "The echoes of what happened have no walls to cling to. The structures that remained standing will only provide anecdotal information at best."

Mey lifted a finger. "Give me one more day. If I find nothing relevant to our quest tomorrow, we will leave Wednesday morning."

That was progress.

Vrog nodded. "Agreed."

Alena

"How do I find a home for sale?" Aliya asked as they entered the department store.

Alena wished Kalugal hadn't used a light shroud that affected only humans so she could see what he'd made Aliya look like. He'd said that he made her appear more ordinary but not completely different.

She still attracted attention, probably because she was so tall, but since those were just passing looks that weren't accompanied by murmurs or snickers, Aliya didn't seem to mind, and some of the tension had left her shoulders.

Then again, she was hunching them, so that might have been the reason she looked less tense.

"I'll ask around," Carol offered. "You need to concentrate on buying a new wardrobe."

"Follow me," Jin said. "As a fashion entrepreneur, I know how to spot quality."

Alena didn't plan on getting anything, but she trailed behind them to offer moral support in case Aliya needed it, and since Jin had taken it upon herself to be her fashion adviser, she probably would.

Arwel's mate had the tact of a bull in a china shop. Her comment about Aliya having no one to talk to outside of their group had sent the girl into a melancholy tailspin, and if not for Carol and her talent for storytelling, that bad mood would have ruined Aliya's enjoyment of the day.

"You look bored," Orion said quietly in her ear. "I have an idea of how to alleviate that boredom."

Smiling, Alena leaned against his side. "What do you have in mind?"

He reached to the nearest clothing rack and pulled out a dress. "I want you to try it on."

She laughed. "It's not my size."

"It doesn't matter," he whispered. "You are only going to pretend to try it on while you shroud me and I go in with you."

She rolled her eyes. "This is a department store. There is no privacy in the changing rooms. They are designed like stalls in a public bathroom with the bottoms and tops open."

He looked crushed. "There goes my fantasy."

Carol sauntered up to them. "I don't know what to do about Aliya and the damn apartment she wants to buy. I asked one of the cashiers, and she told me about a nice new neighborhood that's currently under construction. She and her fiancé put down a deposit, and she said that if we want to get an apartment there, we should hurry because they are selling out fast. I was hoping that the cheapest one would be completely out of Aliya's range so she would drop the idea, but the price for a studio or a one-bedroom is within the range of what Kalugal promised her."

A million yuan was only about a hundred and sixty thousand dollars, but it was probably enough to buy a small studio apartment in Lijiang.

"She can buy it and later sell it," Orion said. "Kalugal made her a promise, and if he breaks it, she won't believe anything else we tell her."

"He's right." Kalugal walked up to them. "A million yuan is a reasonable amount as recompense and not a significant amount for me. If it makes her trust us more, I'll help her get it. After she's done shopping, we will drive over to that development and let her choose an apartment."

"You are okay, cousin." Alena pulled him into a quick hug. "Underneath all the bluster beats a good heart."

Wrapping his arm around Jacki, he grinned. "My mate is my heart, and she makes me a better man. Before I met her, I would have just compelled the girl to forget about my slip-up of an offer."

"No, you wouldn't," Jacki protested. "You are an honorable male, and you keep your promises. I have nothing to do with that."

"Thank you." He kissed the top of her head. "I value your high opinion of me."

"Jin is waving us over," Alena said and started walking.

"I want you to see Aliya's new look."

A moment later, Aliya walked out of the changing room in a pair of tight jeans, a white hoodie, white sneakers, and a pair of big sunglasses perched on her nose.

"What do you think?" Jin asked.

"Beautiful," Phinas said, and given his tone, he meant it.

"Great." Jin motioned for Aliya to turn in a circle. "So that's the look we are going for. An international college student."

"Why international?" Aliya asked.

Alena glanced at Kalugal, who nodded. "I'm shrouding what we say as well."

"Because of your height and the fact that your features are not really Chinese. If people think you are a foreigner, they will shrug off your oddities."

"Maybe I should start speaking only English from now on."

"That's not a bad idea," Lokan said. "That will reinforce the perception."

"My accent is terrible."

Alena smiled. "It's gotten a lot better over the past twenty-four hours. You are an exceptionally fast learner."

The girl was like a sponge. Alena had a feeling that given access to quality education, Aliya could excel in any field of knowledge.

Becoming a Guardian was not her only option.

Annani

"Mistress Ronja." Ogidu bowed. "Please come in."

"Thank you." Ronja's smile was full of secrets as she walked into Annani's living room. "Good afternoon, Clan Mother."

"Good afternoon." Annani rose to her feet and embraced her friend. "Every time I see you, you look better than the time before. Is it the physical activity, or is it the love?"

"A little bit of both." Ronja's cheeks pinked, but she kept smiling. "Or a lot."

"Oh dear." Annani laughed as she took Ronja's hand. "I want to hear all about it." She led her to the couch.

"There isn't much to tell." Her blush deepened. "Well, that's not true. I finally did what you encouraged me to do, and I'm floating on a cloud." She chuckled. "And not just because of the wonderful effects of the venom. I'm in love." Ronja sighed. "Merlin is the perfect man for me.

He's brilliant, kind, funny, and he's hopeless without me. I couldn't have asked for a better match."

Annani was of the same opinion. The Fates knew what they were doing with these two, and the fact that they were so in love gave her hope for Ronja's successful transition. The Fates had no reason to punish either of the two lovebirds by allowing Ronja to perish. Still, nothing was guaranteed, and assuming that everything was destined for a good ending was overly optimistic and simplistic. Annani's gut, which she usually trusted, was undecided in Ronja's case. It vacillated between being excited about her successful transition and dreading the opposite.

"Congratulations." She patted her friend's hand. "Are you just enjoying yourself, or are you already working on your induction?"

Ronja's smile faltered. "We are not using protection. I figured that it was time to take the plunge and go for it. I have to believe that the Fates arranged for me to be with Merlin because he's so perfect for me and we are great together, so they also have to make sure that I survive the transition."

For some reason, Ronja's hopeful words caused Annani's gut to swing into the dread position of the pendulum's range.

She was excited and hopeful, but she could not help being anxious as well. Ronja was the oldest Dormant to ever attempt transition, and she was taking a big risk because Annani encouraged her to do so, which meant that Annani was responsible for her fate and the fate of her young daughter.

Lisa was only fifteen, and she had recently lost her father. Losing her mother as well would destroy her.

"How is Lisa taking it?"

"She's happy for Merlin and me, but she's also scared."

"Does it bother her that you did not mourn her father for a full year?"

Ronja took in a deep breath. "Lisa encouraged me not to wait, but I'm sure that on some level, it upsets her. She loved Frank. We both did." A tear slid down her cheek. "I still love him, you know. You don't stop loving a person when they are gone. I didn't know it was possible to be in love with a new partner and still love the one you lost." She pushed a strand of hair behind her ear. "That's not true. I knew that it was possible. I loved Frank when I married him, but I also still loved Michael. I don't think I ever stopped loving him even though he'd hurt me."

Annani smiled sadly. "The heart has a boundless capacity for love. It is like the universe that keeps expanding like a balloon."

Ronja crossed her legs. "I remember Michael explaining to David and Jonah that the universe is like dough with raisins. When placed in an oven, the dough begins to expand, and the distance between the raisins embedded in it grows proportionally in all three directions."

"I have to agree that I like the dough analogy better, especially since the universe is supposedly flat." She sighed. "Scientists constantly develop new theories, and it is hard to keep up. I will have to brush up on some reading when I return to the sanctuary. While I am here or in Scotland, I prefer to spend time with my large and beautiful family."

"Can I ask you a question?"

"Of course."

"Why do you live in the sanctuary? Kian and Amanda are here in the village, and Alena might soon join them. Sari is in Scotland. If I were you, I would choose the village as my home."

"I like having my own place," Annani admitted. "And I believe that my children prefer it that way as well. I had the sanctuary built exactly the way I wanted it, and it is a paradise under a dome of ice. It is like a fairyland." She waved her hand, signaling Ogidu to serve the tea and the canapés she had asked him to prepare. "You should come to visit me, with Merlin and Lisa, of course."

"I would love to." Ronja sighed. "If I survive the transition, I will reward myself with a trip to your sanctuary."

"It is not an if but a when. When you transition, I will send one of my Odus with the jet to pick you up. I hope that you will stay for a while."

Perhaps that was the solution to Alena's absence. Annani could invite people to visit her in the sanctuary. She could have a rotation of guests so there was always someone with her, and she would never get bored.

Or maybe she could convince Orion to move in with Alena and stay in the sanctuary. The problem was that Kian might not approve for security reasons.

Then again, if they were trusting Orion with Alena, then they should trust him with knowledge of the sanctuary and its general location. Alaska was vast, and they had made finding the sanctuary as impossible as the technology of the time allowed. Things were changing, though, and either they would need to fortify the sanctuary's defenses and detection countermeasures, or she might be forced to abandon her beautiful fairyland sooner than later.

Aliya

After paying for the lotions and hairbrushes they'd gotten in the cosmetics section of the department store, Jin handed Aliya the shopping bag.

"Do you get periods?" she asked.

Aliya looked over her shoulder to where the rest of their group was scattered, smelling perfumes and checking out makeup. Well, the ladies were. The guys either trailed along or stopped in the men's fragrance section.

Fortunately, they weren't close enough to hear Jin's embarrassing question.

"Why? Don't you?" Aliya asked much more quietly.

"Not since I turned immortal," she said just as quietly. "We only ovulate on demand. And I'm asking so I know whether we need to get you feminine products."

Jin was refreshingly blunt, but she took some getting used to.

"I get periods only twice a year, and the last one was two months ago."

"That's not so bad. When I was still human, getting periods every month was a major drag. I took the contraceptive shot just to get rid of them."

"You are so lucky that your people can activate the dormant genes. If not for your dormant mother, you would have been born human."

On the way to the city, Carol, Alena, Jacki, and Jin had taken turns telling Aliya about immortals, about how they were different from the Kra-ell, about their ability to activate Dormants, and about how Jin and Mey's mother must have been one, which was why they'd been born with the godly genes.

Aliya still didn't understand half of what they'd told her, but it appeared that the female descendants of the gods could transfer their immortality to their children no matter how diluted their blood was.

It was most unfortunate that the same wasn't true for the Kra-ell.

A hybrid and a human could only produce human children, which was why Jade had forbidden the hybrid males to have them.

Mey and Jin's father must have defied Jade and had a secret affair with a human outside of the compound. The girls wouldn't have been given up for adoption at the same time if they'd been born inside its walls. Jade would have given each one away as soon as she'd been born.

They'd been the lucky ones, though. They'd been adopted by a nice couple who loved them very much.

"So, what's next?" Jin asked. "The jewelry store?"

"I think I have everything I need."

"You need a suitcase to put everything in." Jin tugged on her hand. "Come on. The others are getting tired of following us around."

"Let's go." Aliya gave her a smile.

After their initial rough start, Jin had turned out to be a good friend. She wasn't as soft and polite as Alena, or as good a storyteller as Carol, but her temperament suited Aliya's better. Perhaps the blood they shared made them more alike.

It might be nice to have a friend who was at least a little bit Kra-ell.

"Thank you for everything you're doing for me," she murmured under her breath. "And I'm sorry about hurting your mate."

Jin chuckled. "I've already forgotten about it, and so did Arwel. Besides, don't thank me, thank Kalugal. I've been very happily spending his money."

Jin had paid for everything with Kalugal's credit card, and Aliya had lost count of how much she'd spent. It must have been at least three thousand yuan. It might not be much for Kalugal, but it was a fortune for Aliya.

She'd bought so many things, of which the ten pairs of panties were the items she was most happy about.

Perhaps she could excuse herself and go to the bathroom to put one pair on. The leggings Jin had loaned her were comfortable and looked good on her, but they didn't leave much to the imagination, and Aliya felt as if she were walking around half-naked.

To their credit, the eyes of the males in her group never traveled below her collar bone, but other men had been staring at her crotch and her ass, and she'd been too embarrassed to ask Kalugal to extend his shroud to cover those parts of her as well.

In addition to the panties, she now also owned five bras, which in her opinion was a waste of money. Her breasts were so small that they didn't need support, but Jin had insisted that she needed them for modesty to cover her nipples when they got cold and stuck out like a pair of very small knobs.

Aliya had also bought ten T-shirts, but only because a pack of ten cost as much as three if she'd gotten them separately. Jin had been against it, saying that the pack of ten was cheap because the department store wanted to get rid of T-shirts no one wanted, but Aliya didn't care that the designs weren't great. Having ten T-shirts felt like such a luxury. Besides, she planned on using the uglier ones as undershirts instead of the bras. The other items filling her shopping bags were five long-sleeved shirts, three pairs of jeans, two pairs of leggings, two sweaters, four hoodies, two pajama sets, a coat, a scarf, a pair of gloves, and three pairs of shoes—four if she also counted the slippers.

She also had two pairs of sunglasses, a bottle of perfume, and some other toiletries that Jin had insisted every woman needed.

"How much money did I spend so far?"

"You have plenty left over. Don't worry about it."

"Can Kalugal pay for the apartment with that plastic card?"

"Most people can't, but he can. He's very rich."

"What does he do?"

"To get rich?"

Aliya nodded.

"He's an investor. He buys stock and sells it, he also finds promising new start-ups and buys them, and God knows what else. I'm sure that there are some shady deals and other skeletons in his proverbial closet."

Aliya didn't know what stock was, or what kind of deals were done in a closet that had skeletons hidden in it.

"I didn't understand that."

"It's not important." Jin sauntered over to Arwel. "Is it time for lunch? I'm famished."

He lifted his hand and looked at his watch. "It's almost time for dinner. Are you done?"

"Aliya thinks that she has everything she needs, but I need to go over everything we've gotten before we leave the shopping district. Where are Carol and Jacki and the others?"

"Over there." Arwel pointed with his chin. "Let's get them and find a place to get something to eat."

Alena

As they neared the development seller's office, Alena lowered the limousine's window. "This is going to be a very nice neighborhood once it's finished."

The buildings, which ranged from six to eight stories tall, were separated by large areas that would most likely become lawns and playgrounds. Those that were completed had large windows, generous balconies, and architectural elements that made them look similar but not the same. A neighborhood like that wouldn't have looked out of place in California or Nevada.

Aliya peeked out the window and frowned. "It's too nice. I don't think I have enough money to buy an apartment here."

"Yes, you do," Carol said. "The clerk at the store told me that you can probably get a one-bedroom apartment for under a million yuan. She and her fiancé just put a deposit on a two-bedroom apartment that was selling for one point two million."

"How much is that in dollars?" Jacki said.

"One hundred eighty-four thousand." Kalugal didn't need a calculator to come up with the figure. "In Beijing, you would pay ten times as much for a nice new apartment. We are fortunate that Lijiang is one of the most affordable cities in China despite being such a popular tourist destination."

As soon as their two limousines parked in front of the sales office, an agent rushed out with a puzzled expression on her face. "Can I help you?"

"Yes, you can," Kalugal said in Chinese and walked over to her. "Do you speak English?" He offered her his hand. "I speak Chinese, but some of my friends don't."

"I speak English." She smiled nervously. "I apologize, but there must have been some misunderstanding. This is the Lo-cur site. The Luckar luxury development is on the west riverbank. I would be happy to give your driver the correct directions."

Kalugal gave her one of his charming smiles. "There is no confusion. I'm looking for a modest apartment for my niece." He motioned for Aliya to come forward. "The young lady fell in love with Lijiang and wants to settle down here."

The realtor's eyes shone with excitement. "Then you are in the right place." She offered him her hand. "I'm Wei."

"A pleasure to meet you, Wei."

"This neighborhood is perfect for young couples who want to start a family. Would you like to see what's available?" She looked over the rest of their group. "Is anyone else interested in purchasing an apartment? It's a great investment opportunity. Lijiang is growing fast, and the demand is rising. In a few years, these apartments are going to be worth much more than they are today."

"Interesting," Kalugal said. "Let's see what's available first and take it from there."

"Do you have anything that's under a million yuan?" Aliya asked.

"I sure do. We have a studio that is offered at eight hundred and fifty, and a one-bedroom that is only one hundred thousand more. Which one would you like to see?"

"Can I see both?" Aliya looked at Kalugal. "If that's okay with you, Uncle."

"Of course it is. I want you to be happy, my dear."

Alena stifled a chuckle. Kalugal loved performing, and he relished every opportunity to do so.

"Is everyone in your group coming to see the apartments?" Wei asked.

"If it's not too much bother." Kalugal fell in step with her. "We were in the city for some shopping, and we heard about this development from a lady who worked in the department store. She was so enthusiastic about the apartment she and her fiancé put a down payment on that we decided to follow her recommendation and visit the place right away. She said that it's selling out quickly."

"It is," Wei confirmed. "It's a beautiful development, and it's affordable." She sauntered closer to him. "As I said, it's a great investment opportunity, and many people are buying apartments because they expect the prices to go up."

"Why is that?" Kalugal asked. "Are new industries coming to Lijiang?"

"Airbnb," she said conspiratorially. "Lijiang is becoming more and more popular with tourists, both domestic and international, and the local authorities have eased up on regulation regarding short-term rentals."

"Interesting." Kalugal smoothed his hand over his goatee. "My niece is not going to be here full time, so she might make some extra money by renting her place out to tourists when she's away."

"Definitely." Wei called the elevator. "I'm afraid not everyone in your party will fit in. Some will have to wait for the elevator to come down. The studio is on the eighth floor, number 823, and the one-bedroom apartment is number 827."

"No problem." Kalugal motioned for Jacki, Shamash, Welgost, and Phinas to join him and Aliya. "We will go first."

As the elevator door closed behind them, Alena let out the chuckle she'd been holding in. "Kalugal should have been an actor. He's happiest when he's performing."

"I noticed," Lokan said. "He amuses himself by pretending to be different people."

When the elevator returned a few minutes later, the three remaining couples and Ovidu got in.

Oridu remained standing by the elevator to guard it.

On the eighth floor, they followed the sound of Kalugal's voice into the apartment.

"It's small," Jin murmured. "But it's big enough for one person."

"Let's see the other one," Kalugal said. "And if you have a two-bedroom apartment available, we would like to see it as well."

"It's over my budget," Aliya said.

"I know, dear. But two-bedroom apartments rent out better on Airbnb."

"What's Airbnb?" Aliya whispered.

"It's a way for people to rent out their homes to tourists for short durations," Orion said. "I used to stay in hotels during my travels, but now I prefer the convenience of having a kitchen, more room, and more privacy, so I use Airbnb whenever I can."

Kalugal grimaced. "I prefer hotels where I know that the bedding is properly laundered. Besides, I like having concierge and room service available."

Smiling, Orion leaned against the doorjamb. "I guess my preferences are more plebeian than yours."

Aliya looked confused. "I don't know what you are talking about. Can someone explain to me how you find these people who rent out their apartments?"

Kalugal patted her arm. "I'll explain everything on the way back to the hotel. We don't want to keep Wei waiting." He turned to the realtor. "When will these apartments be ready for move-in?"

"In about three months."

"Excellent." He smiled at Aliya. "That works perfectly for us."

Aliya

Aliya lay on the couch in Jacki and Kalugal's suite and looked at her purchases of the day. They were neatly stacked on the coffee table with the price tags still attached to them and grouped according to their function. She was supposed to put them in her new suitcase, but she wasn't ready to do that yet.

She'd never had so many clothes or shoes, and even though Jin had laughed, saying that those were just the bare necessities, to Aliya it was an abundance.

But that was nothing compared to owning a brand new two-bedroom apartment in a new development.

It wasn't the one she'd seen earlier today. That had been a model apartment that the realtor used for showing prospective clients the various layouts.

Hers was still in the process of being built, and it would be ready only in three months, which would give her enough time to decide whether she wanted to stay in the immortals' village or go back to China and live alone in Lijiang.

Had it really happened? Had Kalugal purchased for her a home that cost over a million yuan?

She still couldn't believe his generosity. It was true that his excavations of the ruins and the tunnels had caused her to lose the only home she'd had, but it hadn't belonged to her, and he didn't have to compensate her for it. She was well aware that he'd used it as an excuse to get her things, and that the million yuan hadn't been seriously offered.

He'd made a mistake, and she'd used it to get something she shouldn't have, and yet he'd stood by his offer and paid for the apartment.

Kalugal was either an extremely honorable male or he had a hidden agenda for her. But what could it be? She had nothing to offer him or the clan, not even her womb. Her offspring wouldn't be long-lived, let alone immortal. The Kra-ell were in some ways similar to the immortals, but they didn't carry the godly genes of immortality. The only reason Jin and her sister were immortal was that their mother was a dormant carrier who had transferred the gene of immortality to her daughters.

Despite what Alena had said about finding her a nice immortal male, none of them would be interested in her for anything other than casual sex because she couldn't give them immortal children.

The only one who might find her desirable was Vrog.

It seemed that he was her only option whether she liked him or not, and that was no option at all.

Her memory of him was so vague that she didn't remember whether he was handsome. What she remembered best about him was a conversation she'd overheard Jade having with Kagra.

Kagra had questioned Jade's decision to let him run the tribe's business in Singapore, and Jade had replied that he was smart and loyal to a fault and that she trusted him completely.

To her, smarts and loyalty were the two most important qualities, followed closely by tenacity and generosity. If Vrog had all four, Aliya would give him a chance even if he wasn't handsome.

She should have asked for a picture of him.

As the door to Jacki and Kalugal's bedroom opened, Aliya pushed up on the pillows. "Can't sleep?" she asked Kalugal.

"I'm just getting Jacki a glass of water." He opened the refrigerator and pulled out a large bottle of water. "Do you want some as well?"

She shook her head. "I know that I've already thanked you, but I feel like I need to thank you again. I'm shocked by your generosity."

"Stunned, astonished, or flabbergasted would be better words." He walked over to the couch and motioned for her to scoot and make room for him. "Frankly, I'm a little shocked myself. I don't know why I feel so protective of you. I think that at some point, I started to believe the lie I told and thought of you as my niece." He smiled. "I wanted my niece to get the best deal possible, and the two-bedroom was a better deal than the one-bedroom or the studio."

"I don't feel right about accepting it from you," she admitted. "I was sure that at the last moment you were going to back out. I never believed that you would go through with it. Now I don't know what to do. The right thing would be to give it back, but I can't bring myself to do that. I never owned something so valuable."

He nodded. "I understand your dilemma. If I were in your shoes, I would probably feel the same. The thing is that I'm a hundred percent sure that you will choose to stay in the village, and that this apartment is going to end up being rented out. If it makes you feel better, you can donate the proceeds from the rental to the charity I help fund."

"Is that the one the clan runs for the victims of trafficking?"

He nodded. "That's where the largest chunk of my charitable donations goes, but Jacki also sends money to different causes that involve children."

"I will consider it. If I get a job in the village and don't need the money from the rent, I'll donate it."

Kalugal grinned with satisfaction. "You are an honorable female, Aliya." He offered her his hand. "And I accept your deal."

"And you are an honorable male." She shook what he offered. "I will never forget what you have done for me, and I will find a way to repay you. Jin said that if I become a Guardian, I'll make a lot of money. I would be able to pay you back for the apartment. But it's not just about the money. I owe you a debt of gratitude."

Orion

Orion put his hands on Alena's waist and drew her to him. "I love you." He took her lips in a kiss that was meant to be soft and loving but quickly turned hungry and demanding.

By now, he knew her well enough not to worry about his inner predator scaring her or turning her off. Despite her mellow demeanor and good manners, Alena was a predator herself, and she loved it when things got a little rough. With her, he could finally let loose the beast inside of him and let it have its fill without worrying that he might hurt her.

They were very much alike in that respect.

They both had polished to perfection the civilized side they showed the world and reserved their immortal wild side for where it belonged—the privacy of their bedroom.

Just as he was about to pick her up and carry her to bed, his phone pinged with an incoming message, but he ignored it in favor of more important things.

Pushing on his chest, Alena planted her feet firmly on the floor. "Aren't you going to check who it is from?"

"Nope." He tried to lift her again.

"What if it's from Geraldine or Cassandra, and they need you urgently?"

"They would have called."

"Just check it. The bed is still going to be there in the next thirty seconds."

Stubborn woman.

"I'll check it on one condition." He pointed at the bed. "You wait for me in there. Naked."

"That's two conditions."

"And your point is?"

A smirk lifting one corner of her mouth, Alena purred, "Pull out your phone, and I will fulfill both and more."

She was planning something naughty, and he was all for it.

As he pulled the device from his pocket, Alena turned around, crossed her arms in front of her, and whipped her sweater over her head.

The bra was next, and when she turned her head to look at him over her shoulder, she caught him staring at her with the phone suspended midair.

"Check the message, Orion."

"Fine." Reluctantly, he did.

"It's from Cassandra. She asks if I'm awake and if I can call her."

"Call her."

"I'm sure it's nothing urgent."

"Just call her." Alena reached for the robe that she'd left draped over the bed's footboard. "I'll grab a quick shower in the meantime."

That was a change of plans that he could live with. He'd grown fond of their water play. "Don't rush. I'll join you there when I'm done."

Taking the phone to the chaise lounge, he dialed Cassandra's number. "What's up?"

"Is it a bad time? We can talk tomorrow."

Now she tells me. "It's okay. I'm sure you didn't call to ask me how the weather was over here. What's going on?"

"How *is* the weather?"

His niece had never been good at polite chitchat.

"It's nice during the days and cold during the nights. What do you need, Cassandra?"

"You were the one who arranged the cushy antique gallery job for Leo, right?"

"That's correct."

"So you must know the owner."

"I do."

"Can you ask him to send Leo on a long acquisition trip starting as soon as possible?"

He didn't need to ask why. "Aren't you waiting for me to return to compel Darlene's silence?"

"We are going to use another compeller, and it would be beneficial if Leo wasn't around for at least a few days after we release her memories, so she has some time to think things through in peace. The guy is a controlling jerk, and she can't think straight when she's busy keeping him happy."

Geraldine had given him a summary of their last meeting with Darlene and the not-so-shocking revelation about Roni's real father. Orion had suspected that as well, but because Roni and Leo looked a lot alike, he'd dismissed those suspicions.

"Who's the other compeller? Is Eleanor back?"

"We are taking Parker. Onegus cleared it with the boy's parents, and we are going to run a test before we release her memories to make sure that he can compel her. It's a good test for him as well."

"If his parents agree, then who am I to object. I can call the gallery owner and ask him to send Leo to Pennsylvania. I was supposed to go, but I canceled my plans so I could go with Alena, but Leo can take my place in the estate auction. It's a large estate, but the auction will take only one week. I'll have to come up with several other destinations for him, so he'll be gone an entire month. That should give Darlene enough time to make up her mind."

"That would be awesome, but are you sure? The guy is not too bright. He might overpay for worthless things."

"Don't worry about it. Either Marcelo or I will direct him."

"You're on the other side of the planet. It's going to be nighttime where you are."

He chuckled. "I'll manage. Anything else I can do for you?"

"Yeah, let me know when Leo leaves."

"I will. How is everyone doing?"

"We are good. Geraldine and I are anxious about Darlene. I really want her to leave that jerk and join us in the village. She deserves a second chance, and since she's suffered a lot, the Fates should compensate her with a truelove mate. I'm just trying to figure out who that might be. I think I need to start being more social and invite people over so Darlene can meet eligible bachelors, but I suck at being a hostess. What do I know about entertaining people?"

He laughed. "Not much, but you are Cassandra Beaumont, and you can do anything you set your mind to. I have faith in you."

"Absolutely. I just need to cut back on the hours I work to make time for that."

"You've been saying that a lot. Have you done anything to make it happen?"

"I'm making progress. I've gotten a little better at delegating responsibilities to my team. I'm also doing better with reining in my frustration when others can't do what I want them to do in the time I want them to do it."

"I'm proud of you."

"Yeah, yeah. Say hi to Alena for me."

"I will."

When Cassandra ended the call, Orion wrote an email to Marcelo, checked it once for typos, and sent it.

It was ten at night at Lugu Lake, which meant that it was six in the morning on the West Coast, and Marcelo would probably see the email when he opened the gallery later today, and by then, Orion would have to come up with more destinations for Leo. But there was plenty of time until then, and right now, he had a sexy lady waiting for him to join her in the bathroom.

Planning Leo's month-long acquisition trip could wait.

Alena

Alena rested her head on the tub's lip and closed her eyes. It had been a long day, and a warm tub was just what the doctor ordered, as humans liked to say.

That reminded her of Merlin, which reminded her of Ronja, and she wondered how things were going with that. When she'd spoken with Annani last night, there had been no news on that front, but then things might have moved along without her mother knowing about it.

Ronja and Merlin were spending a lot of time together, and they were attracted to each other. They couldn't keep it platonic for long.

Fates willing, Ronja would transition successfully.

Alena offered up a prayer to Ronja's health and long life. Lisa needed her mother, and so did David, even though he was a grown man.

Heck, Alena was over two thousand years old, and she still needed her mother. It was hard enough to imagine living apart from her even if they could see each other every day, harder yet to imagine living in the village while Annani returned to the sanctuary, and inconceivable to never see her mother again.

Suddenly cold, Alena lowered herself into the warm water. Feeling an overwhelming need to hear her mother's voice, she regretted leaving her phone in the bedroom.

It was early morning in California, but her mother was an early riser, and she should be awake already.

Pushing up, she leaned over the tub's lip and listened to the sounds coming from the bedroom. It seemed that Orion was done with the phone call, and all Alena could hear were rustling sounds. Was he taking off his clothes?

If he walked naked into the bathroom, she might forget all about calling her mother.

"Could you please bring me my phone?" she called out.

"In a moment."

"No rush. Take your time." She slid into the water and floated in the large bathtub.

Did the Chinese have a preference for tubs over showers? The tub was easily big enough to accommodate two people, even tall ones like her and Orion, while the shower seemed to have been installed as an afterthought.

"Here is your phone." Orion sat on the edge of the tub, his eyes traveling hungrily over her body. "Who do you want to call this late at night or this early in the morning California time?"

Thankfully, he was still partially dressed.

"My mother. I have a sudden urge to hear her voice."

"Only her voice? You're not going to video chat with her?"

"Why do you ask?"

"Because I want to get into the tub with you, but not if you are video chatting with your mother."

"Annani wouldn't mind, but don't worry, we hardly ever use the video feature. We are old-fashioned, or just old."

"Do you feel old?" His eyes roamed over her breasts, her belly, her legs. "Because you sure don't look old to me."

She wanted to say that she didn't, but the truth was that sometimes she did. Two thousand years was a very long time.

"I don't feel old now." She smiled. "After all, I'm about to call my mother."

He leaned down and kissed her on the lips. "There is something about mothers that always makes you feel like a kid."

"Ha, maybe that's why I stayed by her side for so long. She makes me feel young."

It was true, but for a different reason. Annani was young at heart, adventurous, impulsive, passionate, and being around her was uplifting.

With a sigh, Orion let his eyes roam over her nude body once more. "I'd better not be with you in there while you talk to your mother. I won't be able to keep my hands to myself, and you'll get distracted. I'll take a shower while you call her."

For a moment, Alena considered making a game out of it and challenging Orion, but she knew she would lose. Besides, making out while talking to her mother would be disrespectful.

As he went into the shower, she called her mother.

"Alena, my dear. Is everything alright?"

"Everything is great. We took Aliya shopping today, and Kalugal bought her an apartment in Lijiang."

"Why did he do that if she is coming with you to the village?"

Alena chuckled. "Kalugal didn't mean to get her an apartment, but he painted himself into a corner he couldn't get out of. He told Aliya that she could spend as much money as she wanted, provided that she did it in one day."

Annani laughed. "And the smart girl took advantage of his open-ended offer and got herself an apartment."

"Precisely. Kalugal didn't want Aliya to feel as if she was being given charity, so he said that she should consider it compensation for the home she lost because of us."

"What home? You told me that she lived in the tunnels under the archeological site."

"That was what he meant. She can no longer live there because we discovered her hiding place, and Kalugal's partner is going to excavate the place. Anyway, Aliya challenged Kalugal, asking if she could spend a million yuan, and he said yes, not expecting her to want to buy a home. But he'd given her his word, so he couldn't take it back. To Kalugal, it's not a lot of money, but to Aliya, that's a life-changing amount."

"Did it at least make her less suspicious of us?"

Alena laughed. "I think it made her even more suspicious. Wouldn't you be wary of a stranger buying you a home?"

As Orion stepped out of the shower with his wet hair dripping over his muscular chest, Alena got distracted for a moment.

He stopped by the bath and mouthed, "I'll wait for you in bed."

"I would if he was single," Annani said. "But Aliya knows that Kalugal is mated."

Blocking the microphone with her thumb, Alena whispered, "Don't fall asleep."

"I couldn't even if I wanted to." He let the towel drop, giving her an eyeful of his proud erection.

Her mouth watered. "Don't start without me."

"I can't promise that." He wrapped his palm around his shaft.

"Alena? Are you there?"

Tearing her eyes away from the mouthwatering sight, Alena moved her thumb off the microphone. "Aliya doesn't know what a mated bond is. I don't know how much she knows of the outside world, but you and I know that plenty of married humans keep mistresses on the side, and if they are rich, they buy or rent a place for them."

"I forgot that the Kra-ell do not have truelove mates. They live in a sort of commune, and the females share the men between them. Those are not loving relationships that can result in a bond."

"If they are similar to us, they might be capable of bonding. I think that in their case, their cultural constraints overpowered their physiology. Emmett seems to be in love with Eleanor, and his Kra-ell half is more dominant than his human half. But speaking of bonding, how are Ronja and Merlin doing? Any news on that front?"

"Oh, yes. She and Merlin began the process, and I have my fingers crossed for her."

"It's about time." Alena let out a breath. "Although I would be lying if I said that I wasn't concerned. At least with you there, her chances of pulling through are pretty good."

"I hope that will be enough."

"Other than that, all we can do is pray, and I have already beseeched the Fates on Ronja's behalf."

"I pray every day for her," Annani said. "Thank you for calling me, Alena. It gave me great pleasure to hear your voice."

"Same here, Mother."

"Good night, daughter of mine. Give Orion my regards."

"I will." Alena smiled as she ended the call.

She was going to give Orion much more than that.

Orion

Orion stroked himself leisurely as he waited for Alena to finish with her phone call. His intention was to keep the embers warm but not let the fire ignite until she joined him, but with the sight of her wet pink nipples imprinted on his mind, it was difficult to pace himself.

When she came out of the bathroom with a towel wrapped around her lush body and licked her lips, he gripped himself tighter. "Come here," he hissed from between his elongated fangs.

"Oh, I am." She sauntered over, dropping the towel on the way.

He sucked in a breath. "You are so incredibly beautiful."

A soft smile brightening her gorgeous face, she straddled his legs and leaned down, and when she parted her lips and took him into her mouth, he jerked up.

"Alena," he whispered her name as if it was a prayer.

Taking him deeper, she looked at him from under her blond lashes, her eyes full of feminine satisfaction at the pleasure and awe that must have been written all over his face. She didn't replace his hand on his shaft with her own, and as he gently pumped into her, he put his other hand on the back of her head, threading his fingers into her thick hair.

It took only a few moments of gliding in and out of the wet warmth of her mouth for him to near the point from which there would be no return, and for a brief moment, he considered letting her finish what she'd started.

After all, the night was still young, and this wouldn't be the end of their lovemaking. He knew it would be heavenly, and he wanted it, but it would also be a wasted opportunity to plant his seed in her womb.

Orion's chance of having a child with Alena might be so slim that it didn't justify the sacrifice, but as the saying went—hope springs eternal.

"I'm not going to last long like that." He forced himself to withdraw from the heavenly heat of her mouth, pulled her up his chest, and kissed her hard before rolling her onto her back and rising above her.

Her eyes glowing, she lifted her head. "Kiss me."

As he took her mouth, his tongue going where his erection had been, he had a moment of regret for stopping her, but he was a man on a mission, however hopeless that mission was.

When he swept his hand down to her breast, she groaned into his mouth, and when he teased her nipple, a throaty moan left her lips. Letting go of her mouth, he moved down to lick at the hard peak and then at its twin. As he kept kissing and licking, his hand traveled down her body, and when he cupped her center, he found her more than ready for him.

Slipping a finger inside her, and then another, he pumped them in and out to prepare her for a much bigger girth. Greedily, she arched up to take more of his fingers inside her, and that combined with the wet heat of her sheath was an invitation he couldn't refuse. In a quick move, he shifted up, rolled her over to her stomach, and entered her from behind.

The connection was electrifying, and as he started moving, she turned her head and looked at him. "Kiss me."

He did, but when the urge to go faster and harder made it impossible to keep their mouths fused, he had to let go.

Gripping Alena's hips, Orion surged in and pulled out. With his thrusts becoming faster and harder, he felt his climax nearing and pulled out. As pleasurable as it was to pound into her from behind, her soft bottom cushioning every thrust, he wanted to be face to face with her when they both climaxed. Rolling her over, he entered her from the front.

In moments, they were both climbing toward the edge again, and as Alena cried out her climax, her nails scoring his back and her head turned to the side, offering him her neck, Orion let himself tumble off the cliff.

With a hiss, he sank his fangs into that welcoming expanse and erupted into her at the same time.

His orgasm seemed to last forever, and when he was finally spent, he shuddered.

Surprisingly, Alena didn't black out, and as her arms closed around him in a gentle embrace, he felt loved, he felt cherished, he was home.

Arwel

⟨⟩

As the limousine bumped up and down and side to side on the unpaved path, Arwel was thankful for the stability of modern explosives. He'd found a building-supply store in Lijiang that carried them, and he didn't even have to thrall anyone to sell them to him.

Evidently, the use of explosives was common, and their sale was not restricted.

Still, with all that shaking, he was sure Aliya would become nauseous, and they would have to stop for her to have a breather and calm her stomach like they'd had to do during yesterday's trip, but the girl seemed to adapt quickly, not only to rides in a fast-moving vehicle, but also to her new circumstances.

She looked good in a pair of trendy jeans and a hoodie. The hoodie concealed her thinness and her too narrow waist. If not for the shape of her eyes and her unusual height, she could have passed for a college student. With sunglasses on, only the height remained, and that wasn't such a big deal. Unless she suffered from a case of trigger-happy fangs like Vlad had before mating Wendy, she didn't need to worry about scaring people or being pegged as an alien.

Aliya had quite the temper, though, and that was a problem, especially since her aggression was quick to follow. Perhaps she could wear a face mask to mitigate the fangs issue, but even dark sunglasses couldn't conceal the red glow from her eyes.

Ignoring the shaking and rattling, Aliya looked out the window and didn't take part in the conversation going on around her.

Arwel wondered what was going through her head.

The little emotion she emitted since he'd first encountered her had soon changed from fear and anger to resentment and suspicion, then had morphed into surprise and gratitude, and finally had settled on a general state of pensive wariness.

Was she upset about going back to the tunnels that used to be her home?

Was she debating what to reveal and what to keep concealed?

Or maybe she was debating whether she should try to run away or go with them to the village. Although at this point, that was water under the bridge.

Before making the wire transfer to pay for her apartment, Kalugal had gotten her to commit to giving the village a three-month try. If in ninety days she was unhappy, he'd promised to put her on a plane back to Lijiang.

Aliya wasn't the type to go back on her promise, so running didn't seem likely.

Shifting his gaze to his mate, Arwel wondered about her unusual silence. Jin had an opinion on most things and wasn't shy about expressing it. Was she still thinking about serving as their communication conduit to the world outside the tunnel?

When they were minutes away from the riverbank, he turned to her. "So, what's your final decision? Do you want to tether someone and stay topside while we go in, or did you scrap that idea?"

"What do you think? Should I?"

Arwel arched a brow. Usually, Jin didn't ask anyone's opinion, including his. "It depends on your objectives. If you want to stay out of the tunnel and avoid encounters with creepy-crawlies, and if Alena chooses to do the same, then you can tether Lokan or Kalugal and stay behind. Naturally, I'll stay with you. But if you are curious and want to go in, I think that there is no need for you to give up on it. The excavation workers know that we are going in, and if we don't come out at the end of the day, they will know to come to look for us. We are also better prepared this time."

Yesterday, they had all gotten appropriate clothing and footwear in Lijiang, made from materials that wouldn't snag and tear on any sharp edge. They each had a brand-new hardhat with a flashlight attached, a backpack with two durable water bottles, snacks, and more flashlights. Those who were trained in combat also carried an assortment of weapons, including explosives to blast through places that were blocked. He'd also gotten a rope and a harpoon. In short, Arwel was ready for almost anything.

"I want to go in," Jin said after a few moments. "And so does Alena."

"I'm glad." Jacki turned to look at them. "It would have been boring without you. What are we going to find there? Some more illegible scribbles on the walls?"

As all eyes turned to Aliya, she shrugged. "That's all I found during the fourteen years I lived in these tunnels and explored every centimeter of them. So, I don't think there's more to find. But Kalugal insisted that there must be."

"I know there is." Kalugal patted his stomach. "My archeological sixth sense tells me that I'm right, and we are also meeting a geologist who is going to check the soil." He rubbed his hands. "I'm excited about today. I know we will make new discoveries."

"By the way," Jin said. "Did anyone hear from Herb?"

Kalugal turned in his seat. "He went back to the States."

"When?"

"Yesterday. He sent me a text message and said that I should feel free to call him with whatever questions I have about ancient Eastern languages. He suggested that we meet again."

"Are you going to take him up on his offer?" Jacki asked.

"Of course. I enjoyed talking to him, and since I'm moving some of my archeological interests to the east, I might need him."

"What about the other digs you have going on?" Arwel asked.

"They go on," Kalugal said. "I'm not done looking for clues about our ancestors. I just added the Kra-ell ancestors to the mix." He smirked. "I like to keep things interesting."

Orion

"Where are we meeting the geologist?" Orion asked when they walked through the ancient outpost's gate.

"In the tent," Kalugal said. "Jianye made some improvements while we were shopping yesterday. He said that he'd made the tent comfortable for the ladies. I wonder what he did."

They found out when their group got inside. The tables with the artifacts had been pushed to one side of the tent, and the area that was cleared now served as a place to sit and eat. A long table was covered with a paper tablecloth, and several folding chairs were arranged on both of its sides.

Right now, only one person was sitting at the table, and he rose to his feet.

"Professor Kal Gunter?" His eyes darted to Orion, dismissed him as the possible professor, and moved to Lokan, who apparently fit the image better.

"Mr. Bingwen Zhao." Kalugal stepped forward and offered the geologist his hand. "Or is it Doctor Zhao?"

Looking embarrassed, the young man pointed to a strange device that he'd left on the table. "I'm still working on my doctorate." He lifted the device. "But this has been stealing too much of my time. My brother and I have been working on this since we graduated from MIT."

"How exciting. Did you graduate at the same time?"

"Yes, we are twins."

Orion stifled a chuckle. Kalugal had told them on the way about the twin brothers and their promising start-up, and yet he'd pretended not to know that. Was it a negotiating strategy?

Did he want to appear uninterested so he could get a better deal out of the brothers?

They'd invented a portable device that analyzed soil quickly and accurately. Kalugal had said something about an electron beam microscope or an electron probe, but as usual, anything scientific flew right over Orion's head.

The business part of it, however, he had no problem understanding. Kalugal wanted to invest in the twins' start-up, and he planned to fund the commercial development of their device in exchange for a majority share-holding in their company, the way he did with all his start-up investments. The guy liked to be in control.

"What's MIT?" Aliya asked quietly.

"It's a very prestigious university," Lokan said. "The Massachusetts Institute of Technology produced many important scientists and innovators and is currently ranked first in the world."

Aliya regarded the young man with renewed appreciation. "He must be very smart."

"I'm sure he is," Orion said.

"So, Mr. Zhao." Kalugal motioned for the guy to follow him. "Have you done any initial tests before we arrived?"

"Yes." The guy frowned. "The readings I get indicate the presence of a mineral that my device can't identify, but then we haven't programmed all the possible compounds yet, just the ones that are commonly found. I will have to input its special pattern of iron and carbon into the database and see what comes up. I can't do that from here because of the interference."

"That's interesting." Kalugal smoothed his hand over his goatee. "Is it possible that this peculiar mineral is responsible for the interference we are experiencing here?"

The scientist nodded. "It produces a powerful electro-magnetic interference."

Kalugal inclined his head. "What are your thoughts on that, Mr. Zhao?"

The guy opened his mouth, then closed it, fighting Kalugal's compulsion with his mighty brain, but even a brilliant scientist like him couldn't resist a powerful compeller like Kalugal. "I think that the islet the trading post was carved from was created by an extraterrestrial meteorite."

Kalugal looked doubtful. "Meteorites come from above and usually create a crater, not a new islet. New land is usually created by volcanic eruptions."

"A really big meteorite or asteroid strike can cause deep deformations that can lead to volcanic eruptions, but this is not the case here. The crater is too small. Frankly, I don't know what happened here, and I would like to investigate it further."

"Was there a reason you hesitated telling us about it?"

The guy's face reddened. "The competition in the scientific world is brutal. A discovery like that could mean a lot for my career."

"I see." Kalugal smiled apologetically. "But I can't allow you to do that. In fact, I want you to sell me your device and forget what you found here."

Fighting the compulsion, the guy swallowed. "I can't sell this. My brother and I invested years in developing it."

"And you will continue to do that with my help. I just want to test this device on a little side project. Show me how to operate it, and tomorrow, we will teleconference to negotiate the details of my investment in your company." He smiled at the guy. "I assure you that I have no interest in reverse engineering it and manufacturing it myself. That's not how I operate. I identify a potential, provide the funds, and let others do the work."

Kalugal must have used compulsion again because the guy handed him the device and spent a good hour explaining how to use it.

In the meantime, Jianye entertained them by explaining what the various artifacts were and how old he estimated them to be.

When the geologist left, Kalugal handed the device to Shamash. "Is everyone ready to do some investigating?"

"I am." Jin huffed. "But if all we are looking for are more dusty housewares from hundreds of years ago, I'm going to be very disappointed."

"What did you expect to find?" Jianye asked, his defensive tone indicating that he was offended by her comment.

"Something written," she said. "Something that can tell us about the people who lived here. Or weapons. Swords, arrows, knives. How did these people defend themselves?"

"I hope to find that too," Jianye said. "But we can also learn a lot about the people who lived here from the things they used."

"Of course." Jin gave him a perfunctory smile as she slung her supply backpack over her shoulder. "Wish us luck."

Aliya

"Touchy," Jin muttered under her breath as they exited the tent.

"Jianye is passionate about what he does," Alena said. "You offended his profession."

Jin nodded. "Sometimes I speak before I think, and then I regret what comes out of my mouth."

"They repositioned the tent," Aliya said. "There is more room between it and the entrance to the tunnels."

The hole in the ground had been roped off, and triangular red flags had been hung from the ropes to warn people against a sudden drop. The boulder was more or less where they'd left it.

"Should I tell Jianye that I like what he has done with the place?" Jin asked as she peered down the hole.

Aliya glanced down to see what had gotten Jin excited.

A good quality ladder was attached to one side of the opening, the kind that had rails on both sides and looked more like stairs than a simple ladder. Below, the chamber was illuminated with strong floodlights that were connected with thick extension cords to the noisy generator that had been bothering her since the excavation project had begun.

Well, it was not going to bother her for much longer. After today, she would probably never return to these tunnels again, and she would definitely not miss them.

If the immortals' village didn't work out, she would make a life for herself in Lijiang. It was a beautiful city, and so was the new neighborhood where her apartment was located.

She would have to find a job, but first she needed to learn to control her temper.

As Jin had shown her, it didn't take much to explain away her other oddities. The sunglasses covering her strangely shaped eyes could be explained by a rare eye disorder that made them overly sensitive to light, and her height wasn't as big of a deal in a large city as it had been in the Mosuo village. After she'd gotten her new clothes and put them on, Kalugal had stopped shrouding her to prove that she didn't need to hide.

People had turned their heads to look at her, and she heard one kid say that she must be a basketball player, but that was the extent of it.

She could get a job as a cleaner. It probably didn't pay much, but she was used to living on practically nothing, so she could do with very little. The important thing was that she would have a roof over her head that wasn't made of stone, and that she would no longer freeze at night or go hungry.

"Aliya, you're next," Carol said.

Without giving it much thought, Aliya jumped down. She didn't need a ladder to go down seven meters.

"You shouldn't have done that," Jin said quietly. "Jianye saw you jump."

"So what? I've seen human kids do that. It's not such a big deal."

"Maybe not, but you need to be mindful when you're around humans. The less you stand out, the better. Don't draw any additional attention to yourself."

"Is that what you do?"

Jin snorted. "I try. Luckily for me, I don't need to leave the village often, so I can act as I please most of the time."

That village was starting to sound really good, and Aliya promised herself to give life there a fair chance.

Once everyone had made it down to the big chamber, Kalugal motioned for them to gather around him. "You are all probably wondering what I'm going to do with the device Shamash is holding, and why I went to such lengths to acquire it."

Lokan took the device from Shamash and examined it. "You think that the Kra-ell had something to do with that strange mineral, and you hope that this device is going to lead us to them."

"Close. I don't think we are going to find any live Kra-ell, but we might find traces of their vessel." Kalugal lifted Jacki's backpack off and handed it to Phinas. "For an alien mineral to be in such big concentration here, the scouting crew Jade talked about must have landed here. If that happened around two thousand years ago, any metals would have disintegrated by now and penetrated the soil, which would explain the high concentration of it and the electromagnetic interference. If we find where its concentration is the strongest, we might find the exact spot where they hid their pod."

"But if everything disintegrated, what do you expect to find?" Jin asked.

"If any part of the pod was made from glass, we can find shards of that. Glass never disintegrates. Everything else does."

"What if that alien mineral is like glass?" Aliya asked and immediately regretted it.

Her education had stopped at eighth grade. What did she know about minerals and metals and other science stuff?

"Good point," Orion said.

"Indeed." Kalugal nodded. "The other reason I bought the device is that I need to erase all that Mr. Bingwen

Zhao found out and recorded in it. We don't want anyone other than us finding out about the Kra-ell or even suspecting that any aliens have ever landed on Earth."

Mey

ey's legs were starting to cramp.

She'd been sitting in the lotus position for hours, listening to so many echoes that the stories had all become a big blur in her mind and her concentration was wavering. Letting go for a few moments to rest, she allowed her thoughts to wander.

Those echoes might have been irrelevant to her investigation, but they had been very relevant to those who'd lived them, and they made Mey melancholy.

Or maybe it was just exhaustion weighing her down.

She'd pushed herself hard, keeping her focus for longer than ever before, but nothing important had come up.

Mey hated thinking of the life stories she'd witnessed as unimportant. She was in a unique position to witness people's life dramas, big and small, and she wished she could record them in some way, immortalize the people who had lived them.

Mey supposed that was why Toven wrote about his lovers in his journals. It was the only way he could immortalize those mortal women who'd left a positive impression on him.

Human life was so depressingly fleeting.

Which reminded her that she should visit her parents, and she should do that soon. They weren't getting any younger, and both of their daughters were living abroad.

Talk about guilt.

They had adopted two girls, hoping to one day enjoy grandchildren who would come to visit, and who would spend the holidays with them. They hadn't banked on those girls turning immortal and becoming practically infertile.

She and Yamanu had been faithfully following Merlin's protocol, drinking the vile potions every morning, keeping positive attitudes, avoiding stress...

Yeah, right. Chasing Kra-ell phantoms shouldn't have been stressful, but the circumstances in which they'd disappeared were anxiety-inducing.

With a sigh, she opened her eyes, unfolded her legs, and pushed up to her feet. She was too tired to continue, and there was too much on her mind. She wouldn't be able to reach the meditative state again unless she rested properly and put something in her belly. But the best way to chase away the blues was to make love to her mate.

Heck, just being around Yamanu was a mood booster. He had such an upbeat personality that it was impossible to stay down with him being so up. No wonder the girls in the halfway house loved him and his karaoke nights, which he'd missed out on lately because of the two missions.

It was time to go home.

When she opened the door, Yamanu gave her a pitying smile. "No luck, eh?"

"I think Vrog is right. I've been sitting there for hours, and I've only seen that one echo of Jade and Kagra's fight. All the other ones were created by humans."

"He'll be glad to hear that. The guy is itching to get to that hybrid female, and I can't blame him. If I were him, the moment I heard about her, I would have been on the first flight leaving for Lugu Lake."

"I want to try the laundry again when they close for the day. That's the only place I didn't spend much time in yet. Maybe I'll get lucky."

Yamanu arched a brow and leaned closer to whisper in her ear, "How about I take you to our room so you can rest, and we can both explore how lucky we are to have each other?"

"You read my mind."

Vrog intercepted them on their way to the staff quarters. "Given your exhausted expression, I assume that you had no luck today."

Mey nodded. "This evening, I want to try the laundry again, and if there is nothing there, we can leave tomorrow morning."

A grin spread over his face. "That's music to my ears. I've already made all the necessary preparations, but I was afraid you'd find something new, and we would need to stay longer."

Shaking his head, Yamanu put a hand on Vrog's shoulder. "Aren't you forgetting why we are here? We seek answers about your people. You hear about one hybrid girl and suddenly all the others are unimportant?"

Yamanu was teasing Vrog, but the guy took him seriously.

"The others are just as important to me as Aliya, but at some point, we need to accept that nothing further will be discovered and that it is futile to continue."

Given Yamanu's grin, he wasn't done teasing Vrog. "So says the man who's waited for his mistress to return for twenty-two years."

Vrog let out a breath. "When I started the school, my intention was to preserve and grow the funds the tribe had left behind and wait for those who might have survived to return. But in time, the school itself became my life. I think I stopped waiting a long time ago."

Vrog

Vrog wondered if what he'd just said was a lie.

Had he really stopped waiting? Or perhaps his old hopes had been replaced by new ones of a better future that included a relationship with his son and possibly a mate of his own?

Before finding out about Vlad, the hope of finding survivors of his tribe was what had kept Vrog going, which was why he'd clung to it despite the improbability of it ever happening. Now that he had something else to live for, it was tempting to let go of his quest.

But that would be wrong. Perhaps it was irrational, but he believed that as long as he kept waiting and hoping, his tribe wasn't really gone. The moment he gave up, it would be forever lost.

Given Yamanu's doubtful expression, he hadn't fooled the guy. "Whatever makes you happy, my man." The

Guardian circled his arm around his mate's waist. "We are going to take a little nap. See you at dinner."

"Have a good rest." Vrog inclined his head. "Is it okay if Morris and I drive to the airport and load the safes onto the jet?"

"Sure. Take Jay with you. You have valuable stuff in those safes."

"Thank you."

Vrog doubted that a Guardian's protection was necessary, but he'd learned that nonchalance was just another facet of arrogance and it never hurt to take extra precautions.

Even though he was at least twice as strong as Jay, the Guardian probably carried a concealed firearm, which would always trump muscle.

"How large are the safes?" Morris fell in step with Vrog.

"A square meter at the base and about a meter and a half tall. There are two of them."

"Do you have a truck to transport them?" Morris asked.

"I can borrow the gardener's truck."

Jay shook his head. "A van would be better. Two safes on a truck would attract too much attention. People will think you have valuables inside."

"We can cover them with a tarp," Morris said. "And tie a rope around them so it doesn't fly off."

"That was what I planned to do." Vrog opened the door to the administrative building. "Can either of you shroud?"

"We can't shroud a moving vehicle." Morris followed him up the stairs.

Vrog chuckled. "I mean now. I don't want my staff to see me carry safes out into the truck. First of all, because no one is supposed to be that strong, and also because they would wonder why I'm taking them out. I'd prefer not to have to explain." He opened the door to his office.

"Won't they realize that they are gone?" Jay eyed the two safes. "Everyone who walks into your office will see that."

"If anyone asks, I can tell them that I transferred them to my personal quarters. No one goes in there."

"Not even the cleaner?"

"I can thrall her."

Jay shrugged. "I can shroud you and the safe, but I can only make you invisible. I'm not good at creating illusions. Morris will have to keep people out of the way. How far is it to the truck?"

Vrog grimaced. "A good five-minute walk. I have a dolly downstairs, so I don't have to carry it all the way."

Morris scratched his head. "You know what would be much less complicated? Getting those documents into these boxes." He pointed at the stack of flattened cardboard resting on top of the safes.

"I'm afraid those are not secure enough. They will not protect the documents from water or fire damage. The only reason they survived the fire that destroyed the compound was that Jade had the foresight to keep them in safes."

Morris looked at him as if he was dimwitted. "You can get stronger boxes that are watertight and fireproof. Theft is not an issue, so those are the only things you should be concerned with."

That was true, but he didn't have time to order those kinds of boxes and have them delivered before leaving for Lugu Lake.

"I checked the delivery time, and it will take three days for them to arrive. If we plan to come back here after the lake, I can leave the documents here."

Morris and Jay exchanged glances.

Jay shrugged. "I'm not the boss, so I can't tell you whether we will or not. Can we get those boxes in Beijing? I can drive over and pick them up for you."

"I checked. The boxes I want need to be shipped from the factory. What they have in the stores is not good enough."

"They probably are," Morris said. "You are not transporting fragile works of art. If you're willing to compromise, getting those lower-quality boxes would solve a lot of your problems."

Letting out a breath, Vrog leaned back in his chair and weighed the pros and cons.

Morris didn't have an emotional attachment to the files, and he was thinking logically. Vrog, on the other hand, was too anxious about moving those files out of his office to think straight.

It was the only tie he had to the past, the only clue that could potentially lead the clan to whoever had survived that attack or to the perpetrators, and that made those files invaluable.

His anxiety wasn't so much about losing the ledgers as it was about them being a dead end. As long as he hadn't used them to investigate the fate of his tribe and hit a brick wall, his hope, however dim, still lived. Once that last avenue was exhausted, and nothing was found, it would die. But perhaps that would be better.

He would finally have closure.

Arwel

❧

"**A**re you sure that you know how to operate this device?" Lokan leaned over Kalugal's shoulder. "I'll figure it out."

The geologist had taken nearly an hour to explain to Kalugal how the thing worked, and even though Arwel had heard the entire conversation, he wasn't able to help because most of it had been too complicated for a layperson to understand.

The question was whether Kalugal had understood or just pretended that he had. The guy had a huge ego, and admitting that he couldn't master everything on his first go was inconceivable to him.

"I need a flat surface to put it on." Kalugal lifted his head and looked at the rectangular block of stone in the center of the big chamber. "That will do."

He walked over, put the device down, and pulled out his phone.

"There is no reception here," Jacki reminded him.

"I know. I took a few notes while Zhao explained."

Jin let out a breath. "That's going to take a while." She walked over to the stone altar and hopped on.

"You shouldn't sit up there," Jacki said. "If my hunch is right, this used to be an altar."

"So what?" Jin opened her backpack and pulled out a candy bar.

"So it might have been used for making sacrifices. That's why I don't want to touch it."

Jin took a bite out of the candy bar, wrapped up what was left, and returned it to her backpack. "In that case, you should definitely touch it. Maybe you'll get a vision of what they did in here."

"Yeah." Jacki grimaced. "That's what I'm trying to avoid. Funerals creep me out."

"I'll hold your hand," Jin offered. "We might gain some insight into this mystery." She shifted her gaze to Aliya. "Any thoughts on that?"

"I don't think this altar was built by the Kra-ell. Our tribe's altar was much smaller, and it wasn't in the middle of a large chamber."

"What did it look like?" Jin asked.

"Like an oven." Aliya made a domed shape with her arms. "And it was this tall." She indicated the height from the ground. "People had to kneel in front of it and lower their heads."

"Did you ever pray there?" Jacki asked.

"It wasn't used for praying, and I wasn't old enough to participate in any of the ceremonies." She looked at the rectangular slab of stone again. "This was probably built by the people who lived in the outpost."

"Oh, what the heck." Jacki let out a sigh. "You are right. I should give it a try." She put a hand on the altar, and when nothing happened, she added the other one.

"No vision." She smiled up at Jin. "Scoot. I want to sit down."

Kalugal paused his tinkering with the device. "Don't jump. I'll lift you."

Jacki rolled her eyes. "I thought that you weren't listening."

"I always listen to you, my love." He put his hands on her waist, lifted her, and set her down on the platform.

"So you were okay with me touching this thing and getting a vision but you were not okay with me hopping up on a three-foot-tall altar?"

"Visions are not dangerous to you or our baby. Jumping up and down is." He turned back to his notes.

Leaning back on her forearms, Jacki looked up. "This was definitely used as a funeral pyre. There are scorch marks on the ceiling."

Jin joined her in the reclined position. "You are right. When we were here before, it was too dark to see, but with the light Jianye put down here, it's very clear."

Following their gazes, Arwel looked at the pattern on the ceiling and had to agree with Jacki's assessment. The darkened area on the otherwise yellow and light gray stone corresponded with a contained fire, and not one that consumed the entire chamber.

Except, if the altar had been used for animal sacrifices, the pattern would be similar to that of a funeral pyre.

He was about to make a comment when Jacki's eyes rolled back in her head and she slumped into Jin, who wrapped an arm around her in time to prevent her from sliding off the slab and hurting herself.

"Jacki?" Kalugal turned to his mate. "What's wrong, love? Are you having a vision?"

She didn't respond for the longest time, but since they could all hear her breathing, they just waited along with Kalugal for her to open her eyes.

Alena

Poor Jacki.

She'd been so afraid of touching the altar, and if not for Jin's goading, she would have been spared having an unwanted vision.

Alena thanked the Fates for not making her clairvoyant. She was so much better suited for the gift of fertility and couldn't imagine losing control like that, with the vision taking over her mind whether she wanted to see it or not.

It must be so scary and disorienting for Jacki to lose her connection with the real world, getting thrust into the past or the future with no prior warning.

Alena would have preferred carrying and delivering a new baby every year of her adult life than going through a terrifying experience like that even once.

Two thousand babies would have been a bit much even for her, though. She would settle for just one more with

Orion—a little boy with black hair and blue eyes and his father's gentle nature.

Their child would be perfect.

As Kalugal took Jacki from Jin and sat on the ground with her cradled in his lap, they all waited in anxious silence.

When Jacki groaned a few minutes later, they all released relieved breaths.

She opened her eyes and smiled at her mate. "That was so worth it. Wait until you hear what I saw."

"I'm just glad that you're okay. You've been out for several minutes." He took in a long breath. "You've never been out for so long before, and I got worried. The Fates got an earful from me."

Jacki put her hands on her belly. "I stayed inside the vision because I wanted to see more. I hope that you didn't cuss at the Fates in your head. We need to stay in their good graces, and we don't want them to become vindictive."

"I don't cuss, love. I threaten and then offer bribes."

Lokan chuckled. "Excellent negotiation tactic, brother."

Alena didn't know whether Lokan's comment was sarcastic or heartfelt, but Kalugal took it as the latter.

"Thank you. It takes one great negotiator to recognize another."

Jacki shook her head. "Now that you're done stroking each other's egos, do you want to hear what I saw?"

"Yes, my love." Kalugal kissed her temple. "Please tell us."

"So I was right, and this altar was originally used to hold funeral pyres." She paused for dramatic effect, glancing at her companions, who had formed a large circle around her and Kalugal. "That's how the Kra-ell dealt with their dead." She paused again, waiting to see their reaction to her revelation. "I saw a Kra-ell funeral service."

Alena didn't know what to think of that. Was the additional puzzle piece confirming the Kra-ell scouting team story a good thing?

"Was the dead person male or female?" Orion asked.

"Male."

"Did you see signs of injury on him?" Arwel asked.

She shook her head. "The male looked old, so I assume his death had been of natural causes, and some of the attendants looked old as well."

"How many people attended the funeral?" Carol asked.

"I counted twelve, not including the deceased, and there were no females. They all wore long robes, but the hoods were down, so it was easy to see that they weren't human. They stood around the altar and chanted prayers." She chuckled. "They reminded me of the Klingons. Not in the way they looked, but in the way their language and their chanting sounded. It was somber and very male. It was pretty obvious that those males were warriors. If they were the members of the scouting team who arrived thousands of years before the others, then it seems like their team was made up entirely of males. But from what I've heard about the Kra-ell society, that doesn't make sense. There should have been at least one female in charge of them."

"The females might have not attended the funeral," Aliya said. "As far as I know, none of the Kra-ell died during my eight years on the compound, so I'm only speculating. But I know that in the Mosuo society, the men are in charge of burials."

"The women still attend, though," Jin said. "It would be disrespectful to the dead if they didn't."

Aliya shrugged. "Maybe their females were older and died before the male Jacki saw on the pyre."

"Or maybe the simplest explanation is the correct one," Arwel said. "The scouting team was most likely comprised of males only. Kra-ell females would have been deemed too precious to put at risk. The males were supposed to prepare a safe environment for them once they landed."

Kalugal shook his head. "There had to be a female, and probably more than one, for those Kra-ell to influence the lifestyle of the Mosuo people. I don't see how that could have been the case if the team was exclusively male."

Aliya

༻

Aliya should have felt something for those ancient Kra-ell—pity for how lonely they must have been, regret over their extinction, or anger about their suspected betrayal of their fellow travelers—but she felt nothing aside from mild curiosity.

She had as much in common with that scouting team as with these descendants of the gods. Their ancestors might have shared the same corner of the universe, and Kalugal had told her that the gods and the Kra-ell might have a common ancestor, but they were very different, and they didn't face the same challenges. They could have long-lived offspring, while she most likely couldn't.

It was better not to have children at all than to outlive them. Perhaps Jade hadn't been cruel when she'd forbade the hybrid males from fathering children with humans. She'd been merciful.

"You know what has just occurred to me?" Jin hopped back on the slab, leaned her elbows on her knees, and rested her chin on her hands. "Mey and I might be related to these Kra-ell and not someone from Jade's tribe."

Arwel shook his head. "Jade said that they arrived thousands of years ahead of the rest. If their lifespan is indeed about a thousand years, then the original team is long gone, and if they fathered hybrid children, those are gone as well. The children of the hybrids were born human, so that was the end of the line for them." He shifted his gaze to Aliya. "Did you ever hear Jade talk about the actual lifespans of the purebloods and the hybrids?"

As all eyes turned to her, she shook her head. "All I knew was that they were long-lived compared to humans. How do you know it's supposed to be a thousand years?"

"That was what Emmett told us."

"He must know then," Aliya said. "But an average lifespan doesn't mean that everyone lives to be exactly one thousand. The average lifespan for humans is eighty-something years, but some die much younger while others live to be much older. So if some of those Kra-ell lived for twelve hundred years and others for eight hundred, the average was one thousand. Jade said that the scouting team landed two thousand years before the others, so if one or two of them lived longer than one thousand, and his son lived that long as well, he could have fathered Jin and her sister."

"I still say that there must have been a female leading them," Kalugal said. "And if there was, then she could have produced more purebloods. It's very likely that they didn't die out after all."

Aliya shook her head. "Jade assumed that they had. Which means that they didn't have a pureblooded female with them."

"Or maybe she was past her childbearing years," Carol said. "They are not immortal, so a six-hundred-year-old Kra-ell female would be the equivalent of a sixty-year-old human woman and would no longer be fertile."

Kalugal nodded. "That makes a lot of sense."

Carol smiled and fluffed her curls. "I only look dumb."

"You don't look dumb, love." Lokan wrapped his arm around her waist. "You are one of the smartest, most cunning people I know, and anyone who underestimates you is a fool."

"Thank you." She lifted on her tiptoes and kissed the underside of his jaw.

"There is still another possibility," Lokan said. "What if one of those original purebloods hooked up with a Dormant? She transmitted her immortal genes to her daughters, and they to their daughters, and so on, and maybe those genes were altered by the unique Kra-ell genes, and that's how Jin and Mey came to be." He turned to Jin. "You and your sister might have been born to a descendant of that original Dormant who had hooked up with a Kra-ell pureblood or hybrid."

Her arms folded over her chest, Jin frowned. "That's possible. Our Kra-ell features didn't manifest until after our transition. So you might be right about the Kra-ell special genes hitching a ride on the immortal ones." She inhaled and then sighed. "I thought that Mey and I had all the answers as to why and how we turned out the way we did after our transition. We thought that we'd been fathered by a hybrid from Jade's tribe. But now there is that." She waved her hand over the chamber. "I wonder how many other hidden Kra-ell descendants are out there."

Hope bloomed in Aliya's chest. What if there were more people like her? Could she make it her mission to locate them?

Where would she even start?

The Mosuo were the best candidates, but if in order to preserve the Kra-ell genes, the mother needed to be a Dormant, then she doubted that there were any hidden Kra-ell gene carriers among them.

Hopping up onto the stone slab, Arwel sat next to Jin and wrapped his arm around her back. "I wonder if there is special affinity between Kra-ell and Dormants like there is between immortals and Dormants. It seems odd that out of the entire human population, a hybrid Kra-ell male found a dormant female, and another one found an immortal female. It's like two needles in a haystack somehow attracting each other."

"Like magnets," Jin said.

Shifting in Kalugal's arms, Jacki turned to her mate. "Did you figure out how to work that device? Or did I distract you?"

"I figured out what I was doing wrong. I need to keep feeding it new samples and clean the lenses between tests."

"Then let's go." She pushed to her feet and offered him a hand up. "We need to find where that mineral is present in the highest concentration. Now that I know they were here for sure, I want to find material proof of them."

"Are you sure you're up to it?" He pretended to let Jacki pull him to her, but Aliya knew that he hadn't let her bear any of his weight. "Don't you need to rest a little longer?"

"I'm fine." Jacki dusted her pants off. "And if I get tired, I'll ask you to carry me."

"Deal." He grinned as if she'd just offered him a great prize.

These immortals were strange, and their relationships were even stranger. The couples behaved as if they were attached at the hip.

It was nice, but Aliya couldn't imagine having to endure that twenty-four hours a day, every day. She needed her freedom, she needed to roam and hunt, and she needed to do it alone without an overprotective mate hovering over her.

Orion

Kalugal blew out a frustrated breath. "I wish this thing worked like a metal detector."

Their progress had been excruciatingly slow, and Kalugal wasn't the only one who was frustrated. They all were.

Orion felt especially bad for Jacki, who needed more frequent stops to empty her bladder, which required Kalugal to escort her to one of the side tunnels for privacy.

Aliya had reassured them that the tunnels were free of booby-traps, but Arwel insisted on double-checking, especially whenever stairs were involved. That alone slowed them down to a crawl.

Then there was the device Kalugal had bought from the geologist, which required stops at every fork to take a sample of the soil, put it into the device, and wait for it to analyze it.

"Can't we continue tomorrow?" Jacki leaned against her mate's side. "And by we, I mean you and your men. When you find something, you can come to get us."

"We are getting close." Kalugal's eyes remained glued to the readout on the device's screen. "The concentration of the mineral has been increasing the further down we go."

"We are reaching the end of the tunnel system," Aliya said. "There are only two more forks, and they are not very long. I say we finish this today and be done with it."

Orion was impressed. The girl's use of English was improving at an exponential rate. Even her accent was slowly becoming less noticeable.

He was a quick learner of languages, but she was even faster.

She also knew these tunnels inside and out and had led them to every scratch and mark she'd discovered over the years that could possibly indicate a Kra-ell presence.

Kalugal and Lokan had taken many pictures of everything she'd shown them, and the only thing still keeping them in the tunnels was the strange unknown mineral and Jacki's vision of the Kra-ell funeral ceremony.

They'd either lived in these tunnels or had used them for something, and Kalugal was determined to find more clues.

"How long are those two forks?" Jin asked.

"Together with all the small offshoots that terminate in dead ends there is about a kilometer left. I don't know how long it is in miles."

"It's a little over half a mile," Lokan said.

"Let's go." Kalugal handed the device to Phinas. "I'll check the mineral concentration in both, and we will call it a day."

The next corridor, which was how Orion had started to refer to the tunnels, had many branches on both sides, but as Aliya had told them, they were short and terminated in dead ends.

"I think these used to be the Kra-ell living quarters," Jin said. "What if each of these short tunnels led to a private room, but they were walled off for some reason? Maybe they didn't burn all of the bodies, and this is their crypt?"

"Creepy." Jacki shivered.

Orion was surprised to see Arwel nod. "The same thought occurred to me." He turned to Kalugal. "I would like to check one of these to see if there is a hidden opening. Do you want to finish your mineral detecting before we attempt it? Or do we take a break and try that first?"

"We can split up," Kalugal said. "I'll continue with Jacki, Phinas, and Welgost, while the rest of you can check out Jin's idea." He lifted a finger in warning. "Be careful, and don't even think about using explosives. This whole thing could come crashing down on us."

"I want to come with you," Lokan said. "Carol and I are fascinated by the device and the mystery mineral."

"Yeah," Carol said. "I don't get how it can disrupt our phone signals but lets us take pictures and play music. When I put my earphones in, I expect to hear some background noise, or static, or not anything at all, but the music plays perfectly."

Orion had been wondering the same.

"I'm afraid that my scientific knowledge isn't that extensive," Kalugal said. "I will have to ask the geologists when I speak with them tomorrow."

"What about me?" Aliya asked. "Who do I go with?"

"Stay with them." Kalugal winked at her. "They might need your strength to help them dig through." He turned to Welgost. "Since Lokan is coming with us, you should stay with Alena. I promised her brother to keep her safe."

"No problem, boss. I'll stay to protect Alena." Welgost cast a sidelong glance at Aliya.

Was the guy interested in her?

Phinas hadn't flirted with Aliya during their trip to Lijiang, and Orion had wondered whether she'd said something to discourage him, or he'd lost interest.

"Why can't I stay with them too?" Jacki asked.

"Because you are my mate." Kalugal took her hand. "I want you by my side."

"Ugh." She rolled her eyes. "You are such a mother hen. You want me where you can see me."

"I want you with me so I can protect you, and I don't have to worry about you." He led her down the main tunnel with Phinas trailing behind them.

Arwel unstrapped the hammer from his belt. "It's going to get dusty in there, so I suggest you stay out here."

"I can help you dig." Aliya followed Arwel.

"So can I," Orion said and then looked at Alena. "On second thought, I should stay out here with you."

"Don't be silly." Alena gave him a little shove. "You'll be only a few feet away." She threaded her arm through Jin's. "We are going to watch you be all manly, taking turns swinging that big hammer."

"Yeah." Jin waggled her brows. "Give us a good show."

Alena

"Come sit with me." Jin lowered herself to the ground and opened her backpack. "Do you want to share a candy bar?"

"No, thank you." Alena stood at the entrance to the offshoot and watched Arwel, Orion, and Aliya pat the stone walls and knock on them.

Welgost and Shamash were more than happy to stay out in the main artery with them.

"This sounded hollow." Arwel motioned for the other two to step back.

When they moved nearly to where Alena was standing, Arwel swung the hammer at the wall. At first only a few chips flew off, but as he kept going, larger chunks got loose, which encouraged him to keep on swinging.

Alena moved aside so as not to block Jin's line of sight to her mate, for which she'd gotten a smile and a nod.

After several minutes of that, Arwel paused, and Orion took over.

Standing with her arms crossed over her chest, Alena drank in the sight of him working, his arm and leg muscles bulging under his clothing, the determination on his handsome face, the fluidity of his movements. He worked as though demolition had been his primary occupation and he was an expert in it, when she knew for a fact that he hadn't done any menial labor in years.

"I don't think there is an opening there." Candy bar in hand, Jin pushed to her feet and joined Alena. "But if they keep hammering at it, they might create one."

"My turn," Aliya called out.

Orion hesitated for a moment, but then handed her the hammer and stepped back. "Go for it."

Alena was stupidly proud of him for overcoming his chivalrous instincts and not playing the macho game with Aliya.

"This should be interesting." Jin shoved the rest of the candy bar into her mouth.

As Aliya swung at the wall, the impact was so powerful that Alena feared the hammer would break. It was a large tool that was designed precisely for what they were doing, but it wasn't designed to be wielded by powerful immortal males and an even more powerful hybrid Kra-ell female.

"Go, Aliya!" Jin cheered the girl on. "Show them what you can do!"

As big chunks of stone started flying off, Arwel and Orion retreated further out, but after about two minutes of swinging, Aliya lowered the hammer and handed it back to Arwel. "I need to balance power with endurance. When I use all of my strength, my endurance suffers."

There was a small hole where Aliya had been hammering at the stone wall, and she crouched to peer at it.

"Do you see anything?" Jin asked.

"Yeah, I think that there is a cavern on the other side." She pulled out a flashlight from a loop on her belt. "It's not big, and as far as I can see, it's empty."

"That's a relief," Jin murmured. "I was afraid we were going to find a skeleton."

Shamash, who until now hadn't said much, chuckled. "After a thousand years, even a skeleton would turn to dust."

"That's not true," Alena said. "They've found ancient graves with the skeletons intact and even some hairs. They even found skeletons of dinosaurs, and they lived on Earth long before the gods got here."

"I think the dinosaurs were a genetic joke," Jin said. "Maybe the ones who created the gods played around with different species, created the giant dinosaurs, but then realized that they needed too much food to survive, so they annihilated them."

Alena had never been schooled outside of what her mother had taught her, but she'd read a lot, and she remembered that there were all kinds of dinosaurs, big and small, but with the racket Arwel was producing, having a conversation meant yelling, and she decided to keep her comment for later.

After several more minutes of swinging the hammer, Arwel finally stopped. "I think Aliya can squeeze through and let us know what's in there."

She was no doubt the slimmest among them.

Looking down at her new clothes that were already covered in dust, Aliya frowned. "I'll get dirty."

"That's okay." Jin walked over and patted her arm. "We will all need to have our clothes laundered. But if you are squeamish about going in there, I can try to squeeze in."

Aliya looked at her down her nose. "You won't fit. I'll do it."

"If you insist." Jin waved a hand.

As Aliya carefully wiggled her long, thin body through the narrow opening, Orion dusted off his pants and walked over to Alena.

"I haven't done any manual labor in centuries. It was fun."

Leaning closer, she whispered in his ear, "You looked very sexy swinging that hammer."

"Oh yeah?" He nuzzled her ear. "How sexy?"

"I'll show you later tonight."

Aliya

❦

As the light on Aliya's hardhat illuminated the small chamber, she regretted not finding it fourteen years ago when she'd escaped into these tunnels. At some point in time, it had served as someone's bedroom, and the stone platform that must have been the bed was long enough for a tall Kra-ell male.

Naturally, that was no proof that the cavern had been used by a Kra-ell, but the precision with which it was cut out from the stone indicated tools and technology that wouldn't have been available back then. She knocked on it to make sure that it was indeed a slab of stone and not clay, that could have been poured into a mold to create such a precise and smooth rectangular shape.

Could those ancient Kra-ell melt stone? Because that was what it looked like.

"Aliya?" Arwel peeked through the opening. "Are you alright in there?"

"I'm fine, but I think you should see this, or you won't believe me." She described the stone platform and carved-out ledge that could have been used as a table or a desk.

"Take a picture of it with my phone." He handed her the device.

Somehow in all the excitement of buying a home, she'd forgotten to buy herself a phone, but Kalugal had promised to get her one at the immortals' village.

"Do you see the red button on the bottom? You press it when you want to take a picture."

It took her a moment or two to figure out how to operate the camera, and after snapping several pictures, she handed Arwel his phone back. "Before I squeeze myself out of here, look at the pictures."

The others must have huddled around Arwel as he flipped through the photos because suddenly there was more light on the other side of the stone wall.

"You can come out," Arwel said.

When she squeezed through the opening, he handed her a water bottle. "Drink. I haven't seen you taking one sip yet."

She was touched that he'd noticed and that he cared.

"Thank you. I forgot that I had a bottle."

"We should get Kalugal and his contraption here," Alena said. "What if that stone furniture is made of the mineral he's tracking?" She pushed a strand of hair behind her ear. "Maybe these Kra-ell had a 3D printer and used that mineral to build things from."

"Fascinating idea," Jin agreed. "What if they used that instead of metals to build their equipment? Stone doesn't disintegrate as fast, and we might find more traces of them."

As a sudden boom rocked the tunnel, they all braced their hands on the stone walls.

"What the hell was that?" Jin asked.

"I don't know." Arwel grabbed the hammer. "It came from the direction Kalugal and the others were headed. They might be in trouble."

As he started running, they all followed, their boots thundering on the ground. It didn't take Aliya long to overtake Arwel and sprint into the tunnel the boom had come from, but it was difficult to pinpoint sounds in the underground because of the echoes, and she couldn't be sure that it hadn't come from the other one. "Arwel!" she yelled over her shoulder. "Take the other tunnel!"

When she reached the end of it, she knew right away that it wasn't in the same place as it had been before, and not just because of the dust still settling after the ceiling had collapsed ahead.

"Are you okay?" she yelled.

When there was no response, panic seized her. These people were immortal, so they couldn't be dead, but what about the pregnant woman?

What if Jacki lost the baby?

Frantic, Aliya started pulling away stones.

"Over here!" she yelled. "They are trapped!"

How could that have happened? She'd been through these tunnels hundreds of times, and nothing had ever collapsed or even crumbled, except for where she'd dug to hide a trap, but it wasn't in this area.

What if they blamed her for what had happened to their family? Kalugal and Lokan were Alena's cousins. Would she hate her and seek revenge?

Would she lose her new friends?

The prospect distressed her much more than she'd expected, and as her vision blurred with tears, she averted her eyes when the others joined her.

"Kalugal!" Welgost yelled, his voice booming through the tunnel and echoing off the walls.

"Maybe it collapsed long after they passed it," Jin said. "Maybe they can't hear us."

Aliya wished that were true, but there were only a few meters on the other side of the blockage, if at all. The ceiling could've collapsed over the entire remainder of the tunnel, burying the five immortals under tons of rocks.

Kalugal

As consciousness returned, Kalugal first checked on Jacki, who was stirring under him, and then on his brother who was right beside him, sprawled over Carol, who was also stirring to consciousness.

"Are you hurt, love?" Kalugal's ears were still ringing from the boom that had preceded the ceiling's collapse, and when he tried to move to make room for Jacki, he discovered why they weren't crushed under a pile of stones.

He only had scant inches of maneuvering, and his hardhat was gone, but the light from his glowing eyes was enough to see what was above him. A big chunk of stone was wedged at an angle between the walls of the narrow tunnel, saving them from getting flattened.

"I'm okay," Jacki murmured. "The baby is okay too. I think. What happened?"

"The tunnel's ceiling collapsed," Lokan said.

"Phinas?" Kalugal called out. "Are you okay?"

His answer was a faint groan, but he was alive.

"How badly are you hurt?"

When there was no answer, Kalugal lifted his head as much as he could and peered around. "Lokan, can you see him?"

"I can't. He's not with us under this boulder. I think he's buried under the debris."

"Hang on, Phinas," Kalugal called out. "The others will get us out." He dipped his head and sniffed Jacki to make sure that she wasn't bleeding.

When he couldn't detect the scent of blood, relief washed over him.

They'd been incredibly fortunate, and he still couldn't understand how and why the ceiling had collapsed. Aliya had told them that she'd been through these tunnels hundreds of times and that there were no traps or booby-traps anywhere in this area. The only traps in the entire maze had been the ones she'd built herself in the tunnels leading to the underground lake. That was where she'd made her home, and that was the area she'd protected.

Did it have anything to do with the alien mineral? The reading he'd gotten in this tunnel was the strongest so far, indicating that there was a large deposit of it nearby, but him taking soil samples shouldn't have triggered anything. He'd barely scraped the equivalent of a thumbnail worth of stone for the test.

The device he'd gotten from the geologist was probably smashed together with Phinas, but whereas Phinas's body would self-repair, the same wasn't true of the device.

Not that he cared.

Kalugal wanted his wife, his brother, his sister-in-law, and his second-in-command to be out of there and back in the hotel.

Hopefully, the others were okay and could dig them out.

"Do you hear that?" Lokan asked.

Kalugal's ears were still ringing from the boom, but he heard faint scraping.

"I hope those are not rats," Jacki said.

"What I hope is that the others are not buried under collapsed ceilings like we are," Carol said. "And that they will get us out of here soon."

With the ringing in his ears getting fainter, Kalugal thought that he heard someone call his name, and even though he might have imagined it, he called back, "We are here! Phinas is hurt! The rest of us are fine!"

"Hang on. We are getting you out."

That had sounded like Arwel, but it was hard to tell. Hopefully, the guy was wise enough not to use the explosives he'd brought along.

"Don't use explosives!" Kalugal shouted.

When there was no answer, Jacki shifted under him. "I hope he heard you."

"Do you think that Aliya had something to do with this?" Jacki asked. "Maybe she knew that there was a trap here?"

"I don't think so. I would have sensed guilt in her. I talked with her last night, and we reached an understanding. She said that she was willing to give the village a try, and she sounded sincere. I would have smelled guilt if she was planning something like this. We could have been killed."

"She's not like us," Lokan said. "Perhaps pretending to be friendly while plotting murder is considered honorable in the Kra-ell culture."

Kalugal was familiar with cultures like that among humans, so there was something to what Lokan had said. And yet, his gut told him that Aliya had been genuine when she'd thanked him last night and told him that she owed him a debt of gratitude. He was sure she had nothing to do with the tunnel's collapse.

Alena

When Alena heard Kalugal's answer, the vise squeezing her heart lost its grip, and as her heart expanded, profound relief overcame the confines of her ribcage.

Immortals were very hard to kill, so she'd known that her family would survive, but she'd feared for Jacki's baby. She'd worried about the amount of damage their bodies had sustained and the pain they must be in, and she'd agonized thinking about how long it would take them to recover and how much they would suffer.

Immortals could even regrow limbs, but it took a very long time and was painful as hell.

She'd been praying for them, and hearing that four out of the five were okay was incredibly good news.

She prayed for poor Phinas and his speedy recovery. First, though, they had to get him out, and their progress was excruciatingly slow. The men and Aliya worked tirelessly to clear a small area near the top, but they had to be careful not to further destabilize the tunnel.

The problem was that the blockage went deep, and even though they'd chipped away at the mountain of rock, they'd barely made a dent in it.

Alena, Jin, and Shamash were in charge of moving the stones further away, and the rest were taking turns pulling them out.

Kian had been right. She shouldn't have left the Odus behind. If they were with her, they would have greatly expedited the rescue.

"We should get the Odus here." She helped Jin lift a large boulder and carry it further back into one of the smaller offshoots. "I know it will take time to get them here, but we might not be able to do this without them."

"You're right. But since they obey only you or Arwel, you need to go get them."

Arwel wouldn't be happy about that, but he would have to deal.

"Do you even know how to get back to the surface?" he asked when she told him her plan.

"I do."

"It will take you three hours to get back here. We might get them out by then."

"There is only one road leading up here. I'll ask one of Jianye's men to take me, so you will have the limousines

254

at your disposal. If you are already on your way to the hotel, our paths will cross, and I'll ask the guy to turn back."

Surprisingly, Arwel nodded. "Take Orion with you. I don't want you going unprotected."

"You need him here." She cast Orion an apologetic look. "I'll be okay. I'm not exactly helpless, you know. I can thrall and shroud with the best of you."

"Kian will have my head, but you are right. Go."

"Be careful." Orion stopped to give her a quick kiss.

"I always am."

As she sprinted toward the large chamber, Alena thought of what to tell Jianye. If she told him that Kalugal and the others were trapped under an avalanche of rocks, Jianye would rush down with his men to help, and that would only impede their progress. Even with tools, the humans couldn't do what the immortals and Aliya were doing.

She should come up with a plausible story for why she needed an emergency run to the hotel. She could thrall him, but then she would have to thrall the driver as well. A good excuse would be the easiest way to handle the situation.

Someone needed medication, something that was very important but didn't require a doctor or a rush evacuation to a hospital.

"Carol forgot her insulin at the hotel," she told Jianye. "I need to get it to her as soon as possible. Can one of your men drive me?"

"Of course. But wouldn't it be better if Carol went back to the hotel? She would get her medication faster."

Damn, he was right.

"She can't administer it by herself. I need to do that, and there is still enough time for me to get it and come back. Kalugal also wants me to bring along the two men he left behind. Please hurry. I don't have time to explain." She added a little thrall just to speed things up.

"Right away." He turned to one of his men and spoke in rapid Chinese. "Hu will take you. "

"Thank you."

Orion

As it turned out, Alena had been right, and they were still working on getting to Kalugal and the others when she returned with the Odus, who for some reason were dripping wet.

"What happened to them?" Orion asked. "Why are they wet?"

"They are too heavy to cross over the rope bridge. I had them wade through."

It didn't seem to bother the cyborgs, and they went to work right away, allowing the rest of them to take a breather.

"How are they doing in there?" Alena asked.

"They are uncomfortable, and Jacki is desperate to pee, but the good news is that Phinas is responsive, which means that he's doing better. He's communicating with them."

Orion took the bottle of water she handed him and leaned against the wall to guiltily gulp it down. Kalugal and the others were trapped under a big chunk of stone that was the size of an ancient foundation stone. The thing was wedged diagonally between the tunnel walls, which created a small cavity near the ground where the two couples were trapped. They'd been working for the past two and a half hours to clear the stones piled on top of the boulder, but they still had a long way to go, and in the meantime, they couldn't even get water to those trapped on the other side.

"The Odus are incredible," Aliya watched with awe. "We need to help them move the rocks out of the way."

"Back to work." Orion handed the bottle back to Alena and pushed away from the wall.

For the next hour or so, they all worked in tandem, and surprisingly, the first one they were able to get out was Phinas.

The Odus performed an incredible feat of acrobatics to pull him out. After moving stones out of the way, Ovidu lowered Oridu by the ankles into the hole they'd created so he could reach Phinas and take him into his arms. When Oridu had Phinas, Ovidu pulled them both out by Oridu's ankles.

The maneuver was their own initiative, which made Orion wonder whether they were sentient already. What were the chances that someone had programmed them to know what to do in a situation like that?

None.

Phinas groaned in pain, and as they laid him down on the blanket that Alena had had the foresight to bring with her, she got to work on him. "Is anything broken?" she asked.

It was a rhetorical question since Phinas's legs were twisted in odd angles.

"My legs." He lifted his head to drink from the bottle she held to his lips. "I need a doctor to set them before the bones fuse the wrong way."

"We will get you to a doctor as soon as the others are out."

He nodded. "The bones are probably already fused. The doctor will have to re-break them."

Jin crouched next to him. "Can you hang on, or should we evacuate you before we get the others out?"

"I can hang on. Go help them."

"Master Arwel." Ovidu walked up to the Guardian. "Oridu and I will try to lift the boulder, but someone needs to pull Master Kalugal, Mistress Jacki, Master Lokan, and Mistress Carol out while we are holding it." The Odu looked at Aliya. "It should be Mistress Aliya. She is slim and strong."

"Tell me what to do," Aliya said.

How did the Odu know that Aliya was strong? Had someone told him?

Instead of addressing Aliya, Ovidu explained his plan to Arwel. "We will lift the stone, Mistress Aliya will get under it and pull Mistress Jacki out. She will hand her to you or one of the other masters. Then she will pull Master Kalugal out and hand him to Master Welgost. After that, she will get Master Lokan and Mistress Carol."

Orion leaned to whisper in Alena's ear, "I might not know anything about cyborgs, but that seems like an intelligent plan to me. Your Odus might be sentient already."

Kalugal

~~~

As the hotel staff finished setting up the table in Kalugal and Jacki's suite, Kalugal lifted his glass. "I want to thank everyone for your valiant efforts today. I'm grateful to all of you and especially to Aliya, who I've been told kept on pulling out stones even when her hands were bleeding and the skin on her fingers and palms was practically shredded." He glanced at her bandaged hands and cringed. "Unlike us, her healing takes longer."

"I'll be okay by tomorrow," Aliya said. "The numbing salve the doctor gave me helped a lot with the pain."

"I'm glad, and I'm forever in your debt."

She shook her head. "It was nothing. I would have done that for a stranger. I owe you much more than you owe me."

"Let's call it even," Kalugal offered.

"Not acceptable."

He knew better than to press the issue. Aliya was prideful, and he was risking hurting that pride.

The poor girl had feared that they would blame her for the tunnel's collapse, and he wanted to reassure her that no one thought it had been her fault.

Well, Jacki had voiced her suspicion when they'd been trapped, and so had Lokan, but Kalugal had explained that Aliya couldn't have rigged the place without risking her life as well. Besides, even though she was smart and resourceful, she didn't have the know-how or the tools to engineer it.

But even if she had, she wouldn't have done it after he'd bought her a home. She was an honorable female.

With her bandaged hands, eating would have been a challenge if not for Shamash, who had found fresh blood for her, which she was now sipping through a straw.

"I'm also grateful to Ovidu and Oridu." Kalugal inclined his head in their direction. "Without your help, it would have taken much longer to get us out."

"Mistress Alena commanded us to help in any way we could," Ovidu said. "It was our duty and our pleasure to obey her wishes, master."

"Nevertheless, I'm grateful." Kalugal turned to his second. "I'm sorry that you got hurt, but I'm glad that two broken legs were the extent of your injuries, and I wish you a speedy recovery."

Phinas lifted his glass. "I'm glad that this is over and that Jacki and the baby are okay. When I was lying trapped in there, the pain was secondary to my worry."

"Thank you." Jacki's chin wobbled. "We were so incredibly lucky. It's just now starting to sink in."

Kalugal gave her hand a gentle squeeze. "We are all shaken. I suggest that we spend a few days resting and enjoying the hotel's amenities and leave either Sunday night or Monday morning. By then, everyone's scrapes and bruises will be healed, and Phinas will be able to walk."

"I will walk by tomorrow," Phinas said.

"Until you do, you need someone to take care of you," Jacki said. "I suggest we bring a cot into our suite so we can keep an eye on you during the night."

As much as Kalugal valued Phinas, Welgost or Shamash could do that. Aliya was already sleeping on the couch in their living room, and he didn't want Phinas there as well.

"I'll help you," Aliya offered. "You will need someone to carry you to the bathroom, and I'm strong."

Phinas looked horrified. "I appreciate the offer, but I could never impose on a lady like that."

She gave him a baleful look. "I'm stronger than you. There is no loss of face in letting someone take care of you."

"I know, and as I said, I appreciate your offer, but I'd rather one of my men helped me. Besides, your hands are injured, and you need help yourself."

She lifted her bandaged hands. "It's just skin. My hands are still strong, and I can still carry you."

"I have a better idea," Alena interjected. "Oridu can move into Phinas's room and assist him with everything he needs."

"Thank you." Phinas gave her a grateful smile. "That would be the perfect solution. Oridu doesn't need to sleep, and he'll always be available to help me."

It was impossible to compete with that, and Aliya accepted defeat.

"I still can't understand why the tunnel collapsed," she said. "I've been there many times during the years, and it never showed any signs of weakness. Are you sure that no one felt the earth move? It could have been a small earthquake."

"I checked." Kalugal reached for the dan dan noodles, signaling that it was time to eat. "No seismic activity has been detected in the past few days, including today." He put some on Jacki's plate and then on his own before passing the platter to Alena. "I've been thinking what could have caused it, and I have a theory. I think that the place was rigged, but only when the weight of those standing in that tunnel exceeded a certain limit. That's why Aliya could walk in there safely."

"That kind of makes sense," Jacki said. "Those who rigged it knew to walk in there only one person at a time. It was meant to stop invaders. But the question is, what were they protecting? There must have been something important on the other side or deeper down."

"Correct." Kalugal smiled at his smart mate. "I was following the mineral's concentration readouts on the device. It was weaker in the other offshoot and stronger in the one that collapsed."

"So what now?" Lokan said. "We can't continue the investigation because we don't have the device, and the passage is blocked. But even if we get a new device and clear that passage, there might be more rigs along the way. We can't risk it."

"I agree." Kalugal put his chopsticks down. "I need to talk with the Zhao twins and see if they can combine their invention with a burrowing robot and a robotic arm that would take samples and check them on the spot."

"That would take years to develop," Lokan said.

"I'm not in a hurry." Kalugal reached for another platter. "I'd rather wait than risk lives. I've already told Jianye to keep his people out of the tunnels and proceed with caution with the rest of the outpost."

"Poor Jianye." Jin chuckled. "Since you've erased his and his men's memory of the entire incident, he has no idea why you are being so cautious and probably thinks that you're nuts."

Kalugal shrugged. "He can think whatever he wants. As long as he needs my funding to continue, he will do as I say and keep his crew safe."

Geraldine

❧

"**I**t has been so long since I drove a car." Geraldine clutched the steering wheel with sweaty palms.

Shai cast her an indulgent smile. "We are in a deserted church parking lot. It's the perfect place to practice. Take your foot off the brake pedal and put it gently on the gas."

Taking a deep breath, Geraldine lifted her foot and moved it the few inches to the right. Hovering it over the gas pedal for a couple of seconds, she finally gathered the courage to lower it and apply the slightest pressure. When nothing happened, she pressed a little harder, and the car lurched forward. Immediately taking her foot off the gas pedal, she slammed it on the brake.

"Try it again," Shai said in a calm tone. "But this time, don't take your foot all the way off. You need to find what the right amount of pressure is."

Sweat beading on her forehead, she clutched the steering wheel so hard it groaned under the pressure.

Great, so now her super-strength decided to show up. When she'd needed it to move furniture or heavy planters, it had been nowhere to be found.

The last time she'd driven a car had been years ago, and that car had been very different than Shai's shiny new vehicle with all of its modern amenities and special clan modifications. It felt as if she'd never sat in the driver's seat before.

Gritting her teeth, she moved her foot to the gas pedal, and when the car lurched forward, she eased it just a bit, and the car moved slowly forward.

"You're doing great," Shai encouraged. "Keep the slow pace."

She chuckled. "I have no intentions of going any faster."

The speedometer hovered between ten and fifteen miles per hour, and it was the perfect speed for her first time behind the wheel of a modern car.

After she'd circled the sprawling parking lot several times, her grip finally loosened. "I'm getting the hang of it."

"Yes, you are. Keep going until you feel confident enough to increase the speed a little."

"Okay." She let out a breath. "Maybe it's for the best that the shipping of my car got delayed. By the time it gets here, I will be comfortable enough to actually take it out on the road."

"In three weeks, you will be driving all over Malibu."

She doubted that. "How come the shipping was delayed?"

"The shipping industry can't keep up with the demand. I'm glad that it's delayed only by two weeks." He chuckled. "Kian should have seen it coming and invested in trucking, storage facilities, and other shipping enterprises. Everything is in short supply—containers, chassis to put the containers on, trucks, truck drivers, warehouse operators, warehouse space, and everything else that goes into transporting goods."

"Is it because people buy more and more things online?"

"That's one of the reasons. The other is that manufacturers prefer not to store inventory. They call it just-in-time manufacturing. It's less costly and more efficient for them to manufacture and ship it right away. Another problem is the workforce. Members of the current generation don't want to be warehouse operators and truck drivers."

"Why? I thought that those jobs paid well."

"They do, but they can't drive a truck if they smoke pot, even if they do it on the weekend when they are not driving because it comes up in the testing days after. It was a bad decision, and I hope they will relax the rules a little. It's like Prohibition era all over again."

"Is marijuana use so widespread?"

Shai shrugged. "I was surprised to read that as well. Since the testing started, thousands of truck drivers have lost their jobs, and there aren't enough takers to replace them." He leaned back in his seat. "When self-driving trucks get approved, that will no longer be an issue. Warehouse automation is also on the rise, but in the meantime, we need to be patient and not expect our goods to be delivered as fast as they used to be."

With Shai distracting her with his explanations about the shipping industry, Geraldine hadn't noticed that she'd increased the speed and was comfortably circling the parking lot at twenty miles per hour.

"Your tactic worked." She cast him a quick sidelong smile. "I wasn't paying attention and went faster."

He smiled back. "Are you ready to take it out on the road? This time of day, there are hardly any cars on it."

"Heck, why not? We are immortal, right?"

He laughed. "Stop worrying. You are not going to wreck the car. We have dinner with Darlene at your old house tomorrow, so you can't get into an accident. It will ruin our plans."

He was teasing, of course, and it was working. She was even starting to enjoy herself. As Cassandra liked to say, it was all in the attitude. If she believed that she was a good driver, she would be, and the opposite was true as well.

Geraldine stopped at the parking lot exit and watched the road for a few moments before easing onto it. "By the way, I don't have to get there early tomorrow, so you don't have to cut your workday short. Cassandra has arranged for everything. A cleaning crew will be there this afternoon, and she ordered tomorrow's dinner from a catering service that brings everything and even sets up the table."

Shai shook his head. "Your daughter is a force of nature. She even found a way to get rid of Leo for the entire month. It was a brilliant move to call Orion and have him arrange with the gallery owner for Leo to go on an acquisition expedition."

Geraldine's heart swelled with pride. "Cassy is very resourceful. When she wants something, she finds a way to make it happen."

Shai sighed. "I hope Parker is not going to fail, for his sake more than for Darlene's. If his compulsion doesn't work, we can wait for Orion's return to compel her silence, but it would crush Parker's ego. From what I've observed, compellers tend to be arrogant people, and I think that confidence has a lot to do with their ability. I don't want Parker to lose his mojo."

Eleanor

⌒⌒⌒

E leanor sat across from Colonel Crowley and a higher-up who'd only offered his last name, which was Wolfe—a name that fitted him so well that she'd doubted he'd been born with it.

"The job is yours, Dr. Takala." Wolfe regarded her with his beady eyes. "You came to us at a pivotal time. Dr. Roberts' untimely death left the program without a leader, and we are fortunate to have you step in. You are not only qualified, but you're also familiar with the program, know each of the program's members, and have been involved in their recruitment as well as some of their training."

"Thank you." Eleanor stifled the urge to ask him how much the job paid.

It was irrelevant, she was not in it for the money, but it still mattered to her. She deserved to be paid at least as much as Roberts. Being offered the same salary would vindicate her for having been kicked out of the program and offered a pittance of severance pay.

Then again, perhaps she should be grateful to the old bastard for kicking her out. If he hadn't done that, she wouldn't have infiltrated Kalugal's stronghold, hooked up with Greggory, and turned immortal.

"How soon can you be available?" Crowley asked.

"I can start tomorrow."

Wolfe grinned like a hyena. "Excellent." He extended his hand to her. "Welcome aboard, Dr. Eleanor Takala."

She liked the prefix and wished it were deserved. Perhaps one day, she would take a break from everything and get a doctorate in whatever. Philosophy or ancient languages, or something else that was totally useless but fun to learn.

She shook his hand. "Before I start, there is an issue I need to discuss with you."

"Right." Wolfe pulled his hand away. "You're probably wondering about the pay. I don't know how much Roberts was paid, but I'll have my secretary check and prepare a formal job offer with the same compensation package."

Triumphant drums sounded in Eleanor's head, but she affected a bored expression. "With all due respect, Roberts might have founded the program with Simmons, but I can do better than both of them. I was the one who brought in all the talent. After I was forced to leave, they failed to recruit anyone new."

"I'm well aware of that," Wolfe acknowledged. "I'm willing to renegotiate in six months."

"That's an acceptable offer, but my pay wasn't what I wanted to discuss with you. In my informed opinion, the program is not doing well because you keep the members underground. That's a big mistake."

Wolfe leaned back and crossed his arms over his broad chest. "And why is that?"

"My theory is that paranormal talents operate on some sort of frequency that science hasn't discovered yet. Those who are sensitive enough to pick up on it, harness it and use it need to be surrounded by nature, and in my experience, as close as possible to the ocean. If you go over the files of our strongest talents, you'll see that most of them lived near a beach or at least spent their summers there. I bet that everyone's talent would manifest stronger when in close proximity to the ocean."

"That's an interesting hypothesis, and I'm willing to send a request to find a new location for the program. Perhaps the naval base has space."

That was where the Echelon spyware was located, and it would have been a perfect location for her to move the program to, but her agenda was to move them to Safe Haven.

Perhaps she could do both.

"That would be a wonderful temporary solution because I don't want them to spend even one more day in that underground crypt. It's killing their talents. But the base is far from perfect. These people need quiet, they need serenity, and they need to feel connected to nature."

Wolfe narrowed his eyes at her. "It seems to me that you have a specific place in mind."

"I do. Have you ever heard about a spiritual retreat called Safe Haven?"

"I can't say that I have."

"It's located on the Oregon Coast, right on the beach, and there is nothing for miles in every direction. There is no better place for honing paranormal talents. We can get our own corner of the property that will be completely separate from the rest of the retreat, and I can get it at a bargain price. On top of that, I suspect that I'll be able to recruit more talent from the spiritual retreat's attendees. Paranormals are drawn to the mystical. They search for answers."

"That's a brilliant idea, Eleanor." Wolfe uncrossed his arms and leaned forward. "And the timing is perfect since we need the space the paranormal research is taking for a different project. Moving it to Oregon is a terrific solution, provided that we can safeguard the research. It is, after all, top secret."

That was twice that Wolfe had said research instead of program.

Eleanor's hackles rose. Had it been a slip of the tongue?

No one was supposed to know about the founders' plan to breed super babies, and even they hadn't called it

275

research. Their term for it was the leap, or some other nonsense like that.

"What kind of research are you referring to?" she asked. "I was under the impression that the paranormal division was about spying on America's enemies, not conducting research."

Wolfe smiled his creepy smile again. "For a smart and ambitious woman, you are surprisingly naive, Dr. Takala."

"I only know what I was told."

"You didn't have the security clearance before, but now that you are heading the program, you need to know what it is really about. The so-called missions they were supposedly training for were just a cover for the real reason the talents were recruited."

The puzzle pieces were starting to fall into place, and the emerging picture was scary as hell. "You were after what made them different."

"Precisely. We want to know what makes these people sensitive, as you coined it, to that mysterious frequency. We hired a new doctor to replace Roberts, and he will continue the research, but he already informed me that he needs fresh talents."

"And that's why you hired me. I was the best at luring paranormals into the program."

"You are a hundred percent correct."

Kian

"William is here. We will talk tomorrow." Kian ended the call with Arwel and motioned for William to take a seat at the conference table.

"Is anyone joining us?" William asked.

"No. Do you prefer my desk?"

"Here is fine." William pushed his glasses up his nose. "Any news from China?"

"Plenty. Both teams are returning Monday."

William frowned. "That's early. What happened?"

"A lot. But the most important discovery was a hybrid female that escaped the massacre of Jade's tribe. She was a young girl at the time, and the attacking Kra-ell thought she was human and let her go with the other humans. She lived among the Mosuo until she grew up and started looking too alien. Since then, the poor woman has been living alone in a tunnel system under an ancient outpost. The team is bringing her to the village."

William's frown deepened. "Vrog and Emmett could easily pass for humans. In what way does the hybrid female look alien?"

"Arwel said that she has a temper and can't control her fangs and glowing eyes well, which in the Kra-ell's case turn red. He also said that the shape of her eyes is very alien-looking."

"That could be solved with sunglasses."

"Precisely. Anyway, Vrog is flying over to see her tomorrow. We might be hosting a Kra-ell couple in the village."

"I have a match waiting for him, and he knows that. Is he going to cancel?"

"I don't know. But given that a hybrid Kra-ell female was found, he might. Just don't tell the lady yet. Who knows, maybe there will be no chemistry between Vrog and Aliya, and he will want to participate in the virtual adventure with the clan female."

Kian assumed that William knew who the clan female was, but he wasn't going to ask. The whole point of Perfect Match was anonymity.

"Is Aliya the reason they are cutting their trip short?"

"She's not. They had an accident earlier in the day." Kian relayed what Arwel had told him. "Kalugal forbade any excavation in the tunnels, and his plan is to end the archeological dig of the outpost soon as well. He suspects that more tunnels are rigged."

William nodded. "The question is by whom, the ancient Kra-ell who died out, or someone else who hid something in those tunnels."

"Arwel mentioned some device that Kalugal wants to develop to search those tunnels remotely, but I don't have details. You'll have to ask him when he returns."

"You seem happy that they are cutting their trips short."

"I am." Kian chuckled. "I like all my ducklings under my wings, and especially Alena. I know she's well protected, and I also know that when she travels with our mother, she's in more danger than she's in now, but I can't help the uneasy feeling I've had throughout their trip. Perhaps it was a premonition."

William arched a brow. "Alena wasn't hurt, so if you had a premonition, it was about your cousins and their mates."

"True. I'm just so relieved that they are coming home." He raked his fingers through his hair. "I'm turning soft. It must be old age, or maybe it's fatherhood."

"I think it's fatherhood. Until not too long ago, we didn't all live together, and you were fine with that. Many of our programmers lived in the Bay Area, and Arwel and Bhathian were stationed there."

It seemed so long ago that Kian could barely remember those days.

"I wasn't fine. I always wanted everyone to live in the same place where I could protect them. That was why I built the keep. But until Mark's murder, I had no reason to order everyone to move into the building." Kian's good mood took a nosedive. "I wish we didn't have to lose him to prove to our people that they were not safe, and that hiding in plain sight was not enough."

"True that." William took his glasses off and used his shirt to clean them. "I like living and working in the village, but I also liked it in the keep, so I'm not a good example. But I think most of our people love living here."

"It's easy to get used to good things. And this is not only good but getting better. The new section of the village is almost ready, and Callie informed me that she's going to run the restaurant. We are going to have gourmet fare in the village."

William's eyes started glowing. "Now, you got me excited. When is it going to open?"

"I assume she'll need a couple of months to get everything she needs, hire staff, and train them. She plans on offering Atzil a position, but I doubt Kalugal would let him go." Kian leaned back and crossed his arms over his chest. "We've gotten distracted. You came here to talk about your progress with finding Toven, not the future of fine dining in the village."

William sighed. "That was a much more pleasant topic, at least for me. I'm afraid that facial recognition is not the way to find Toven. I did as you suggested, and I ran a looser search for men who look like Orion but are not an exact match. I've gotten thousands of results. Roni and I went over them, but none looked close enough to Orion to be Toven. So I ran Orion's picture and asked for an exact match. I didn't even find Orion, let alone Toven. Orion must be using a foreign driver's license or passport as his identification, and Toven is probably doing the same thing."

"Let's check." Kian glanced at his watch. "It's early in the morning over there. I'll text Orion. If he's awake, he'll answer now, and if not, he'll answer later."

The answer came back right away. "Orion uses mostly his Swiss passport as his identification."

"Is he a Swiss citizen, or is it a counterfeit?"

"He's probably a citizen." Kian typed the question.

His phone rang a moment later.

"Thanks for calling, Orion."

"I'm a Swiss citizen, and I have several other passports as well that I use from time to time. Why the questions?"

Kian told him about William's results. "The facial recognition seems to be a dead end. The only thing left is trying to find Toven through his publishers."

"There might be one more thing we can do," Orion said. "I asked Mey if she's willing to come with me to Paris and listen to the echoes in the residence Toven was renting when I met him. It's a long shot, but beggars can't be choosers."

"Did you ever go back there?"

Orion chuckled. "Many times. It was always rented out, and in recent years, it's been offered on Airbnb, so I will have no problem getting access to it. In fact, we can stay there while Mey listens to the echoes."

Emmett

Eleanor entered the hotel suite, kicked her heels off, flung her purse on the table, and plopped down on the couch. "Houston, we have a problem."

Emmett sat next to her and took her hand. "They didn't hire you?"

"Oh, they hired me. They even offered me the same pay as Roberts was getting, which felt really good. And they even agreed to move the program to Safe Haven when the facilities there are ready. In the meantime, they suggested moving the program to the naval base."

"That's where Echelon is located," Peter said. "That's perfect."

"I know. I couldn't have asked for a better outcome of this meeting, but none of that is the problem. Turns out that the paranormal spying division was a cover-up for what they were really doing, which was conducting research on the talents. They want to know what makes them different. What if they discover their godly genes? The government has access to gene sequencing equipment that the clan does not, and their chances of discovering what makes some people have paranormal talents are much better than Bridget's."

"We need to stop the program," Peter said.

"It's not that simple." Eleanor sighed. "Is there any alcohol left in the mini-fridge? Because I really need some."

"Housekeeping replenished the supply this morning." Peter walked over to the fridge and pulled out three little bottles. "What's your pleasure?"

"Can you mix a screwdriver for me?"

"Coming up." He pulled out a bottle of orange juice.

As he mixed the drink, Eleanor continued. "I spent the entire drive back here thinking about what to do. If we get the talents out, they will find new ones and keep testing. We can't allow that to happen."

"How are we going to stop them?" Emmett asked.

"We will feed them fake information." Eleanor took the drink Peter handed her. "We get the program moved to Safe Haven, and we take control of that doctor. We need him to give us the results of all the research Simmons and Roberts did, and if there is anything that even hints that these people have alien genes, we will need to hack into the database and change those results."

"What if the doctor is immune?" Peter asked.

"Then we get him replaced. As the new director, I can fire him for whatever reason like Roberts did to me."

She let out a breath. "Kian doesn't know how lucky he is that he has me on this mission. No one else could have solved this mess."

"We need to call him." Peter sat on her other side.

"I wanted to call him on the way here, but I decided to run my plan through you first and see what you think."

"I think your plan is solid, but the big question is whether Roni can hack into highly secure military data, which I assume is how they classified this research."

"If he can't, I'll make the doctor corrupt the data somehow." She took a long sip from the drink. "I've read somewhere about a clever cyber sabotage of a system that was offline. Top, top security. They infected the scientist's laptop with a virus that stayed dormant until the guy went to work and hooked it into the system. The virus traveled from the laptop into the offline servers and went to work. It didn't do anything noticeable, but it corrupted the data slowly over time, until one day, the whole thing crashed."

"How did they get the virus onto the scientist's laptop?" Emmett asked. "Did he use it online?"

"I don't remember. I should look up that story again."

"Or just call Roni and ask him," Peter said. "I'm sure he knows about every major hack ever perpetrated."

"I don't know about that." Eleanor waved a dismissive hand. "I bet the best hacks never made it to the news."

"The hacker community is not that big," Peter said. "They know when someone manages something big, and they usually know who that is."

Eleanor shrugged. "Perhaps you are right. What I need to figure out now is how to get the two of you into the base."

"We can be new talents," Peter suggested. "Roni has already created fake identities for us."

She eyed him as if he'd lost his mind. "Are you nuts? I'm not letting that doctor anywhere near you with a needle."

"He's not going to do anything to us because Emmett and I will thrall the crap out of him."

Eleanor slumped against the couch cushions. "I need to check whether he's susceptible to compulsion. If he is, then he's most likely susceptible to thralling as well, and then we can proceed with your idea."

Kian

William was getting ready to leave when Kian's phone rang again. Expecting it to be Orion, he didn't even look at the display. "Did you think of something else that can lead us to Toven?"

"Was I supposed to?" Eleanor asked.

Kian chuckled. "My apologies. I didn't check the caller ID, and I assumed you were the person I spoke with before. How are things going in West Virginia?"

"I got the job. I'm now officially the paranormal program's new director, and I start tomorrow."

"Excellent work, Eleanor. Congratulations."

"Thank you, but that's not why I'm calling. During my job interview, I've learned new and alarming information."

That didn't sound good. "I'm listening."

287

"Turns out the program is not a renewal of the government's previous paranormal investigation that was all about spying on the Russians using paranormal talents. That was just the cover story. What they are really after is researching paranormals and learning what makes them different. Now that my security clearance has been upgraded, I was finally told the truth, but I beat myself up for not realizing that before. I pride myself on being cynical and questioning everyone's motives, but I didn't question why Roberts was constantly taking blood samples from the trainees. I assumed that it had to do with the drugs they were giving them to enhance their performance, or the super babies they hoped to breed, but that didn't justify the frequency of those tests. It had research and experimenting written all over it."

"Don't feel bad. I should have realized that as well, and I'm as cynical as they get." Kian let out a breath. "They had four confirmed Dormants to run their tests on, and they have equipment we don't. We need to find out what they know."

"My thoughts exactly. I plan to compel the new doctor they assigned to the program and get him to give me all the relevant information. If there is anything in there that flags abnormalities, I'll have him erase those test results and plant fake ones. I will probably need Roni's help to give the doctor instructions on how to tamper with the data. And if that's too complicated, he can create a computer virus that I'll have the doctor introduce into the system. It's not going to be a big loss if all of their research results are corrupted."

"That's arguable. If we can get access to it, we might learn something, but that's a secondary consideration to ensuring that they don't find out anomalies in the talents' genetic make-up. In any case, I'll tell Roni to provide you with all the assistance you need."

"Thank you. I also pitched them the Safe Haven idea, and they seemed all for it. The big boss, Wolfe, even offered to move the program to the naval base until Safe Haven had the facilities ready for them. The question is whether I should keep pushing it or tell them that the owner changed his mind about leasing it to the government."

"Why would you do that?"

"Because we don't want them breathing down our necks."

"We need to be in control of that research, which means that your stint as its director is going to be a long-term thing. I assume that you don't want to stay in West Virginia for years to come."

"You assume correctly. Safe Haven it is. When do you think you will have it ready? To get final approval on that, I need to at least show them the architectural plans, timeline to completion, and asking price."

"I've already asked Gavin to work on ideas for the place, but he hasn't shown me anything yet. I'll talk to him, and once the plans are finalized, I'll get the Safe Haven project going on a fast track, so it will be ready as soon as possible for the program."

"I need an approximate timeline to completion and asking price as soon as possible. If we want this to happen, I need to strike while the iron is still hot."

"I'll get it to you as soon as I can. In the meantime, you can keep using compulsion to make them cooperate."

She chuckled. "The funny thing is that I barely had to use it, and I didn't even have to work hard to convince them that the underground is detrimental to the talents. They took at face value my bullshit explanation about paranormals' need to be close to nature and especially to the ocean to feed and enhance their abilities. Wolfe jumped on the idea. He said that they needed the space in the shelter for some other project."

"I'm curious about what they are doing in that underground city of theirs, but my curiosity will have to wait. Right now, your first priority is finding out what they know and eliminating it if needed. Your second priority is finding someone in the Echelon system so we can gain access to it, and your third is moving the paranormals to Safe Haven. Naturally, if the opportunity presents itself and you need to do things out of order, then by all means, but keep me informed."

"Will do, boss."

Alena

❦

As Alena entered Kalugal's suite, her eyes immediately darted to Phinas, who looked much better, and then to Aliya, whose bandages were off.

"Good morning." Smiling, she waved her greetings while Orion pulled out a chair for her next to the breakfast table. "How is everyone feeling?"

Aliya lifted her hands and turned them around to show Alena. "I'm mostly healed."

Faint scars still marred her palms and fingers, but they would probably be gone in a day or two.

She was dressed in one of her new outfits, her hair was loose down her back and shone like a black velvet curtain, and her cheeks had a healthy pink hue to them.

Plentiful food, good rest, and new clothes had transformed her into quite a beauty despite her oddly shaped eyes. In fact, Alena was growing accustomed to them, and they no longer jumped out at her as they had in the beginning. Maybe it was because Aliya looked less gaunt, so those alien eyes didn't look as disproportionately large in her small face.

"How about you, Phinas?" Orion asked. "Was Oridu a good nursemaid?"

"He was invaluable," Phinas said. "But I won't be needing his services tonight. Later today, I'm going to remove the braces."

"The doctor told you not to put weight on them for six to eight weeks," Aliya said.

"That advice doesn't apply to immortals." Phinas stuffed another steamed bun into his mouth. "Kalugal thralled the good doctor to remember that I had sprained both legs, not broken them."

Alena shuddered. Watching the doctor re-break Phinas's legs had been painful. The doctor couldn't understand how the bones that had been broken in several places were already fused back, just not properly, and Kalugal had to compel the doctor to re-break them. Phinas had tried to be macho and refuse anesthetics, but Kalugal had ended that nonsense quickly, ordering him to stop being an idiot.

Thankfully, Phinas's knees had somehow avoided being crushed. The delicate and intricate joints would have taken much longer to heal. Alena wasn't sure why, but the big leg bones healed very fast in comparison.

"I spoke with Yamanu earlier this morning," Arwel said. "They will be here shortly after lunch." He looked at the table. "Can we squeeze five more people in here? Or should we go back to dining in the hotel's restaurant?"

"I like us dining up here in privacy, and there is plenty of room once we extend the table." Kalugal reached for the teapot and poured himself and Jacki more tea. "There are two extension leaves stored underneath, and I'll ask housekeeping to bring more chairs."

"Are they going to stay long?" Aliya asked.

"They are going home with us on Monday," Kalugal said. "It's good that this is not the height of the tourist season, so I was able to get rooms for them in the hotel."

Aliya fiddled with the napkin, wrapping it around her hand and unwrapping it. "Are Vrog's eyes like mine? I don't remember him well."

"They are not," Alena said. "They look human."

"Lucky guy," Aliya murmured. "No wonder Jade chose him to run the tribe's businesses in Singapore."

"Do you know what those businesses involved?"

She shook her head. "I was just a kid. No one told me."

"I have an excellent idea," Jin said. "Since all of our fingernails look like shit, I suggest we book appointments at the hotel spa and get manicures and pedicures." She cast Arwel a bemused glance. "And that includes you and the rest of the guys."

"I could go for a massage." Kalugal rotated his shoulders one at a time. "For some reason, our self-healing abilities don't include softening stiff muscles. Any idea why?"

"Call Bridget and ask," Jacki said. "I'm all for a massage at the spa and a visit to the hair salon. Since I turned immortal, my hair grows so fast that I need to trim it every week if I want to maintain my hairstyle."

Alena cast a sidelong glance at Aliya. "Would you like to join us?"

"I would, but I shouldn't. Kalugal can't shroud me in there."

"You don't need shrouding," Jin said. "I'll give them so much attitude that they won't even look at you. They will be too busy trying to avoid me."

Aliya chuckled, which startled Alena. She hadn't heard the girl laugh even once. She smiled a little, but even that had looked sad.

Hopefully, Vrog would be able to cheer her up.

Under the table, Alena reached for Orion's hand and gave it a little squeeze. She had always been quick to smile and laugh, but since Orion had entered her life, she'd been doing both much more often.

He made her happy.

Leaning over, he kissed her temple. "I love you," he whispered in her ear.

"How long will those things in the spa take?" Aliya asked.

"A couple of hours," Jin said. "Maybe three. Why, are you in a hurry to go somewhere?"

"I don't want to be in the spa when Vrog gets here. I want to be ready to greet him."

"Don't worry." Jin waved a hand in dismissal. "We will be done long before that."

Aliya

Aliya had never dreamt of being a princess, but she felt like one now. Her nails and toenails had received a professional manicure and had been painted with clear gloss, her hair had gotten a trim, and her skin had never felt as soft or looked as glowing.

There had been a few tense moments when the beautician had commented about Aliya's unusually hard nails, but Jin had done as she'd promised, going on the offensive and telling the woman to just do her job and stop complaining.

"You look good." Jin put her arm around her shoulders and looked at both of their reflections in the mirror. "I can't wait to see Vrog's reaction when he sees you for the first time." She smirked. "I sent Mey a picture of you, but we decided not to show it to him."

That was news to her. "When did you take my picture?"

"When you first got here and still looked like something that the cat dragged in."

Aliya winced. "Are you sure your sister didn't show it to him?"

"Positive. Don't get me wrong, you were pretty in that picture despite your haggard state, but we decided that not knowing what you looked like would help build up Vrog's anticipation."

Aliya shrugged. "I hope he's not disappointed, but if he is, that's his problem."

She'd done her best to look appealing, and if Vrog didn't like what he saw, Phinas was a viable and attractive alternative.

He had backed off during their trip to Lijiang, and she'd thought that he'd lost interest. Admittedly, she'd felt disappointed. But something had changed after his injury. Perhaps he'd had time to think while trapped, and he'd thought about her.

It was a nice feeling to be desired.

The immortal wasn't shy about showing his renewed interest, flirting with her the same way she'd seen the Mosuo boys flirt with the girls but never with her.

Aliya had been just a girl back then, and after she'd fled the village, she'd lived like a hermit vagabond. Thinking about being feminine or desirable had been the furthest thing from her mind.

Still, her body had matured, and she'd become a woman at some point. She just hadn't realized it until now.

Then again, desirability meant different things to different people.

Humans appreciated sweet, soft-spoken women with pretty faces and feminine curves. The Kra-ell valued strength and aggression, and the more of it, the better and more desirable.

She was a hybrid, though, and so was Vrog, and their preferences might be somewhere in the middle.

What did she value in a mate? Was it strength? Intelligence? A sense of humor?

Those were the kind of thoughts she'd never wasted time on before and not just because she'd had no viable options. The purebloaded females hadn't had to choose, and the Mosuo girls could take as long as they wanted to sample lovers until they decided to settle on one. But if she lived in the immortals' village, she would have to follow their customs, whatever they were.

They were monogamous, but perhaps on their way to monogamy, they played around like humans did and tried out many lovers?

Now that she might have to choose a partner, she should know her own preferences.

Out of the group of immortal males, Aliya debated who would have caught her attention if all of them were available. Orion was by far the most handsome, and he was kind and cultured. He was also a powerful compeller, but other than that, he wasn't aggressive at all.

He wouldn't have been her first choice.

Arwel had the most beautiful eyes, and he exuded authority and leadership, but in a calm and collected way. He wouldn't have been her first choice either, but she would have considered him.

Kalugal had everything she wanted in a male, handsome, smart, cunning, innately aggressive, and outwardly cultured, but he was taken, and he was also out of her league. He would have never gone for an uneducated, unfashionable, flat-chested female. Given his wife's ample bosom, he preferred a handful.

The same went for Lokan.

He was gorgeous, and there was a lot of pent-up aggression in him, but he kept it under tight lock and key, and showed the world only his cultured side. That was admirable, and if he wasn't taken, she would have considered him as well.

Shamash was a nice guy, but she didn't find him attractive, so that left Phinas and Welgost. Both were strong warriors, both were handsome, but Phinas was smarter, and he was a leader while Welgost was a follower.

As she and Jin walked into Kalugal's suite, Aliya returned Phinas' smile and nodded, but other than that, she had no idea how to respond to his flirting. She had zero experience.

"Help yourself to some tea and dessert." Jacki motioned at the table.

"Thank you." Aliya sat across from Phinas and gave him another small smile.

"Did you enjoy your massage?"

"I did, but I would have preferred a stronger set of hands on me."

Was it more flirting, and was he hinting that he would have liked her hands on him?

"They are here," Jin announced. "Mey texted me that they are unloading the car and heading to the lobby." She pushed to her feet and pocketed her phone. "I'm going down to greet them. Anyone want to come with me?"

"I'll come." Arwel got up.

Aliya wanted to come as well, but she didn't want to look too anxious to meet Vrog. The Kra-ell females always acted uninterested, letting the males bend over backward to impress them so they would issue them an invitation.

Vrog would expect no less.

Besides, she didn't want Phinas to think that she wasn't interested in him.

"I'll wait here," she said as she pushed to her feet and headed toward the balcony doors.

Phinas might join her there, but she hoped he wouldn't. She needed to calm her nerves.

Except, Kalugal's compulsion made it impossible for her to even put her hand on the door handle. She turned to him. "Am I allowed outside?"

"You are free to come and go as you please," Kalugal surprised her. "You gave me your word that you'd give the immortal village a three-month chance, and I know that you're an honorable woman and would never break your promise."

He had no idea how much his words meant to her.

Her honor was like a shield that Aliya carried around her. It made her feel like a person of worth.

"Thank you." She inclined her head to hide the sudden moisture coating her eyes.

"Do you need company out there?" Alena asked softly.

"Thank you, but I need to be alone for a little bit." Her words had been meant more for Phinas's ears than Alena's, but she didn't want anyone to follow her.

"I understand." Alena gave her a reassuring smile.

As Aliya opened the French doors, stepped outside, and closed them behind her, her lungs expanded to allow a large inhale. She felt free for the first time since they'd captured her, and not just because Kalugal had released her from his compulsion.

It was nice to have people to talk to, people who cared whether she lived or died, but it was also oppressive. Aliya was used to being alone and was comfortable with her solitude. She found the constant company of others fatiguing.

How was that going to work in the immortals' village?

Did they have a hotel? Or would Kalugal and Jackie invite her to stay in their house?

He was a rich man, so his home was probably big and beautiful like the houses she'd seen on television. Would she have a room of her own? Would they let her clean their house to earn her keep?

Later, she would ask him, but for now, she should enjoy the few minutes of solitude before she had to face Vrog and put on an act worthy of a pureblooded Kra-ell female.

Vrog

"**R**eady to meet your dream girl?" Yamanu wrapped his arm around Vrog's shoulders.

Only Jin and Arwel had come down to greet them.

Why hadn't Aliya?

Wasn't she excited to see him?

Perhaps her injuries were more severe than Arwel had reported, and she was too hurt to walk?

To their right, Mey and Jin were hugging and chatting up a storm as if they hadn't seen each other in weeks.

Ignoring the Guardian's taunting, Vrog turned to Arwel. "Is Aliya okay? You said that she was injured in the rescue."

"Her hands are much better already. She even had a manicure earlier."

That was a relief. But if she'd been well enough to visit the salon, why hadn't she come down to greet him?

Keeping his expression neutral, Vrog slung his travel bag over his shoulder. "I'm glad to hear that she recovered so quickly."

"Her injuries were superficial, just cuts and scrapes that would have taken one of ours minutes to heal. Hers took much longer to mend, and the scars haven't faded yet." Arwel took one of the suitcases Yamanu had pulled out from the trunk of the rented car. "I don't remember your healing after Richard turned your face into hamburger meat. Did it take more than twenty-four hours to heal?"

"Most of it was healed in just a couple of days, but it took longer for the bruises and cuts to fade." Vrog fell in step with Arwel as the Guardians started walking toward the hotel lobby. "Why do you ask?"

Arwel didn't stop by the front desk and continued to the staircase. "I wonder if that has to do with your shorter lifespans."

Vrog wasn't concerned with that. He was still a young man even in Kra-ell terms, and he didn't need to worry about his life expectancy just yet.

"It makes sense." Vrog followed him up the stairs. "Do the others know where to go?"

Arwel turned to look over his shoulder. "What's taking them so long?" He waited until Yamanu entered the lobby. "Where are Mey and Jin?"

"They are coming." Yamanu headed their way. "Jin wanted to show Mey something."

Behind him, Alfie and Jay walked in with the rest of their luggage.

The ledgers had remained on the jet under the pilot's care. Morris had assured him that he had nothing to worry about and that he wouldn't let anything happen to them, but Vrog still worried.

The cases they had gotten on the way to the airport were durable, but they were not fireproof, only fire resistant, and Vrog regretted listening to Jay and Morris and taking the files out of the safes.

"Where are we going?" he asked as Arwel continued climbing the stairs.

"To Kalugal's suite. That's where everyone is right now." Arwel cast him an amused smile. "I know that you're anxious to meet Aliya."

There was no point denying it. The empathic Guardian could no doubt sense his excitement. "I am. Is she excited to see me?"

"She's trying to play it cool, but I can tell that she's anxious as well."

Anxious was not the same as excited or happy, but Vrog was confident that he could quickly change that. He would show Aliya that he was nothing like the cruel pureblooded males and the other hybrids she might remember from the compound. They had been savages, while he was a well-educated, cultured male.

Then again, he knew nothing about her except that she'd lived like a recluse for the past fourteen years. She might prefer a more rugged type of male.

On the third floor, they were intercepted by Jin and Mey, who must have used the elevator. As Jin opened the door, Vrog craned his neck trying to get his first peek at Aliya, but she wasn't in his line of sight.

Was she hiding from him?

"Welcome," Kalugal said as they entered. "I ordered lunch, and it's going to be delivered shortly. I hope you're all hungry."

"We are," Yamanu said. "Nice place you got here."

Vrog scanned the suite for Aliya, finally finding her standing on the balcony with her back to the room as if she was not at all interested in meeting him.

Her height and coloring were Kra-ell, but since she was wearing a baggy sweatshirt, he couldn't see her waist, which in the case of pureblooded females was extremely narrow.

Having a tiny waist had been a source of pride for Jade and the others, but in his opinion, it had made them look even more alien and wasn't all that attractive.

Nevertheless, it was obvious that the woman leaning over the railing was Aliya.

His heart sank.

If this was his welcome, he shouldn't expect an invitation from that female anytime soon, or ever.

He'd been prepared for rejection, reminding himself that Aliya wasn't his only option. A match had been found for him, a clan female whose profile and wishes matched his, and he was to join her on a virtual adventure as soon as he returned to the village.

Still, Aliya's dismissive attitude hurt.

Sensing his eyes on her, or maybe just hearing the commotion of the two teams greeting one another, she finally pushed away from the railing and turned around.

As their eyes met through the glass, Vrog felt like he'd been hit by lightning. He couldn't decide whether that was good or bad, but it was powerful, and he suspected that Aliya felt the same.

Her enormous eyes widened and blazed green, which was a dead giveaway of the emotional turmoil she felt. And as she walked over to the glass door and reached for the handle, he looked at her hand and saw the slight tremor she was trying to hide.

Her reaction relieved some of his anxiety, and as she opened the door and stepped inside, he smiled and walked toward her.

"Hello, Aliya." He offered her his hand. "My heart is overflowing with gratitude to the Mother for taking you under her wing and saving your life."

Even though handshaking was not a Kra-ell custom, she placed her hand in his. "I'm also grateful to the Mother for sparing your life. I heard that you were away when we were attacked."

Her palm was calloused, and he held it gently, mindful of the injuries she'd sustained working to save Kalugal and the others. They probably no longer hurt, but he didn't want to take a chance that they did.

"I was in Singapore. When my emails and phone calls went unanswered, I got worried and came back home. I found the compound deserted, and most of it burned to the ground." He swallowed. "I rebuilt it, hoping Jade would return, and in the meantime, I opened an international school on the premises. I knew Jade would appreciate the tribe's money being used for a profitable endeavor."

Aliya nodded. "Alena and Arwel told me about your school."

"Hello, pretty lady." Yamanu snuck up on them, a testament to how absorbed they had been in one another. "I'm Yamanu, Jin's sister's mate." He offered Aliya his hand.

She looked down, and she and Vrog realized at the same time that they were still holding on.

When Vrog let go of her hand, Aliya seemed confused for a moment, but then she shook her head and placed it in Yamanu's enormous paw. "It is nice to meet you, Yamanu. Jin told me a lot about Mey and you."

"I hope only good things." He winked.

Aliya

୧~୨

Vrog was very handsome, more so than Aliya had remembered, but he also looked more human than she'd expected. Was that a good thing or bad?

She wasn't sure. He looked like a teacher, not a warrior, and he talked like one too. His English was perfect, including his accent, and he was very eloquent, polite, and cultured.

The aggression was there, she could sense it just under the surface, and it excited her. The question was how tightly Vrog had it leashed, and whether he was capable of unleashing it.

Did she want him to?

Aliya had no clue. The farthest she'd gotten with her girly fantasies was passionate kisses, which she hadn't experienced but had seen others exchange. As for the rest, she wasn't sure which side of her was more dominant. Would she have to become a snarling beast to get aroused like the pureblooded females had? Or would she enjoy softer touches like the human Mosuo?

The problem was that Vrog most likely assumed that she'd taken plenty of males into her bed and was experienced. Revealing that she was a clueless thirty-year-old virgin would be so incredibly embarrassing.

What if she seduced Phinas first and got it out of the way?

A Kra-ell would expect her not to limit herself to one lover, but if Vrog had adopted human attitudes toward sex, he might not like that.

Kalugal clapped his hands to get everyone's attention. "Lunch is served."

As everyone took their seats, Aliya found herself sitting across from Vrog, which was more awkward than if she was seated next to him. Now, every time she lifted her head, she had to look at him.

"I see that you can eat a variety of foods like I do," Vrog said. "That's very advantageous. Emmett, the other hybrid male who found his way to the clan, can only drink blood and eat nearly raw meat."

"He shouldn't eat an animal's flesh if he can subsist on its blood. That's wasteful and an affront to the Mother."

Vrog smiled indulgently. "Not everyone interprets the Mother's teachings so literally. There are many interpretations of what the nine commands mean. Some say that you shouldn't eat the meat of animals in the wild, but animals that are raised for that purpose are okay. It's also permitted to eat the flesh when there is not enough blood to sustain you. The Mother does not require you to forfeit your life to obey her commands. Your life always comes first. Others interpret the Mother's wishes still differently. Since she doesn't discriminate between her creatures and allows predators to hunt and kill their prey, it could be argued that since we are predators as well, we should be allowed to hunt and kill our food."

Aliya felt her cheeks heat up. "I didn't know that there were so many interpretations of the Mother's will. I was just eight when I was forced to leave the compound, and my knowledge of the Kra-ell ways was limited. I tried to follow them to the best of my ability."

"That's admirable, and your strict interpretation is the traditional one. I think the others were later adaptations, except for the one that puts your own life ahead. To save yourself, you are allowed to break each of the nine commands."

She let out a breath. "So I can still follow it the way I understand it."

"Of course. We are all free to worship in our own way. There is no right or wrong."

She shook her head. "I don't agree. I still think that killing animals for food is wrong unless it's to avoid starvation."

He waved his hand over the table. "But you don't mind that the people around you are enjoying animal flesh. You don't preach to them that it's wrong. Therefore, you accept their right to choose their way."

"They are not followers of the Mother. They are free to do as they please."

"My brother is vegan," Alena said. "You and he share the same opinion. But since he doesn't need blood to survive, he doesn't drink it either."

Aliya allowed herself to smile. "That is a surprise. I imagined him as a fearsome warrior."

Kalugal chuckled. "One has nothing to do with the other. Kian is fearsome alright, but he's also a sanctimonious prick who has to prove that he's morally superior."

Aliya had no idea what 'sanctimonious prick' meant, but she understood that acting morally superior was not a good thing. Was that Kalugal's way of hinting that she was being rude and also a sanctimonious prick?

Alena chuckled. "That's funny coming from you. Kian just chooses not to eat meat if he doesn't have to. You like to show off in other ways."

"That I do." Kalugal smiled. "I like your brother, and I respect him, but I could do with a little less of his holier-than-thou shtick."

Despite his comment about Kian's moral superiority annoying him, Kalugal had sounded impressed by him, and he wasn't a male who was easily impressed. That meant that the leader of the clan was a formidable man, and she hoped that her drinking of blood didn't offend him.

What if he considered it morally wrong?

"You invited me to live in the village, but you have not secured your leader's permission. What if he doesn't allow me in?"

"Don't worry about it." Kalugal waved a dismissive hand. "Kian already approved your visit. Your continued stay is conditional, though. You will have to prove yourself."

"What if he finds me unsuitable in some way and turns me away? Are you going to send me back here even if I don't complete my three-month trial period?"

"Of course. And you still get to keep the apartment I bought you, so in either case, you won't be homeless again." He leaned forward. "But don't worry. Unless you go nuts and start snarling and biting people, Kian is not going to turn you away."

Vrog

Vrog wasn't sure that he'd heard correctly. "I must have misunderstood." He looked at Kalugal. "Did you buy Aliya an apartment?"

"You understood correctly. I did buy her an apartment in Lijiang, so if she's unhappy in the village, she has a home to go back to." Kalugal smiled at Aliya. "I couldn't think of her ever living in caves or tunnels again. Not that I think she would want to come back after experiencing the village, but if that makes her feel less trapped, then it was worth the money I spent on it."

The territorial rage flaring up in Vrog's chest like a bonfire startled him. As a Kra-ell male, he shouldn't feel possessiveness, but apparently his human side had taken over.

The anger was suffocating in its intensity.

It should have been him buying Aliya a place to live, taking care of her, and making sure she had everything she needed. It was his duty, his obligation, not Kalugal's.

The guy was rich, and the money he'd spent on the apartment was peanuts to him, but Vrog could have certainly afforded it as well. He might have not been able to get Aliya even a rundown studio in Beijing, but he sure as hell could have gotten her an apartment in Lijiang.

Kalugal was lucky that Vrog knew for a fact that he couldn't have been interested in Aliya sexually and therefore hadn't gotten her the apartment to buy her affections. The guy was not only mated but also bonded to Jacki, and Vrog knew what that meant to immortals.

If not for that bond, Kalugal would be a dead immortal, and the irony of that statement was not lost on Vrog.

The Kra-ell females might have shared several males, and the males accepted that as a necessary way of life, but that was not the case for him and Aliya. There were no other Kra-ell, pureblooded or hybrid, for them to form a tribe with, and Kalugal was the exclusive property of Jacki.

"You forgot to tell Vrog that I tricked you into it." Aliya cast Kalugal an apologetic look. "And also about the agreement we reached."

Kalugal waved a dismissive hand. "Feel free to fill in the details."

Vrog was very interested in those details.

Aliya exhaled a long breath as if bracing for the explanation. "Kalugal offered to compensate me for the loss of my hiding place. He told me that I could spend as much money as I wanted during our shopping trip to Lijiang. I challenged him, asking what if I ended up spending a million yuan, and he said I could, but only if I spent it all during that one day. I said that there was no way to spend so much money in a few hours, and Jin said that it could be easily done if I bought expensive jewelry. I said that I would never spend money on such a frivolous thing, and then it occurred to me that I could buy an apartment with such an amount. I expected Kalugal to take it back because he didn't mean it, but he stood by his promise and even bought me an apartment that cost more than the one million yuan he'd promised me."

The whole speech was delivered in under a minute, and at the end of it, Aliya sucked in a breath. "I thought that he would back out and say it was just a joke, but I was wrong. Kalugal is an honorable man."

Vrog didn't know how to feel about that. Should he thank Kalugal for his generosity?

Yes, that was the polite thing to do, even though he hated the guy for taking away what should have been his.

"You are very generous. Thank you for taking care of Aliya."

"It was my pleasure." Kalugal refilled Jacki's plate from one of the communal platters. "But it's all going to come back to me anyway. If Aliya decides to stay in the village, which I'm convinced she will, we will rent out her apartment, and the proceeds will go to one of the charities Jacki and I support."

"Only if I find a job," Aliya corrected him. "If I don't, I will rely on that money for my support."

"You'll make plenty as a Guardian," Jin said. "Even during training."

Vrog arched a brow. "You think Aliya wants to be a Guardian?"

"Why not?" Aliya asked. "I would love to help fight those terrible slavers who trick and abduct young women and then sell them as sex slaves. I cannot think of a more honorable thing to do than saving these victims."

It seemed that Aliya's future had been all mapped out for her without his input. Obviously, it was her prerogative, but Vrog doubted Kalugal and the others had presented her with all the other possible options she might consider.

"You don't have to work for money, Aliya."

She tilted her head. "I don't?"

"I founded the school with the tribe's money, and I've been growing it over the years and saving it for Jade's return. But since it doesn't seem that she and the other females will ever get free from their abductors, this money belongs to you as much as it belongs to me."

Aliya gaped at him, and so did everyone else around the table.

Vrog hadn't planned to say that. He hadn't even thought it through before blurting it out, but he didn't regret making the offer. Aliya was entitled to that money as much as he was. In fact, so was Emmett, but since he'd fled the tribe and Jade's rule, that was arguable. It wasn't in Aliya's case. She was a survivor, same as he was, and it was her birthright.

Besides, his generous offer to share with Aliya everything he'd worked for outshone Kalugal's generosity.

"I don't know what to say," Aliya murmured.

Vrog wanted to reach for her hand, but she was across the table from him, so all he could do was look at her with fondness and promise in his eyes. "We can work out the details later, but I just wanted you to know that you have options. Living in the immortals' village and becoming a Guardian is just one of them."

He was so glad that he'd made the offer.

The village was beautiful, and life there was good. Kalugal was right that after spending three months there, Aliya would not want to leave. The offer to share the school with her gave Vrog a fighting chance of convincing her to leave the comfort of the village and join him.

Kian

6~~9

"Come in, Gavin." Kian motioned for the architect to put his plans down on the conference table. "Show me what you have."

Gavin spread the plans out on the table, using the two bottles of water Kian had put there to weigh the thing down so it wouldn't curl back up.

"As per your instructions, I kept it simple so the structure could be manufactured using the 3D printer. As for the finishes inside, I leave that up to Ingrid."

"No problem."

"Grading will be a challenge." Gavin pointed to the area designated for the paranormal division of Safe Haven. "The terrain is rocky, and it will be a bitch to create a buildable pad, which is why I separated the facilities into several smaller structures instead of building one that was large enough to house everything we need. As always, a challenge incites creativity, and creativity offers solutions that turn out to be more interesting and more beautiful than what would have otherwise been done if the conditions were perfect." He smiled proudly.

"I like it." Kian was impressed with what Gavin had achieved in such a short time. What he was showing him was much more than conceptual drawings.

"The small structures are all on different levels, which provides visual interest and landscaping opportunities. Each classroom has its own small building, and the residential quarters are individual bungalows instead of one large lodge. They are small, about eight hundred to one thousand square feet each, but with the abundance of windows and the open space around them, they will feel more spacious. This is the administrative building, which as you can see is about the size of one of these bungalows, and that's the gym, which is slightly larger. The dining hall and kitchen are about fifteen hundred square feet, and there is plenty of space for outdoor dining when weather conditions permit. The bungalow at the top of the hill will serve future potential Dormants and their mates."

"That's less of a concern now that we have Kalugal and Eleanor to compel their silence, but I love having the option." Kian flipped to the next sheet. "Basically, you have kept it to simple rectangles, letting the landscaping and interior design provide the individualized aesthetics and interest."

"Precisely. I will also vary the stucco colors, the shutter shapes and colors, and the roof materials, so it will look like a village that was built over time and not all in one shot."

"Unlike ours."

Gavin shrugged. "You wanted uniformity of design, and you got it. But I introduced enough variety in the different layouts and façades. I knew that you wanted to build the Safe Haven project even faster than what we did here, so I didn't want to complicate it and kept it as simple as possible. All the windows and doors are the same standard sizes, and so are the bathrooms and kitchens. Makes ordering materials and installation a breeze."

"Great work, Gavin. When will the final plans be ready?"

"If there are no changes, I can finish everything in two days."

"Just one thing. How difficult would it be to connect the structures with an underground tunnel system? Winters there are brutal."

"It will be costly, and it will complicate the project."

"Can you give me a time and cost estimate?"

"Sure. I'll need a day or two to do that."

"Try to do it in one. How about the utilities? Is there enough juice left over for the new section?"

"Barely, but since it's not going to house many people, it should suffice. If not, we will have to implement some of what we did in the village, meaning water desalinating equipment and a small nuclear generator."

"I hope there will be no need for that. As it is, I'm spending more than I initially wanted on this project. The lodge renovation has started, and Leon tells me that it's going well, and we are also remodeling the community quarters one room at a time. I expect these people to maintain the paranormal section as well, and I can't leave them living in squalor. I know that they are all into self-sacrifice as a form of enlightenment, but I'm not. Once I'm done with the place, every room and bungalow should be comfortable enough for me to stay in or invite my friends to." He chuckled. "The only one who might find it lacking is Kalugal, but he's welcome to contribute to the project if he wants to visit and lodge in luxury."

"I couldn't agree more." Gavin rolled the plans back and secured them with a rubber band. "Are we using our regular tactics in regard to securing permits, or are we just going to build what we want and plant fake permits later?"

"The second one. No city inspector is going to come all the way out there to check if work is being done. And if one does, we can deal with them. I want this place up and running in a month."

Gavin chuckled. "Of course, you do."

Vrog

After lunch was over and several members of both groups had left while others chatted and made plans for the rest of the day, Vrog seized the opportunity to take the vacated seat next to Aliya.

"Would you like to go for a walk with me?" he asked.

She glanced at Kalugal. "I don't know if I'm allowed."

Even though he disapproved of Kalugal having a say in what she was allowed or disallowed to do, Vrog forced his expression to remain amiable. The demigod might be a big deal in the village, but it wasn't his place to rule over Aliya.

Instead, he offered, "We can ask him."

Aliya cast another quick glance at Kalugal, but he was busy talking with Yamanu and didn't notice. "I don't think he would mind," she said. "But why do you want to be alone with me?"

She was blunt, and Vrog liked that even though he wasn't. "Other than Emmett we might be the only survivors of Jade's tribe. We have a lot to talk about."

"I hope the females are alive," she murmured. "But maybe they aren't. The Mother only knows what those evil Kra-ell are doing to them."

Vrog cast a quick glance around. "The same kinds of thoughts torment me as well. I think it will help us both to talk about it."

"Okay. I'll just get my coat." Aliya rose to her feet.

She walked over to the couch, crouched, and pulled out a suitcase that had been tucked under it. Inside were neatly folded clothes. She lifted out a dark gray puffer coat, closed the suitcase, and tucked it back under the couch.

"Where are you going?" Jacki asked her when she shrugged the coat on.

"On a walk with Vrog." Aliya cast Kalugal a questioning look.

"Have fun." He waved her off and turned back to talk with Yamanu.

When they were out the door, Aliya let out a breath. "Until this morning, I couldn't even touch the door handle. Kalugal used compulsion to keep me from running away."

"How come he released you now? Was it because of your heroic efforts to save him the day before?"

"Maybe. He said that he trusted me not to run because I gave him my word that I would give the village a chance."

"Was he right?"

She narrowed her eyes at him. "Of course he was. I would never break a promise."

"Would you have run if not for the promise you gave Kalugal?"

"When they first caught me, I wanted to run. I didn't know who these people were. I thought that the bad Kra-ell found out about me and came to take me too."

Vrog wanted to ask her about the attack, but he decided against it. The subject was no doubt painful to her, and he wanted this walk to be about them getting to know each other. Some reminiscing about the good times in the compound could be enjoyable, and if she indicated an interest in him, maybe he could start with some flirting.

So far, he wasn't sure what she felt toward him. She was polite, but she wasn't friendly, and what irritated him even more was that she was much more comfortable with the immortals than she was with him.

"When you found out that they weren't Kra-ell, did you still want to run?" He opened the lobby door and held it for her.

Aliya nodded. "I didn't trust them. I didn't know what they wanted from me, and I suspected them of cooperating with those evil Kra-ell." She zipped up the jacket and pulled a pair of gloves out of her pocket. "They lured me with the simplest things. Food to fill my belly, a shower to finally get properly clean, and a soft couch to sleep on. Kalugal compelled me not to run, but I don't think I would have even without his compulsion. Then they took me shopping, and for the first time in forever, I had new things that weren't torn or dirty. And then Kalugal bought me a brand new two-bedroom apartment, and I could no longer suspect them of wishing to do me harm. I had to accept that they were good people and that they were sent by the Mother to find me and give me a home." She turned to him and smiled. "I want to believe that it was a reward for observing her rules and for acting with honor."

His heart broke for the hardships she'd endured. "The village is not your only alternative, Aliya. You could come to the school and live in the staff quarters. I can help you catch up on your education, you can go to a university and study something that interests you, and you don't need to worry about earning an income because half of the school belongs to you. You are entitled to half of the net income."

She shook her head. "It's very generous of you to offer, but I'm not entitled to your school. You built it, and you made it profitable. I'm glad that you found something that you are passionate about, but I need to find what that thing is for me, and I don't think I can get passionate about a school."

"And you think that becoming a Guardian is your true calling? You haven't explored all the possibilities. Being a Guardian is just one option among many."

"It appeals to me. I want to help these poor victims who were sold into sex slavery in any way I can, and if I can get paid for doing that, it's even better." She pushed her hands into the coat pockets. "I can't help you run the school, and even if I could, that's not what I want to do with my life. Besides, I would need to keep hiding and pretending that I'm human, while in the village, I can be myself."

"I understand." Vrog mimicked her and pushed his hands into his pockets as well. "I have a son in the village, and I love spending time with him and his fiancée. But I also love my school." He gave her a sad smile. "It's difficult to be torn between two loves that are on opposite sides of the world."

Aliya stopped walking. "Carol and Alena told me that you have a son who is very nice and dresses like a Goth. I was curious about how you met his mother."

Vrog hadn't meant to reveal having a son so soon, but now he was glad that he had. Evidently, Aliya already knew about Vlad, and if he kept it from her, she would have wondered about his reasons.

All he'd hoped for was to get her to like him before telling her about his son, but from her perspective, that could have been perceived as cowardly or dishonest.

"A long time ago, I had a short fling with a lady who I thought was human. When I discovered that she was immortal, I had already planted my seed in her womb. She refused to abort it, for which I'm eternally grateful to her. She vowed to keep the identity of the father a secret, and we parted ways. I never expected to meet her again or to get to know my son, but the Mother had other plans." He put his hand on her shoulder. "I would like you to meet Vlad and Wendy. I think you will find their company very pleasant."

Aliya

"I like all the immortals I've met so far, and since your son is half immortal half Kra-ell, I'm sure that I'm going to like him as well. You are incredibly lucky to have a long-lived son. You must have pleased the Mother greatly to earn such a boon."

Aliya was keenly aware of Vrog's hand on her shoulder. Was she supposed to allow it? Was it a test?

Observing the pureblooded females back in the compound, she had never seen any display of affection between them and the males. The males were respectful, the females domineering, and most of the time, everyone treated each other with respect. Occasionally, though, tempers flared, or something was construed as an offense or disobedience, and then all hell broke loose. She'd made herself scarce at those times, running back to the human quarters as fast as her legs could carry her.

His hand on her shoulder didn't feel bad, though, so she decided to pretend that she hadn't noticed it and ignore it.

"I don't know what I did to deserve Vlad." He took his hand off her shoulder and resumed walking. "I was very young at the time, and I hadn't accomplished much yet."

Aliya missed the contact. She hadn't had anyone touch her with affection in so long that she hadn't even realized how starved she was for it. Fourteen years had passed since her mother's death, and she had been the only person who'd ever loved her. The only one she'd loved.

"I hope to never have children." Her throat constricting, she looked straight ahead. "I don't want to outlive them."

Her mother's death had devastated her. She couldn't fathom losing a child.

Vrog cleared his throat. "I don't want to appear presumptuous, and I know that we've just met, and it's too early to talk about things like that, but if you find me pleasing and invite me to share your bed, we might produce a long-lived child together. The adult hybrid females of our tribe never invited the hybrid males to their beds because they preferred the purebloods to father their children, but I think there is a good chance that two hybrids can produce a long-lived child."

As Aliya's cheeks caught fire, she kept her eyes on the path ahead, avoiding looking at Vrog. "If you mate a clan female, you can have an immortal child for sure. You already have one. Why take the risk with me?"

"Because we are of the same people. Naturally, you can choose any of the clan males if you like, but they can't give you a long-lived child. The immortal genes only pass through the females of the clan."

"I know that. They explained it to me. Right now, I'm not looking for a mate. I need to find my place in the world first."

That was such a lie.

Circumstances had inhibited her feminine urges for many years, but now that her belly was full, she wasn't cold, and she wasn't afraid of what the next day would bring, they were awakening.

"Of course." Vrog bowed his head. "Forgive me for bringing it up."

Great. Now he thought that he had no chance with her, when nothing could be further from the truth.

Vrog wasn't like the pureblooded males or even the hybrids, but that wasn't a bad thing. He was capable of love, and he was growing on her. She liked his calm manner, his eloquence, his quiet confidence. He was more human than Kra-ell, but surprisingly she found it very attractive. He didn't stir her innate aggression, and that was a good thing too. She didn't want to be cruel like the pureblooded females. She didn't want to fight him and hurt him until he managed to subdue her to prove his worth.

More than anything, Aliya wanted to be loved.

Finally daring to look at him, she asked, "When we leave on Monday, are you going back to your school?"

"I'm not. I'm coming with you." He regarded her hesitantly to gauge her response. "My visit in the village was cut short, and I didn't have enough time with my son. Kian wanted me to take Mey to the school so she could listen to the echoes and possibly find out more about what happened in the compound, but he said that I'm welcome to visit any time. I promised Vlad and his fiancée that I would return."

A weight rolled off Aliya's chest. "I'm glad. Maybe we can spend more time together there. You could introduce me to your son and future daughter-in-law."

If the son was like the father, and his fiancée was as nice as the immortals she'd met so far, she would enjoy their company. Maybe they could even become friends.

"I would like that very much." Grinning, Vrog didn't try to hide how happy her wish to meet his son made him.

His human side was definitely more dominant than the Kra-ell.

"Can you tell me how the clan found you?"

"They didn't tell you?"

She shook her head. "Just bits and pieces here and there. I had a feeling that they didn't want to tell me. Did you do something bad?"

He chuckled. "You could say that. I attacked Stella, Vlad's mother."

"Why?"

"I thought she had something to do with the attack on our people."

"Why would you think that?"

"Because it happened shortly after I met her."

Alena

❧

"What are you smiling about?" Orion asked as they entered their hotel room.

Alena walked into the bathroom and sat on the edge of the tub. "Aliya and Vrog. I think there is a spark there. They went on a very long walk, and when they returned, they both seemed much less tense." She chuckled. "Kalugal probably started to worry."

"No, he didn't." Orion leaned against the vanity and crossed his arms over his chest. "He meant it when he said that he trusted her. I trust her too. She is not the type to go back on her word."

Alena turned the faucet on and checked the water until it reached the right temperature. "You like her."

He nodded. "She's strange, and it takes time to peel off her layers, but under the rough exterior beats a good heart."

"It's a miracle that she hasn't gone insane after living in isolation for fourteen years. Humans, immortals, Kra-ell, and even the gods need a community of people to interact with. We are not meant to be alone."

"She ventured into the Mosuo village from time to time, so she wasn't completely isolated. Besides, one can be surrounded by people and still be alone."

She'd forgotten that until very recently, Orion had lived among humans, and his only contact was a half-sister and niece, who he couldn't allow to remember him.

That must have been so damn lonely, and the talk about Aliya's isolation had reminded him of it.

Alena knew exactly how to cheer him up. Pulling her sweater over her head, she tossed it at him. "That's enough talk about Aliya."

"Agreed." His eyes glowing, Orion sauntered over and kneeled at her feet. "Let me help you undress."

Smiling, she lifted her foot for him to remove her shoe.

He gently gripped her ankle and took off the ballet flat. "Pretty color." He looked at her pink toes.

"It matches the polish on my nails." She wiggled her fingers. "My nails weren't as badly chipped as Jin's or ruined like Aliya's, but they needed some tender care." She sighed. "I wasn't as helpful as they were."

"But you saved the day." He gripped her left ankle and took the shoe off. "If you didn't come up with the idea to bring the Odus, Jacki would have for sure peed her pants because it would have taken us much longer to get them out. Actually, I don't think we could have done it without the Odus."

Alena shuddered. "If I never see another tunnel again, it will be too soon."

He chuckled. "You have to see one every time you enter the village."

She pouted. "I don't see it because the windows of the cars turn opaque, but thanks for reminding me. Now I will have a mini panic attack every time I have to go through it."

"I'm sorry." He lifted her foot and started kissing her toes one at a time. "I promise that in a few moments, you'll forget all about it."

As he kissed her instep, she stifled a giggle. "That tickles."

Smiling evilly, he did the same to her other arch. When she laughed, he kissed it again, and then lifted her with one hand while tugging her pants down with the other.

When all she had left on her body was a bra, he pushed up on his knees and pressed a soft kiss to one swell and then the other before reaching behind her and unhooking it.

She held her breath as he blew on each nipple and then kissed them lightly. Licking and nibbling, he tormented her with pleasure until she was writhing on the edge of the tub. Pulling back a little, he regarded her glistening tips with satisfaction.

"Let's get you into the tub." He lifted her and slowly deposited her in the water.

"Come join me." She scooted to the side. "There is enough room."

He shook his head. "If I get in, we will cause a flood. I have a better plan." He reached for a washcloth and squirted liquid soap on it. "I'll be your devoted servant tonight. I'll bathe you, towel you dry, carry you to bed, and give you a massage."

Alena wasn't sure she could survive all that before throwing him on the bed and having her way with him, but she was willing to play along, especially since it involved Orion's hands all over her body.

He would probably snap before she did.

"I like your plan." She sprawled in the bathtub. Resting her head and arms on the lip of the tub, she closed her eyes and surrendered to his ministrations.

Orion

❦

O rion took great pleasure in bathing Alena, his palm following the trail he made with the washcloth over her smooth skin, caressing gently, intimately.

He wished she'd let him wash her hair, but she didn't want to ruin the hairdo she'd gotten earlier in the spa. It was a shame. He loved massaging her scalp, working the shampoo into the long, luxurious strands of her hair. But even more than that, he loved washing her breasts, her belly, her thighs, her feminine center.

"You're teasing me," she murmured. "You keep doing that, and I'll pull you into the tub and mount you."

He chuckled. "Is that supposed to be a threat?"

"It's a heads up in case you want to undress first and save your clothes from getting shredded."

She sounded deliciously vicious, and he teased her for a little longer just to hear her threatening him again. He had no intentions of taking her in the bathtub. He had a plan, and he was sticking to it.

"Last warning, Orion." She cut him a mock glare.

With a laugh, he reached for the large towel he'd brought over and fluffed it out. "Come on, princess. Time for stage two of tonight's session."

He helped her out of the tub, wrapped her in the towel, and carried her to the bed.

After patting her dry, he tossed the towel aside and laid her on her belly. "Magnificent." He dipped his head to kiss the round swells of her bottom.

She arched up, and he kissed lower, but he didn't linger. Tearing himself away from the intoxicating scent of her arousal, he reached for the lotion and applied generous amounts to his palms.

"You're such a terrible tease, Orion."

"Patience, my love." When he put his hands on her calves, she groaned. "That feels good."

"I've only just started." He began a slow progression, kneading and stroking up her thighs, and then he was cupping her generous bottom. He lingered there, kneading her lush mounds for much longer than necessary, but then this wasn't about relaxation, it was about slow, torturous seduction.

As he moved up to her back, he kissed her spine, and as she wiggled and writhed over the bedding, he nipped her ear. "Patience is not your strong suit, is it?"

"Patience is overrated." She turned around and pulled him over her. "And you are overdressed."

Orion chuckled. "If only people knew what a tigress sweet Alena really is." He took her lips in a soft kiss. "But I'm glad that I'm the only one you show this side of you to."

Her glowing eyes softened. "I love you, and I know that you love me in all of my facets, the sweet and the spicy. I'm free to explore the other sides of me that have been stifled in favor of the one everyone expects to see."

His heart swelled with love and gratitude for the incredible gift she was giving him and would keep on giving for eternity. They were bonded, there was no doubt in either of their minds that their bond had solidified and was unbreakable.

Alena's lips twitched with a smile. "If you're going to keep staring at me instead of getting rid of your clothes, I'm going to do it for you."

"You're full of threats today." He dipped his head and took her nipple between his lips.

Licking it, he smoothed his hand down her belly to her center and slid a finger into her. When she moaned and writhed on it, he added another one. She moaned again, her hands closing around fistfuls of his hair and tugging his head to her other nipple.

He wanted his tongue to go where his fingers were, not to replace them but to add to the delicious torment, but she was holding on tight, not letting go of his hair.

Impatient minx wanted to get straight down to business, but he would have none of that.

Perhaps he needed to issue a threat of his own.

"Let go of my hair, Alena. Until I make you come with my mouth, I'm not getting rid of my clothes."

When she let go right away and spread her thighs for him, Orion laughed. "Now I know how to get you to cooperate." He slid down her body and positioned himself right where he wanted to be.

"Took you long enough to realize that." She lifted her head and gazed at him, amusement and desire dancing in her eyes. "I'll do anything to get you naked."

"Anything?" He treated her to a long lick.

"Anything." She let her head drop back on the mattress.

Alena

❧

Would it always be like this? The insatiable need to be joined? Their bodies hungry for each other, their minds never wandering too far off the other?

In one way or another, Orion was always on Alena's mind. Everything she did, she considered how it would impact him, would he approve, not because he was demanding or hard to please, but because she loved him and wanted to be the best version of herself for him.

When his mouth replaced his fingers, and he slid his hands under her bottom to lift her, like he was raising a platter so he could feast, her core clenched in anticipation.

He delved deeper, taunting and teasing, giving her just enough stimulation to bring her close to the edge but not to topple over.

Panting, she clutched at the bedsheets next to her, her hips churning on the mattress as much as his grip allowed. She braced for a prolonged torment, but then he let go of one side, plunged two fingers into her, and closed his lips around the bundle of nerves at the top of her cleft.

The climax tore through her like a tornado, and he helped her ride it out—his fingers plunging in and out of her, his tongue lapping at her juices, hungry groans leaving his throat.

When she collapsed, exhausted from the powerful orgasm, he pressed one last gentle kiss to her folds before leaving her for a split second to get naked.

"Finally." Alena cracked her eyes open just as Orion prowled on top of her.

Her male was magnificent. His lean body was made of powerful muscles and smooth, olive-toned skin, his long hair fell forward, framing his gorgeous face, his blue and violet eyes were aglow, and his fangs were fully extended.

She wrapped her arms around his torso and arched up to rub herself against his hard shaft, coating it with the copious juices from her climax.

Baring his fangs, Orion growled and with one powerful surge, joined them.

Alena cried out at the sheer perfection of it. Her inner nerve endings were still overstimulated from the powerful orgasm he'd given her, and as he withdrew and plunged in, she climaxed again.

The look of satisfaction on his face was precious.

"You're mine, Alena, and I can't believe how fortunate I am to have you give yourself to me."

"And you are mine, Orion. And I also thank the Fates every day for the gift of you."

It was a sweet moment, and she was going to remember it forever, but she needed him to move.

As if reading her mind, Orion started with shallow, gentle thrusts that lasted for about thirty seconds, and then he gripped her hips and gave her what she needed.

They were making a racket, and the Odus in the next room over could hear every screech of the bed's legs on the floor, every bang of the headboard on the wall, and every moan and groan leaving her and Orion's throats, but Alena didn't care.

Heck, she didn't care if every immortal in the hotel heard them.

When they both hovered over the edge and Orion hissed, she turned her head, elongating her neck for him, and when the bite came, she didn't try to hold on to reality and let herself soar on the clouds of euphoria.

Orion would keep her safe, and when she floated down to earth, he would be there to catch her.

Darlene

❧

As Darlene entered the hair salon, Judy, her stylist, waved her over to her station. "What a nice surprise to see you here today." She unfurled a big nylon cape and motioned for Darlene to take a seat. "I wasn't expecting you for another two weeks. Do you have an event or a special occasion that you need to look pretty for?" She draped it over Darlene's front and closed it at the back of her neck.

"Yes." Sort of. "I'm invited to dinner with my cousins tonight, but that's just an excuse. I feel like I need a change. Maybe a new hair color? Or perhaps a more youthful style?"

Standing behind her, Judy fluffed up her hair, brought it all forward, and then combed it to the side. "Let me bring you a few style journals to flip through."

"Okay."

Darlene had hoped that Judy would know what to do, magically transforming her into a beautiful young woman with the help of her styling shears.

Right. Only a surgeon's knife could perform such a magical feat. She'd been spending too many hours on that plastic surgery website, looking at before and after images, and wondering whether she would ever have the courage to go for a facelift or a nose job.

Heck, a boob job and a tummy tuck could probably improve her looks more than anything she could do to her face.

Except, she was too much of a coward to do any of that, and Leo would never let her spend the money anyway.

She'd been feeling odd lately, like something was missing from her life.

She also felt resentful toward Leo and had a hard time hiding it.

Well, she always felt that, but lately it was more than usual. She was short-tempered, argumentative, and after one too many snapping comments, Leo packed up his things and left, telling her to calm the fuck down and call him when she was back to normal.

Supposedly, Leo's boss was sending him on a month-long acquisition trip for the gallery, but Darlene doubted that. It was a cover story for what he was really up to, which was most likely shagging a young mistress.

She had no proof that he was cheating on her, but with the way things were between them lately, it was a safe bet that he was.

"So here is what I think." Judy handed her a journal already open on a page. "This hair color." She pointed to the auburn-streaked shoulder-length hairstyle. "With this cut." She thrust another journal into Darlene's hands.

The style was much shorter than what she had now, but it looked young and pretty and was precisely the look she was going for. Not that there was any chance she would look like the model, but she hoped it would be an improvement.

"I like it." She handed back the two journals to Judy.

"Don't you want to flip through them? Maybe you'll find something that you like more? I want it to be your choice."

For some reason, Judy's words brought about a sense of déjà vu. Something about red and blue pills and having to choose one.

She must have dreamt something, and her brain had stored pieces of the dream but not the entire story, so she had no reference to figure out what it meant.

Looking up at the stylist, she smiled. "You've been coloring and cutting my hair for years. I trust you."

She'd been going to the same hair salon for over twenty years, and not because Judy was such a great stylist.

Darlene clung to the familiar and hated changes, even simple ones like going to a new hairdresser.

"Thanks." Judy took the magazines and put them back on the waiting area's table. "You will look great. I'm going to mix the color and be right back."

As Darlene waited for Judy's return, she looked in the mirror at the other hairdressers and their clients. She knew most of them, not by name, but she knew their faces. Most were like her, loyal clients who'd been coming here for years, and yet she'd never engaged any of them in conversation, never asked what their names were, and never took part in the chatting that went on around her.

Was it any wonder that she was lonely?

Her social skills sucked, and that was why she was so dependent on Leo. She had no network of friends, and her family lived far away, so she had only him.

But that was no longer true.

She had a newly discovered family, her cousins Geraldine and Cassandra, and their boyfriends. They seemed just as starved for a connection as she was, or they wouldn't have proactively sought her company.

She should initiate get-togethers and get Cassandra to invite Roni and his girlfriend as well. Darlene still didn't have her son's phone number and couldn't call him even if she had it.

Roni lived in hiding, avoiding capture by the agents that still watched their house. She'd thought that they were long gone, but according to Onegus, her and Leo's cell phones were monitored, and so was the landline to their house.

Perhaps today, she would suggest their next lunch or dinner meeting, or maybe a shopping spree. With Leo gone, she was a free woman and could do as she pleased. It would be so nice to go shopping without him checking where she was every ten minutes and frowning over every little thing she bought for herself.

Looking in the mirror, she eyed the beautician's station and wondered whether the woman could squeeze her in without an appointment. Her eyebrows could use a professional touchup, and she might even go for the eyelashes and brow tinting she'd been wanting to get for so long and was afraid to.

Ronja

As Lisa left the kitchen to set up the table in the dining room, Ronja marked the calendar she'd taped to the fridge and sighed. It had been six days since she and Merlin had started working on her transition, and nothing was happening yet.

Well, working wasn't the right term for what they'd been doing. It wasn't a hardship to make love to Merlin twice and sometimes three times a day. Fortunately, or maybe unfortunately, he could only bite her once every twenty-four hours, and he usually did that at night, so she could float on the pleasure cloud for as long as she pleased.

Six days wasn't a long time. Merlin had told her that it had taken some of the Dormants two or even three weeks to transition, and they had been much younger than her. She shouldn't start worrying even if she didn't transition in a month. As a confirmed Dormant, there was no question about her having the immortal genes, but her age was an issue, and the transition might not start because her body couldn't take it.

Ironically, she had never felt better than she felt now, not even as a young woman. The venom was Merlin's best miracle potion. It invigorated her, smoothed out her skin, brought luster into her eyes, and had reversed the clock on her sex drive, so she was as obsessed with sex now as she'd been in her youth.

Thankfully, Merlin's work didn't suffer terribly because of their stolen moments of passion. Well, hours was more accurate. They'd just worked longer days, or rather Merlin did. Ronja had to go home to cook dinner for Lisa and spend time with her.

The first morning after Merlin had stayed the night, things had been a little awkward at breakfast, but Lisa had said that she preferred him sleeping over to Ronja spending the night over at his place. Lisa didn't want to be alone in the house, and even though Merlin's place was only two houses down, Ronja agreed with her daughter.

The result was that Merlin's place had turned fully into a lab and a makeshift fertility clinic, and her place was where they chilled in the evenings and spent their nights.

The three of them were becoming a family, and life was good, but her impending transition loomed over them like a dark cloud.

"The table is set." Lisa walked into the kitchen. "You should call Merlin and remind him that it's dinner time."

She chuckled. "That man needs to be reminded to put his shoes on before leaving the house. He's such an absentminded professor."

"That's because he's brilliant." Ronja smiled. "Smart people have so many thoughts circulating in their heads that they don't pay attention to the most basic things."

"Was David and Jonah's father like that?" Lisa pulled out a stool and sat at the counter. "Michael was supposedly brilliant too."

Lisa had been a little girl when Ronja's ex-husband had died. She didn't remember him.

"He was, but in a different way than Merlin. Michael knew a lot, and he was a world-renowned cardiac specialist, but he wasn't an inventor, and his mind wasn't scattered. He had an excellent memory, and he paid attention to detail."

Excruciatingly so.

If anything was out of place, he would notice and make a comment. Ronja remembered how it had stressed her out. Keeping the house in order with twin boys running around was a losing battle, but she and the housekeeper they'd had at the time had done their best. Every night after the boys' bath, they'd stuck them in front of the television in the den, so they could put everything in order before Michael walked through the door.

He never raised his voice or his hand to her or the boys, but his disparaging looks had been nearly as bad. He had a way of making her feel worthless no matter how hard she tried to prove the opposite.

"I don't remember him," Lisa admitted. "But I remember feeling sorry for David and Jonah because he was so demanding and never happy with their achievements. My father praised me for the smallest things." She sighed. "He was a great dad."

"Oh, sweetie." Ronja walked over to Lisa and pulled her into a crushing hug. "This must be so difficult for you."

Lisa nodded. "I miss him, and I wish he were here with us, but I'm not blind. You are happier with Merlin."

It was true, but Ronja couldn't acknowledge it. "I was happy with Frank too, and I miss him. Our love might have been less fiery, but it was warm and fuzzy, and safe. I was contented."

Lisa looked doubtful, but she was smart enough to let it go. "Call Merlin, Mom."

Cassandra

❦

"They will be here in less than ten minutes." Cassandra put her phone down.

For security reasons, they'd sent an Uber to pick Darlene up at her home and drive her to one of the clan's office buildings.

Cassandra had told her that it was where Onegus worked.

He'd picked Darlene up from there and explained that Roni was joining them, which was why she had to leave her phone behind in a locker. It was also the reason he'd given her for running William's handheld bug detecting device over her.

It was a convenient excuse, and it was also partially true.

Roni was there, and his safety was paramount, but even if he wasn't, Cassandra didn't want her house to get compromised. The last thing she needed was for the agents to start monitoring her place.

It wouldn't have mattered if she'd rented the house out like she'd planned to, but she was dragging her feet about it.

That house meant a lot to her and Geraldine, and having strangers live in it just rubbed her the wrong way. It was silly, and it proved that she wasn't as pragmatic as she wanted everyone to believe she was.

"I'm nervous," Parker admitted. "How am I supposed to test whether my compulsion works on her? What if she's the type who goes along with everything she's told to do?"

"That's only true for the man I thought was my father," Roni said. "Darlene always does what he tells her to do. She's not a pushover with anyone else."

"Maybe she feels guilty?" Geraldine suggested. "It might be her way of atoning for lying to him for all these years."

Roni grimaced. "Thanks. So now it's my fault that my mother is punishing herself by staying married to a miserable jerk."

"It's not your fault that you were born as a result of a fling," Sylvia said. "Your mother's decisions and their consequences are on her, not you."

"People." Cassandra clapped her hands. "Let's concentrate on coming up with a good test for Parker. We don't have much time."

"I know how to test her," Roni said. "When I was a little kid, my mother used to sing me this one song that I loved, but only when we were alone. She thinks that her voice is terrible, and if I bring it up and ask her to sing it for me in company, she will refuse. If Parker asks her and she starts singing, we will have our answer."

"That's good." Cassandra moved the vase a fraction of an inch to the right, centering it on the dining table. "Anything else? We need one more as a backup plan."

"I could ask her to tell me the most embarrassing moment of her life," Parker said. "We can pretend to play a game of truth or dare."

"That would have been an excellent idea if we were teenagers." Cassandra patted the boy's back. "Grownups don't play truth or dare."

"It's a backup plan," Shai said. "If the singing one is not conclusive, we can use Parker's idea."

When Onegus's car pulled up in front of the house, Cassandra opened the door and stepped out to greet her sister.

The woman who exited the vehicle looked transformed.

"Oh my, Darlene. You look amazing." She pulled her in for a quick hug. "I love the new hair. And I love your outfit."

"Thank you." Darlene smoothed her hand over her shiny, sleek hair. "My hairdresser suggested the Brazilian blowout. I'm so glad I listened to her."

Cassandra took a step back and regarded her with the critical eye of a fashion executive. "You also dyed your eyelashes and your brows. Well done, Darlene." She threaded her arm through her sister's. "You are on the right path."

"Right path to where?"

Cassandra smiled. "Growth, independence, a new life."

Darlene chuckled. "It's just a new hairdo and professionally applied makeup. I didn't win the lottery."

"Oh, I think you did. You just don't know it yet."

Darlene

Cassandra was a strange woman.

Darlene didn't know why she had formed that opinion about her cousin, but it had been there even before the comment about her winning the lottery but not knowing that she had.

When they walked inside, Geraldine rushed over to her and hugged her as if they hadn't seen each other in weeks. "You look so beautiful, my Darlene. This new hairdo is perfect for you."

"Thanks." Darlene kissed her cousin's cheek and looked over to where Roni was sitting with his girlfriend.

"Aren't you going to give your mother a kiss?"

He got to his feet, walked over to her, and gave her a peck on the cheek. "What's the occasion?" He waved a hand over her new hairdo. "Is it your and Leo's anniversary?"

She tilted her head. "Our anniversary is in March. Did you forget?" And since when had he started calling Leo by his given name?

"I have a bad memory for dates." Roni led her to the dining table, where a gangly teenage boy was sitting. "This is Parker. Parker, this is my mother, Darlene."

"Nice to meet you," the boy said.

"It's nice to meet you too, Parker. Are you Onegus's or Shai's nephew?"

"Parker is the son of a good friend of mine," Onegus said.

He didn't explain why the boy was there, but she assumed his parents were vacationing somewhere, and Onegus was hosting Parker while they were gone.

As everyone sat at the table, Cassandra lifted her wine glass. "To family, and many more family dinners."

"I'll drink to that." Geraldine lifted hers and clinked it with Cassandra's.

When the salute was done, and everyone had clinked everyone else's glasses, Cassandra and Geraldine removed the lids from the chafing dishes. "*Bon appétit*, everyone."

"Wow, Cassandra, you cooked up a feast." Darlene salivated over the selection.

She filled her plate with thin beef slices and steamed asparagus, but she skipped the mashed potatoes even though they smelled divine. Today was the start of her new self, and along with the new hairdo, she would also start watching what she ate and include exercise in her daily routine.

"I didn't cook a thing." Cassandra put a big scoop of the yummy mashed potatoes on her plate. "I ordered catering." She gave Darlene a sly smile. "I love having the family over for dinner, but I don't have time to cook."

"Then it's a wonderful solution." Darlene admired her cousin for her resourcefulness.

If only she could be a little like Cassandra, assertive, determined, a go-getter who went for what she wanted and didn't stop until she got it. But first, she needed to figure out what she wanted.

That wasn't it.

Darlene actually knew precisely what she wanted, but there was no way she could ever get it, so what she needed to figure out was what would be a satisfying substitute for having everything she wanted in life.

Family, friends, something fulfilling to do, and no financial worries. She didn't need to be rich, but it would be nice not to worry about paying her bills.

"Do you remember the song you used to sing for me?" Roni asked out of the blue.

"'You Are My Sunshine.'"

"Yes, that's the one. I wanted to sing it for Sylvia, but I couldn't remember the words or the melody. Could you sing it for me?"

There was no way she was going to sing in public. Leo said that she sounded like a deaf goat. "I could recite the words for you."

"I want you to sing it."

She shook her head. "Maybe when we are alone. I'm too embarrassed to sing in company."

"I want to hear you sing," Parker said. "Sing for me."

Shocked at the boy's audacity, Darlene wanted to tell him to mind his manners, but instead, she found herself quietly singing the song.

"Louder," the boy commanded. "Sing louder."

Her eyes bugging out, she raised her voice even though it was the last thing she wanted to do.

"You can stop now." Parker smiled like a fiend.

"What the hell was that?" she croaked. "What kind of a trick did you use to make me sing? Was it hypnosis?"

"Close. It was compulsion." The kid turned to Onegus. "I've done my part. Now it's your turn."

Geraldine

Geraldine's heart started pounding as frantically as it had the first time they'd told Darlene that she was her mother.

This was round two, and it might not go as well as round one had, which hadn't been great either. Darlene had listened to her explanation, so that was good, but she hadn't forgiven her, and she hadn't warmed to her. She had treated her much better when she thought that they were cousins.

As Onegus switched places with Cassandra and sat next to Darlene, Geraldine had to force herself to take a breath.

"Look at me, Darlene," Onegus said. "I'm going to release the memories I suppressed before, and as they flood back in, it might feel a little overwhelming, and you might get a headache, but the sensation shouldn't last long. I only erased the memories of what we told you during our last meeting."

She narrowed her eyes at him. "What are you talking about? I remember everything that happened during our lunch last week."

He smiled at her. "You remember what I planted in your head to fill up the gap created by what I suppressed."

"How can you do that?"

He smiled. "Instead of explaining everything once again, I'll release your memories, and if you have more questions after that, I'll try to answer as best I can. Ready?"

Looking doubtful and suspicious, she nodded nonetheless. The doubting expression turned to awed, then pained, and then she clutched at her head and whimpered. "You weren't kidding. Not about the pain and not about all the rest."

Her eyes closing again, Darlene slumped in her chair. "Give me a moment. It's all a jumbled mess in my head."

"Take all the time you need," Cassandra said.

As the seconds ticked by, and Darlene's expression vacillated between confused and angry, the change marked by the depth of her frowns, Geraldine couldn't fill her lungs with enough air.

When Darlene finally opened her eyes, she shifted them to Geraldine, and the anger in them didn't bode well. "How could you?"

Geraldine swallowed the lump in her throat. "I explained. I had a very bad accident, and I lost my memory. I didn't know that I had another daughter. I only found out recently."

"I understand about the memory loss, but you pretended to be my cousin." She turned to Cassandra. "You also lied to me." She then shifted her eyes to her son. "You should have told me. You knew all along who they were, and you didn't say anything."

"Would you have believed me if I told you that Geraldine was your mother? You would have thought that we were all on drugs. In order for Cassandra and Geraldine to come forward, we had to tell you about the gods and immortals, but since we believed that you were too old to transition, we decided to spare you the pain of knowing you missed your chance."

"So why are you telling me now? What has changed?"

"Before, we didn't know that we were direct descendants of a god," Cassandra said. "We found out about Orion through Rudolf, and when we caught Orion, he told us that his and Geraldine's father was a freaking god. With a god's blood flowing in your veins, you have a much better chance to transition successfully, even at your age, than Dormants who are younger. That's why we came forward, and that's why we offered you a chance of immortality now and not before."

Slumping in her chair, Darlene closed her eyes for a long moment. "I need a drink. Something stronger than wine, please."

"Coming up." Cassandra rose to her feet and walked to the kitchen. She returned with a bottle of brandy. "Will this do?"

"It's perfect." Darlene lifted her empty wine glass for Cassy to fill.

After taking a long sip, she turned to look at Parker. "You are the compeller they were talking about?"

He nodded. "The other compellers are scattered on missions all over the world, so that left me. You are my first mission." He took in a long breath. "What I did before was just a test to see if I could compel you. Now I need to compel you for real. You will keep everything you learned about gods and immortals a secret and never mention it to anyone unless they are immortals or gods as well." He stopped and looked at Onegus. "Is that good?"

Onegus shook his head. "You need to clarify that she can only talk about immortals with clan members."

"Right." He turned to Darlene. "You can only talk about immortals and gods and everything else they will tell you with clan members."

"How would I know who is a clan member and who isn't?"

"It's simple," Onegus said. "You can only talk to those you know for sure are clan members."

"Is everyone here a clan member?"

"Yes."

"Then go ahead." Darlene waved a hand at Parker. "Compel me."

"I just did."

"That's all? That's all it takes?"

He nodded. "It's in the voice. But don't ask me how it works because I don't know."

"What about the adult compellers? Do they know how they do what they do?"

He shook his head. "The ability is hereditary. We are born with it."

"I see. Well, thank you for coming here and doing this for me. I appreciate it."

Parker grinned. "No need to thank me. Onegus paid me a hundred bucks to do it."

Darlene

⚮

"**G**ood for you," Darlene gave the kid a smile before shifting her eyes to Roni.

The look of hope in her son's eyes gave her pause.

He wanted her to say yes to leaving the human world behind and joining him in immortality, and she wanted that as well, but she still couldn't believe that what they were telling her was true.

Then again, all these people, including her son, couldn't be crazy or part of a conspiracy to separate her from Leo.

She also had personal proof of the paranormal power Onegus wielded. He'd made her memories disappear and reappear by just looking into her eyes.

Onegus could potentially be a powerful hypnotist, but the kid was too young to have mastered the technique, and she'd never heard of the ability to hypnotize being hereditary.

Parker looked perfectly normal and acted like any other teenager. It had been easy to see that he'd been nervous before conducting his compulsion test on her, unsure of himself, but now he seemed relieved, and his confidence was through the roof.

The truth was that she had enough proof to believe everything Roni, Cassandra, and the others had told her, but she was hiding behind her disbelief and using it as an excuse to avoid having to make a life-altering decision.

What if she didn't have to, though? What if she could give living among the immortals a month-long trial while Leo was away?

They were all looking at her expectantly, Roni and Geraldine in particular, but so were the others, even Parker, who wasn't related to her, didn't know her, and had no stake in her decision.

"I know that you are all waiting to hear my decision, and I have to admit that I'm more inclined to say yes today than I was the other time, but I'm really bad with making big decisions on my own and without having enough time to mull them over. Is it possible for me to come live among you during the month Leo is gone and make my decision then?"

Onegus shook his head. "Thralling away a month's worth of memories is difficult and might cause damage to your brain."

"You don't need to thrall me now that Parker compelled me to keep quiet about you."

"That's true." Geraldine turned a pair of pleading eyes at Onegus. "Darlene is my daughter, and she's Roni's mother. She will never betray us. I'm sure special accommodations can be made for her."

Onegus still looked skeptical. "If you decide not to go for it and return to Leo, I can't allow you to have memories of our village. Leo has proved that he can't be trusted, and compulsion is not a hundred percent airtight. You might blurt something out, he might become suspicious, and I can't allow it."

They'd accused Leo of betraying Roni, but she still had a hard time believing it. Then again, she might be using her disbelief again to avoid making a decision.

Leo was a jerk, and she needed to leave him for a thousand and one little reasons even if he hadn't betrayed Roni. All those small insults, put-downs, and let-downs had a cumulative effect, and the resentment she felt toward him had become too much to contain.

She was such a damn coward, though. She had chosen to stay with him not because she loved him but because she was afraid of the alternative and because she had no energy and no confidence to take the necessary action.

If only they would allow her to stay in the village for a little while so the decision would become easier to make.

"What's the maximum length of time I can stay before you have to erase my memories?"

"The standard is two weeks," Onegus said. "I doubt that would be long enough for you. Usually, we only allow it for Dormants who are already in a relationship with a clan male and are working on their induction. In most cases, it takes up to two weeks for the transition to start, and if it doesn't, it means that the person does not have the godly genes."

"It took much longer for Richard," Shai said. "Mey also exceeded the two-week mark, and Kian allowed an extension."

"True, but their circumstances were different." Onegus crossed his arms over his chest. "Both Mey and Richard were willing to stay in the village indefinitely. Mey because she was in love with Yamanu, and Richard because he didn't want to live anywhere else. Darlene still hasn't decided what she wants to do with the rest of her life, and two weeks are not long enough to meet someone, fall in love, go through the induction, and transition."

"She is a confirmed Dormant," Shai said. "She doesn't need to do any of those things right away. All she needs to do is decide whether she wants to stay."

Onegus nodded. "I'm aware of that. But what I was trying to say is that she would have a much easier time with deciding to stay if she found love with a clan male and transitioned."

Darlene struggled to come up with a counterargument, but perhaps there were other options. "What if I come for two weeks, and at the end of them decide whether I want to stay forever or go back to Leo? Or what if I'm willing to take the risk of sustaining brain damage at the end of a month if I go back?" She chuckled. "If I give up immortality for Leo, I should get my head examined anyway. I don't know why I cling to that failed marriage. He's probably shagging someone on the side, and she's warming his bed on this so-called business trip."

"The business trip is for real," Cassandra said. "I arranged for Leo to be sent away for a month so you would be able to make up your mind without him hovering over you. You need time to think."

Darlene nodded. "I do."

With a groan, Roni pushed to his feet and started pacing. "Stop being such a pushover, Mother. What are you clinging to? Dancing around Leo's moods? Jumping when he says jump and asking how high? Don't tell me that you love him."

She swallowed. "I've been married to Leo for over two decades. I don't know how to live without him."

Roni

Frustrated, Roni glared at his mother, who shrank back under his gaze.

Was he any better than damn Leo if he was making her feel smaller? She needed encouragement, not derision.

The problem was that out of everyone in the room, he was the worst at providing support and guidance. Cassandra wasn't much better than him, Geraldine was crumbling under a ton of guilt, and the others didn't want to influence Darlene's decision.

It was up to him.

Letting out a breath, he pulled out a chair and brought it over next to his mother. "I know that it's a difficult decision to make without seeing the village with your own eyes and meeting the people. It was easy for me because I fell in love with Sylvia and would have followed her to the ends of the world, but also because I was basically a prisoner, and anything was better than the isolation I lived in. You don't have a lover in the village, and you're not a prisoner, but you have me, Sylvia, Geraldine, Cassandra, Onegus, Shai, Orion, and plenty of other nice people you can be friends with. None of us can fully compensate for the lack of a life partner, but you will not be alone. You can come live with Sylvia and me, or perhaps with Geraldine and Shai. Geraldine doesn't need to leave for work and can keep you company. Come stay for the weekend, and if after that you decide that you need more time, Onegus will thrall your memories of the place away but leave the rest intact so you can go home and give it some more thought."

He turned to Onegus. "Can you do that? Can you leave some of my mother's memories of us and erase the rest?"

Onegus nodded. "It will take time to sift through them, but two days' worth of memories is not that much. I can do that."

Roni turned back to his mother. "What do you think?"

"I love you," she whispered, tears misting her eyes. "When did you become so grown up and so insightful?"

He chuckled. "I'm still working on it."

"You're doing really well, and I like your plan."

There was a collective sigh of relief, and then Cassandra took over. "So, how are we going to do it?" She turned to Onegus. "I can pick Darlene up in the office building on Friday and take her to the village."

Darlene's eyes widened. "Oh heck, you will want me to leave my phone there again. What if Leo calls me?"

They all exchanged looks and then shifted their eyes to Onegus.

"I can give you a clan phone, and you can forward your calls to it, but they will have to be monitored by the village's security. You can't tell him where you are or with whom."

"What should I tell him?"

"Tell him that your cousins took you for a weekend in a mountain cabin," Cassandra suggested. "He won't be able to verify that."

Roni rubbed his chin. "If you want, I can find out if Leo took a woman on his business trip. If he did, it should make your decision much easier."

Darlene swallowed. "I prefer not to know, but that's a coward's response. I can't be a coward if I want to transition into immortality."

"Damn right." Cassandra clapped her on the back. "It's time to grow some balls, Darlene, and you couldn't have asked for a better instructor than me to show you how."

When everyone laughed, Roni let out a breath. For the first time ever, his mother was choosing him over Leo, or even better, she was choosing herself over them both.

"I'm proud of you, Mom." He leaned to kiss her cheek. "That took guts."

"Not really." She caught his hand and gave it a squeeze. "I keep telling myself that it's only one weekend, and that Leo is probably not cheating on me. Even if I decide to leave him, I don't want to look back on my time with him and berate myself for not seeing him for who he really was. I know it's difficult for you to understand because none of you have spent so many years with your partners. Imagine waking up one morning and discovering that it was all a lie, and that you wasted your life with the wrong person."

Cassandra's eyes softened as she regarded her sister. "When you're an immortal, these decades with Leo will seem like a blink of an eye. Your life is just beginning."

"Or ending." Darlene smiled sadly. "I might not make it. I might die instead of turning immortal."

"That's why I was pushing you so hard," Cassandra said. "I can't tell you too much because that's really sensitive information, but I can tell you that there is no better time for you to transition than now. We have a narrow window of opportunity that I don't want you to miss."

Cassandra was adamant that Annani's blessing was absolutely necessary for his mother's successful transition, and even though Roni was a skeptic, he also wanted Darlene to get all the help she could get, and Annani's blessing had proven helpful. The goddess planned to stay in the village until Amanda's baby was born and probably for a few more weeks after that, which gave his mother plenty of time to find an immortal male she liked and who liked her back.

Perhaps William could arrange a virtual Perfect Match for her? That would speed up the process of finding her a mate. It would also allow her to experience adventures she would have never had the guts to try in real life.

Roni was getting excited. That was the best idea he'd had so far.

During the three hours she would be hooked up to the virtual fantasy machine, Darlene could experience weeks of adventures with a compatible male. It could be just the thing she needed to cure her of her indecision and give her confidence in herself.

Aliya

A liya hadn't slept much, but this time it wasn't because of the television. She'd tried to watch, but her thoughts had kept wandering to Vrog and their walk last evening. They'd talked for hours, first on the walk and later in Kalugal's suite.

Vrog had left only when Kalugal had practically thrown him out because it had been time for everyone to go to sleep.

They'd talked about Vrog's journey from being a novice businessman working for Jade to becoming the head of an international, well-regarded high school. He'd told her about the misunderstanding with Stella, and how he'd been captured by an untrained newly turned immortal who'd outsmarted him.

Vrog's humility was one of the things she liked best about him. He didn't boast, didn't try to make himself look more important than he was, and had no problem admitting his shortcomings.

It wasn't a typical Kra-ell attitude.

Humility hadn't been valued in the compound, and it was a very human quality, although not all humans were the same in that regard.

The heroes and heroines of the American television shows and films she'd watched weren't humble. Well, most of them weren't. Did that reflect on the American culture?

The British were self-deprecating and courteous, but humility seemed to be valued more by the Eastern cultures. That was what she was familiar with, so perhaps that was why it appealed to her.

"A penny for your thoughts?" Jacki sat next to her on the couch.

Aliya frowned. "Is that a saying? Because a penny is not a lot of money, right?"

Jacki laughed. "It is a saying. You have been sitting here all morning, staring at the blank television screen, and you seem to have a lot on your mind. I wondered if you needed to talk."

Aliya shrugged. "I was thinking about the cultural differences between people. Easterners are humbler than Westerners."

"Are they really? The fact that people act a certain way doesn't mean that they truly are that way on the inside. If it's considered rude to boast and polite to show humility, then people would attempt to appear humble even if they are not. In my opinion, people are the same everywhere, and that includes immortals and even the Kra-ell. We all want to be appreciated, loved, and accepted, and no one wants to be ignored, put down, or marginalized. We all want a family, traditional or otherwise, we all want to have our basic needs met, and we want to feel safe."

As Aliya nodded, her stomach growled, and Jacki chuckled. "We all want to be well fed too." She pushed to her feet. "Breakfast should have been delivered already. I'll call the concierge to check what's happening with it. The others will start coming and we don't want a bunch of hungry immortals in one place." She winked. "They are much easier to deal with when their bellies are full."

When a knock sounded at the door, Jacki was still on the phone, and she motioned for Aliya to open it.

Pushing her feet into her new cozy slippers, Aliya walked over to the door and opened it.

"Good morning." Phinas grinned at her.

His braces were off, and he wasn't even using crutches. The immortals' healing ability was truly exceptional.

"Are you all healed up so soon?" She opened the door all the way.

"I wouldn't go dancing just yet, but by tomorrow, I will be good to go." He walked up to the dining table and pulled out a chair for her. "We can drive to Lijiang and find a club."

"I've never been to a club before." Aliya sat down. "What do people do there?"

He sat next to her, his body turned in a way that their knees were almost touching. "They dance, they drink, they talk with their friends." He leaned closer to her, and his eyes started to glow. "They also kiss and make out in dark corners, enclaves, and nooks."

Was he flirting with her?

Aliya had no experience in those things, but it sure looked like he was. But she might be wrong, and this sort of behavior could be commonplace between immortals.

"That sounds like fun. We should all go."

Phinas smiled, but it wasn't a friendly smile. It was predatory, and it stirred something in her. "The offer was for you, not everyone."

"I doubt Kalugal would let me go. He likes to keep an eye on me."

"I'm his right-hand man. He will have no problem with it, but your boyfriend might."

"I don't have a boyfriend."

Phinas's grin was broad enough to split his face in half. "In that case, you should have no problem going to a club with me tomorrow."

"Leave her alone, Phinas." Kalugal walked into the room.

"Why? She's single, I'm single, and we have nothing better to do."

Kalugal turned his gaze to her. "Do you want to go out with Phinas, Aliya? Don't feel obligated to say yes. If you're not interested, just say so."

Was she interested?

Yeah, she kind of was. But she was also interested in Vrog. As a Kra-ell female, she could enjoy both and not feel an ounce of guilt about it, so why did she feel bad about being attracted to Phinas while contemplating a future with Vrog?

They were both fine males, and from having no choices, she now had one too many and didn't know what to do.

"I need to think about it," she said just as another knock sounded at the door and saved her from having to say more.

Vrog

Vrog felt the tension as soon as Jacki opened the door and let him in. Not from her, but from Aliya and Kalugal's second-in-command.

What was going on?

"Good morning." He plastered a smile on his face. "Am I early? Or is everyone else late?"

"You're on time, and everyone else is late," Jacki said. "Including room service. I just got off the phone with the concierge, and he promised me that breakfast was on its way and should be served in the next ten minutes." She motioned for him to take a seat at the table. "Can I offer you coffee in the meantime?"

"I don't want to impose." Vrog inclined his head.

"You're not imposing." Jacki walked over to the suite's kitchenette. "I'll bring the carafe and the mugs to the table, and everyone can serve themselves."

"In that case, I would love some. Thank you."

As Vrog pulled out a chair on Aliya's other side, Phinas's body language didn't escape his notice. The guy was sitting sideways on his chair, facing Aliya, and their knees were almost touching.

"I see that you no longer need to use braces." Vrog pinned the guy with a hard look. "But given your sitting angle, I assume that you didn't regain full range of motion yet."

Phinas wasn't dumb, and he got the message. "Thank you for your concern, but my range of motion is just fine." He moved his legs to where they were supposed to be, beneath the table.

Aliya shifted as well, aligning her body straight with the table and making sure that she was smack in the middle of the two of them.

Aggression swelling inside him, Vrog regretted not being able to challenge Phinas to a fight. He would win, there was no doubt about it, but he was not in the Kra-ell compound, and these days that was not how males competed for a female's attention in the human or the immortal world.

He'd never done that before, but he knew how other males did. Money and status were the aces in their deck of cards, while humor and sarcasm were the jokers. The wild card could trump the ace if wielded correctly. Charm was king, intelligence and eloquence were queen and prince, and brute force was reserved for the plebs.

What card should he open with?

Phinas was a salaried employee, but he had no idea how much Kalugal paid him or if Phinas had been smart managing his money. He was also older and had had more time to amass his fortune. Still, the guy was a fighter, not a businessman, and Vrog probably had more money. As for status, being the head of an international school was much more prestigious than commanding a bunch of former hoodlums.

The question was how to present these advantages without sounding too obvious or boastful.

Perhaps he should start with humor?

"Here you go." Jacki put down the coffee carafe and four mugs on the table. "I'm so glad that this hotel caters to foreigners. I need my coffee in the morning."

Vrog seized the opportunity to flash his prince card. "It is true that China is traditionally a tea-drinking nation, so much so that tea became an integral part of Buddhist practice, and it is said that Zen and tea have the same flavor. But coffee is rapidly gaining popularity. In fact, Shanghai has the most coffee shops in the world and even has a coffee festival. Starbucks has opened over five thousand stores in two hundred cities in China, and they are planning to expand into at least a hundred more."

"How many do they have in the US?" Jacki asked.

"Over fifteen thousand."

"Let me see." Kalugal smoothed his hand over his short beard. "That's one store for every twenty-two thousand people in the US, compared to two hundred and eighty-thousand people per store in China. I say Starbucks still has a long way to go here."

Vrog stilted a smile.

Kalugal was a sophisticated player, but fortunately, he wasn't competing for Aliya's attention. Phinas, on the other hand, had nothing to contribute to the conversation.

Perhaps he should continue to dazzle Aliya and the others with his vast knowledge and intelligence.

"Whiskey is also a rapidly growing segment of the Chinese high-end liqueur market. Urban consumers who consider themselves trendy and sophisticated perceive whiskey as an international drink. And as with all things that carry that designation, the demand for it is growing."

"What about cigars?" Kalugal asked.

"Oh, the cigar market is booming. China is officially the biggest market for Cuban cigars, and that's despite the government's restrictions on tobacco use. There is a huge demand for all luxury products, and cigars are an outward sign of success."

"I should call Kian," Kalugal said. "Perhaps hearing about the whiskey and cigars will tempt him to visit China."

Vrog cast a sidelong glance at Aliya to see whether she was impressed but was disappointed to see her gazing out the window with a vacant look in her eyes.

She hadn't been paying attention, and the only one he'd managed to impress was Kalugal. Was Phinas impressed?

Even if Aliya had found the subjects of their conversation boring, Vrog still considered intimidating Kalugal's second-in-command with his superior intelligence and knowledge a worthwhile endeavor.

Alena

❧

Alena gathered her hair in a loose bun on top of her head and examined her reflection in the vanity mirror. Her cheeks were rosy, her eyes were shining bright, and her lips were curved in a smile that just refused to abate.

She was so stupidly happy that it scared her.

To say that she was in love was an understatement. Her heart was so bloated with emotion that it was close to bursting, and she was so consumed with Orion that she could scarcely think of anything else.

Everything about him pleased her, his gentle demeanor, his innate curiosity, his intelligence, his love for art and his appreciation for beauty in all forms, and it didn't hurt that he had the body of a god and the stamina to match.

They'd made love seven times last night, or rather last night and this morning. They had gone to sleep only a few hours ago, and they were terribly late for breakfast at

Kalugal and Jacki's suite, but Alena couldn't bring herself to care.

"What's the smile about?" Orion leaned over her and kissed her neck.

"I'm happy." She leaned into his touch.

Crouching next to her, he put his hands on her thighs. "I've never been happier in my life. Does that scare you as much as it scares me?"

Alena nodded. "It's overwhelming."

"Is it the bond?"

"Part of it is, but not all. We are just good together."

"Yes, we are." He pushed up and took her lips. "But if we keep this up, we will miss breakfast and end up in bed again, and I'll be neglecting my duty to you."

"Which is?"

"For starters, making sure that you are fed." He pushed to his feet and offered her a hand up. "The others are waiting for us, and they won't start until we get there."

She let him pull her up. "We can't have that. Hungry immortals are antsy."

"Not to mention a hybrid Kra-ell who went hungry for so long that she can't get full no matter how much she eats." He handed her the long sweater coat she'd left draped over the arm of the lounger.

An arm that had seen a lot of action recently.

Right. She needed to shift gears and get her head out of the sex, or they would end up missing breakfast and ordering room service, which wasn't such a bad idea.

"Let's go." She shrugged the coat on and walked toward the door before her hormones had a chance to take over.

Ovidu and Oridu trailing behind them, Alena and Orion held hands as they climbed the stairs to the third floor and walked down the corridor to the presidential suite.

When the door to the suite opened, and a procession of servers with carts rolled out, they moved aside to let them pass.

"I guess we are not late after all." Orion held the door open for her.

"Good morning, everyone." Alena walked in. "I'm glad that we are not late. I was afraid that you were all waiting for us."

"Good morning." Vrog pushed away from the table and approached her with a big grin on his face. "Congratulations." He offered her his hand.

Was he being sarcastic? Was he congratulating her on making it to breakfast?

"Thank you." She shook his hand. "What are you congratulating me for?"

His gaze shifted to Orion, then back to her, and again to Orion. "Forgive me. I forgot that immortal males don't have the ability to sense when they create a life like the Kra-ell do."

There was a gasp, and then all conversations stopped, the silence in the room becoming deafening.

Alena's heart hammered against her ribcage.

Vrog had said that she and Orion had created a life, but that was impossible. How could Vrog possibly know that? But what if it was true?

Pulling her hand out of Vrog's, she put it over her belly. "What are you talking about?"

"Kra-ell males can sense a pregnancy at the moment of conception. You created this life last night. It wasn't there the day before."

Someone inhaled sharply, and someone else started clapping but was quickly silenced.

It felt as if the entire room was holding its collective breath, waiting for her to say something.

Her heart did a somersault, and then happy butterflies took flight in her stomach.

Could it really be true?

Alena had felt that last night was special, but she'd never expected to get pregnant so soon. She'd prayed to the Fates to give her and Orion a child, but even in her most rosy fantasies, that didn't happen for many years to come.

"Are you sure?" Orion croaked.

"I'm positive," Vrog said. "I've never been wrong about a pregnancy yet."

Orion

〰️

Too stunned to react, Orion gaped at Alena's belly. She had her hand on it, already protective of the life growing inside of her.

He wanted to wrap his arm around her and not let go for the next nine months.

Damn, he didn't even know if immortal pregnancies took the same time as human gestation. Were they shorter or longer? More or less dangerous to the mother?

"Are there any risks?" he managed to ask through his constricted throat.

Seemingly stunned and as speechless as he was, Alena shook her head.

"Immortal bodies are very resilient." Kalugal pushed to his feet and walked over to them. "Congratulations, cousin." He pulled Alena into his arms and kissed her on both cheeks. "I know it's a human custom, but I would be delighted if you chose me to be your child's godfather."

"And I his godmother." Jacki got up and walked over to Orion. "Congratulations, Daddy." She hugged him and kissed his cheeks.

The same continued with the others, and the last one to congratulate them was Aliya. "May the Mother keep you and your child safe and healthy." She made a fist and punched her own chest. "Congratulations."

When everyone had returned to their seats, and he and Alena were the only two still standing, Orion took Alena's hands and kissed them one at a time. "Thank you. You've made me the happiest man on earth." Ignoring the oohing and aahing, Orion pretended that they were alone in the room, took Alena into his arms, and kissed her gently on the lips. "I'm grateful beyond words, to you and to the Fates that brought us together and granted us this unexpected boon. I don't know what I did to deserve it, but I promise to spend my eternal life proving that I do."

"Oh, Orion." Alena wound her arms around his neck. "You are more than deserving of this boon. You loved, and you lost your love, but you healed and loved again."

Behind them, someone cleared his throat.

"As touching and lovely as this is, we are all hungry," Lokan said. "Let's celebrate this joyful occasion with a feast."

Smiling, Alena let go of Orion's neck. "I need to be mindful of what I eat now. Once again, I'm feeding a baby." She chuckled. "Wait until I tell my kids that they are about to get another sibling. They will be overjoyed." Her eyes widened. "I need to call my mother."

He put a hand on her arm. "Food first, phone calls later."

"Yes, sir." She beamed at him happily.

"Here." Jacki passed her a platter of steamed buns. "Load up."

"Have some breakfast biscuits." Carol pushed another platter toward Alena.

She laughed. "Right now, our baby is just a fertilized egg. I don't need to eat for two."

As Alena ate and chatted happily with the other ladies about the joys and woes of pregnancies, about raising children, and the joys and woes of that, Orion sipped on his coffee, unable to take a bite. He was elated and terrified at the same time.

He'd been given so much in such a short period of time, and it was wonderful to have and terrifying to lose.

"So, what's next?" Jin asked. "Are you going to hole up in the sanctuary for the duration of your pregnancy?"

"No way." Alena wiped her mouth with a napkin. "We are going to Paris."

Orion arched a brow. "We are? When was that decided?"

"Right now. We need to find your father." She turned to Mey. "Are you up for a trip to Europe and more investigating of echoes?"

Mey glanced at Yamanu. "I am if you are."

"I want to come," Jin said. "I've never been to Paris."

She turned to Arwel. "Can we?"

"I don't see why not. Kian wants to find Toven, and Paris holds the only clue we have so far. Or so we hope. Toven might not have left any echoes in that townhouse."

"I don't think we can come." Carol pouted. "Can we?"

Lokan leaned back in his chair and crossed his arms over his chest. "Paris is still the capital of fashion. I can justify a trip there provided that there is a fashion show going on."

"There is always some show going on in Paris," Jin said. "When do we want to go?"

"I can't leave until Amanda has her baby," Alena said. "She is due in three weeks, and I promised her to be there for her. I can't go right after either. I need to stay for at least a week or two."

"That actually works better for us," Lokan said. "We need to put in some work between vacations."

From the corner of his eye, Orion caught a glimpse of Aliya, who seemed distressed.

Lifting his hand, he halted the discussion. "What's the matter, Aliya?"

"If all of you are leaving to go on a trip to France, what is going to happen to me? Are you just going to leave me in the village?"

"Oh, sweetie." Alena reached for her hand. "By the time we leave, you will have plenty of new friends. And if you still don't feel at home in the village, we can postpone the trip. Amanda would be very happy if I stay longer."

"I'll keep you company," Vrog said. "I'll stay until they all come back."

"I'll be there as well," Phinas said. "I'm not joining Kalugal this time." He cast a quick glance at his boss. "You don't need me there, right?"

"There are no Kra-ell lurking in Paris, and I doubt Toven is a threat." Kalugal took Jacki's hand and brought it to his lips. "Unlike this trip, Paris is going to be decadently luxurious. No dusty archeological sites, no tunnels, and no nasty surprises."

Alena

᠕᠕

"**C**ome sit with me." Alena looked up at Orion and patted the spot next to her on the couch. "I want us to tell my mother together."

"Hold on." Orion sat down and took her hand. "Before you call her, I want to discuss a couple of things."

"Okay." Alena put the phone down.

"I want to get to know all of your children. You said that most of them live in Scotland. Correct?"

"Yes. All except one."

"Then let's include Scotland in our European trip. It can be before or after Paris."

Alena smiled. "Did I already tell you today how much I love you?"

"Many times. So, is it a yes?"

"It's an enthusiastic yes. I would love for you to get to know my children. Forgive me for not thinking about it first. I should have."

Leaning closer, he kissed her forehead. "You are forgiven. The second thing I want to discuss involves the ring that I didn't have time to purchase yet. I want us to get married before the baby is born. I know that marriage ceremonies are not part of your tradition, and that making it official is not important to you, but I grew up in the human world, and it's important to me."

Alena's lips were going to be permanently stuck in an upturned curve because this man was making her so happy. "Annani would love to officiate at our wedding. Do you want a small ceremony or a big one?"

"If possible, I want the entire clan to attend."

"A big one, then. That would make my mother even happier."

He took both her hands in his. "I want to know what would make Alena happy."

"Being with you makes me happy. Everything else is optional."

THE ADVENTURE CONTINUES
MIA & TOVEN'S STORY IS NEXT
THE CHILDREN OF THE GODS BOOK 59
DARK GOD'S AVATAR

TURN THE PAGE TO READ THE EXCERPT—>

JOIN THE VIP CLUB
To find out what's included in your free membership,
flip to the last page.

Dark God's Avatar

Unaware of the time bomb ticking inside her, Mia had lived the perfect life until it all came to a screeching halt, but despite the difficulties she faces, she doggedly pursues her dreams.

Once known as the god of knowledge and wisdom, Toven has grown cold and indifferent. Disillusioned with humanity, he travels the world and pens novels about the love he can no longer feel.

Seeking to escape his ever-present ennui, Toven gives a cutting-edge virtual experience a try. When his avatar meets Mia's, their sizzling virtual romance unexpectedly turns into something deeper and more meaningful. Will it endure in the real world?

Toven

Toven put his wine glass on the side table, propped his slippered feet up on the worn brown leather ottoman, and clicked the television on.

"Are you depressed?" asked the actor playing a sympathetic doctor. "Does your life feel like a long road to nowhere?" He looked directly at Toven. "Neurotap offers hope to those who no longer believe it exists. In clinical trials, seven out of ten—"

Annoyed, Toven clicked over to another channel.

That damn commercial had been popping up on different cable and broadcast stations for days. If he were human, he might have been tempted to give Neurotap a try, but no medication could alleviate a god's ennui, and neither could therapy sessions with the best psychoanalysts.

Philosophizing about the meaning of life with the greatest human thinkers was pointless as well.

He should know.

Toven had conversed with the most renowned philosophers humanity had produced.

Socrates, who had believed that the secret to happiness was found in enjoying less, Confucius, who had advocated meditating upon good thoughts as a way to make the world a better place, and Seneca, who had preached that people should be happy with their lot and not strive for more. Lao Tzu advocated living in the moment, Nietzsche valued power above all, and Kierkegaard explained that life was not a problem to be solved but a reality to be experienced.

Ironically, most of those thinkers had been influenced in one way or another by Toven's own writings, and yet they had arrived at very different conclusions about the human condition and how to best endure it.

Toven agreed with some and disagreed with others, but he'd given up on solving that age-old problem centuries ago. Humans were doomed to their misery, and even a powerful god like him could not help them.

He'd tried, failed, tried again and again, but at some point, he had to resign himself to the fact that humans were bloodthirsty, power-hungry savages. Not all of them, but enough to make everyone else's life miserable.

Out of all the philosophers, Kierkegaard had been the wisest. Trying to solve humanity's problems was futile, and living in the moment and just experiencing life was all that was to be had, even for a god.

A god.

What a joke that was. He should've abandoned thinking of himself as a god eons ago. He was no deity, he was not deathless, he was just the scion of a superior race of people, who had long ago been worshipped by primitive humans.

But the gods were no more, destroyed by his own brother in what had turned out to be a suicide mission, and Toven was all that was left of that superior race of beings.

A rare burst of anger rising in his chest, Toven wished that Mortdh had survived the bombing so he could've killed the murderous bastard himself. His insane, power-hungry brother had dropped a bomb on the gods' assembly to escape his punishment for murdering a god, but the idiot had miscalculated the weapon's destructive range and had been swept away in its deadly wind.

His anger subsiding just as quickly as it had risen, Toven let out a sigh. Killing Mortdh would have been intensely satisfying, but he knew that he would not have prevailed against his older brother. Mortdh had always been more powerful, but since the bastard was dead, Toven could allow himself the fantasy.

Except, Toven was well aware of how absurd even fantasizing about it was.

He was a scholar, not a killer, which was probably the reason for his lack of effectiveness. The pen might be mightier than the sword, but the sword was still necessary to implement and enforce the pen's creations.

Toven had never wielded a tool of death.

Hell, he couldn't even bring himself to end his own miserable life.

Humans didn't realize it, but they had the better deal.

Their short lifespans were like rollercoaster rides, the slate wiped clean with each new rotation. Once they grew bored and disillusioned with life, which was inevitable, they didn't have to suffer long. Their lives ended shortly thereafter, and they were given a fresh start in a brand-new body and no memory of their previous incarnation.

Not all humans believed in the cycle, and even he couldn't be absolutely certain that reincarnation existed. But after witnessing too many cases of humans who'd remembered past lives and could prove that those memories were real, Toven had become a believer, and he envied humans for it.

A god who had lived for over seven thousand years and was tired and bored had limited options to end it all, and Toven was too much of a coward to jump out off a plane or pay someone to behead him.

Instead, he tried to amuse himself the best he could, passing the never-ending time by traveling from one metropolis to another and penning romance novels about love he couldn't feel.

He used to enjoy his human lovers, but even that had become boring. Nowadays, he rarely sought out female company, preferring his solitude and the realities he created in his head to pleasures of the flesh that no longer excited him.

It took someone very special to stir even the slightest emotion in him.

As a loud car commercial began playing, pulling him out of his head, Toven groaned.

Why did he even bother watching television? It wasn't as if he was really interested in what was happening in the human world. The players and costumes kept changing, as did technology, but history kept its cyclical ebb and flow, and humans seemed to learn nothing from their ancestors' mistakes.

Was it morbid fascination that prompted him to follow global affairs? Or was it hope that humanity would one day break out of the cycle and reach the enlightenment he'd tried to steer them toward and failed?

Hope springs eternal.

Apparently not only humans fell victim to hope's allure. Toven had thought that his had died a long time ago, but perhaps a kernel of it still lived in a corner of his dark heart. Perhaps that little spark was what kept him from hiring a killer to behead him and end his misery.

As the car commercial finally ended and the news program tune started playing, Toven put the remote down and lifted his wine glass.

"In today's news, a Bayview resident is accused of…"

Toven switched to another channel. He wasn't interested in local drama.

It was time to move to his next destination.

The San Francisco home he was renting was lovely, but he didn't like staying in one place for too long, and he was looking forward to the change in environment his next stop would bring. The old-world charm of the Victorian house on Webster Street had inspired a historical romance, while the ultra-modern seventy-second-floor Park Avenue apartment in Manhattan would hopefully inspire a contemporary novel.

As a loud commercial for a cleaning product started, he clicked over to the next channel and yet another commercial, but the stunning visuals snagged his attention and he lingered to watch more.

Toven assumed that what was being promoted was a computer game, but as a pretty young lady walked in front of the screen and presented a service that was not about playing a game on the computer but rather playing inside of it, Toven's interest was piqued.

It was a fascinating idea.

"Are you a busy professional with no time to search for your soulmate?" she asked in a sexy, slightly raspy voice. "Are you tired of surfing endless profiles on dating apps and going out on disappointing dates?" Several snapshots of humorously overdone disastrous first dates flashed across the screen. "If so, then Perfect Match Virtual

Studios has the answer for you. For more details, go to www.PerfectMatchVirtualFantasy.com. Your dream partner is only a few keyboard clicks away."

Intrigued, Toven pushed to his feet and walked over to the desk to retrieve his laptop.

Back in the armchair, he typed the URL into the search box and started reading the online brochure explaining the service. Could it be for real? Surely it was impossible to turn into someone else for the duration of the virtual adventure. A computer couldn't take over a person's mind and let them live out a fantasy. The brochure claimed that in the span of three hours, weeks of virtual adventure could be enjoyed. They promoted their service not only as the safest and most scientific way to find a soulmate, but also as the best vacation solution for busy people.

If genuine and not paid for, the numerous testimonials confirmed the service's claims, singing its praises. People were finding their perfect matches, and if the wedding photos of happy customers weren't fake, the number of featured couples was impressive.

Others were going on adventures with their spouses, rekindling their passion by either choosing beautiful avatars to represent them or going in as themselves.

It wasn't cheap, but the one thing Toven had no lack of was money. The savages he'd tried to civilize had paid him tribute in gold, and while it was the only tangible good he'd gotten from wasting centuries trying to improve their lives, there was lots of it.

There were many adventures in a variety of environments to choose from, and the service promised a perfect match with a real person who was interested in the same sort of adventure.

Toven wasn't hoping for a soulmate, and he'd been on enough real-life adventures not to crave fake ones, but what appealed to him the most was the promise of stepping out of his own mind and becoming someone else for a spell.

Mia

Mia turned the cream-colored envelope around, looking for a hint of what was inside, but other than the hand-scribbled *Happy 27th Birthday* there was nothing, not even a Hallmark logo or that of one of the other greetings card brands.

Patting the envelope didn't help either. It didn't feel like a gift card, which was what her friends had gotten her for her 26th birthday, or cash, which was what her grandmother always put inside the cards she'd gotten for her at Walgreens.

Margo and Frankie were smiling like a couple of fiends, so it was probably a gag gift.

"What is it?" She narrowed her eyes at her besties.

"Open it," Margo said.

Frankie waved the waiter over. "Another round of margaritas, please." She winked at Mia. "You're going to need it."

Mia rolled her eyes. "Did you get me a subscription to Boys Down Under?"

The three of them were obsessed with the Instagram sensation. They'd been tempted to subscribe to the private channel nearly every time the guys posted new pictures of themselves in provocative poses. Those who paid for premium access got to see more than just a sliver of muscular chests peeking from unbuttoned shirts, but Mia wasn't sure that she was ready to see more, especially if the guys exposed anything other than their abs and pectorals. She wasn't into pornography.

Frankie looked at Margo. "Damn, why didn't we think of that? That could have been so much cheaper."

"Indeed," Margo pretended to agree. "Next year, that's what we are getting you."

Laughing, Mia opened the envelope, and as she pulled out the card and saw the logo embossed in its center, her eyes widened. "You got me a Perfect Match adventure? Are you nuts? These cost a fortune!"

"It was on sale," Frankie said. "They opened a new studio a few blocks down from my office building. There was a big sign on the front window that they were offering fifty percent off to the first one hundred customers. I was sure that it was no longer available and that all one hundred were sold out." She waved a hand. "You know how everyone and their grandma is talking about it."

Mia laughed. "You're right. My grandma talks about it nonstop. She says that she's not interested in the hookups, and she just wants to try the Russian spy virtual adventure, but I think that she's full of it. She wants a hookup with 007. I know that she's been fantasizing about it ever since the Perfect Match commercials started."

"What does your grandpa have to say about it?" Frankie asked.

"You know him, he just smiles half-indulgently, half-sufferingly and goes back to his newspaper or his television show." Mia looked at the card. "But even at half off it is still a very expensive gift."

Frankie waved a dismissive hand. "Margo and I split the cost. You can pay us back by telling us all about it after you're done. And if you find your perfect match, I'm going in there and buying a token at full price for myself even if I have to sell my vintage record collection to pay for it."

"It's just an advertising gimmick." Margo lifted her margarita and licked the salt from the rim before taking a sip. "To be able to find people their perfect matches, the Perfect Match Virtual Studios people would need to have hundreds of thousands of profiles in their database, which they can't have because their service is so costly that only the wealthy can afford it. But if I had the money, I would love to experience a virtual hookup, or two or three, in some exotic location just for the fun of it."

"You know what the best part is?" Frankie leaned forward. "Time moves differently in the virtual world. In the span of three hours, you can have a two-week romantic vacation with enough sex to last you for a year."

Mia forced a smile. "Awesome."

What Frankie had really meant to say was that in Mia's case it would have to compensate for the four preceding years, and unless she could afford another trip to cyber world, probably even more going forward.

Besides, there was no guarantee that she would enjoy it. The service was hyped up by a big advertising campaign and celebrity endorsements, but that didn't mean it was all that. It only meant that there was a lot of money behind the national chain of virtual adventure studios. Or was it international by now?

"Hey, maybe we should follow their website so we'll know where and when they open their next branch." Margo pushed her half empty margarita aside. "Maybe we can get more tokens at half off."

Mia lifted her purse from the back of the chair and put the envelope inside. "If my children's books gain some traction, I will buy you each a token for your next birthday."

Margo's lips twisted in a grimace. "Your illustrations are brilliant, but the stories suck. You need to find a different writer or write them yourself."

"I can't. That's the deal I have with my publisher. I'm just the illustrator."

Her agent had told her that they'd loved her illustrations but hadn't liked her stories, and the condition for a publishing deal had been that they provide the writer. The guy was okay, better than she was at coming up with compelling stories, but the books lacked something. They just weren't exciting, not to the kids, and not to the parents reading them to their children.

The publisher had said that her stories weren't happy enough, but they weren't supposed to be. Not everything in life was happy. In fact, most of it was not, and pretending otherwise was dishonest. Children should not grow up in a bubble, unprepared for life's challenges. Thinking that life was fair and that everyone got their happy ending was just setting them up for disappointment.

Margo lifted her margarita, took a sip, and as she put it down her expression was somber. "Just be careful with the type of adventure you choose, Mia. Don't go for the Russian spy one. Go for something sweet and romantic."

"You don't have to remind me. I know."

Too much excitement might kill her.

Literally.

Four years ago, it almost had.

Kian

Kian closed the last of the files Shai had put on his desk and handed the stack back to him.

His assistant rose to his feet. "I'm going down to the café. Do you want me to get you something?"

"Only coffee, please. I'm having lunch with Syssi at home later." Kian swiveled his chair around and looked out the window at the village square below.

At this time of day, the café was teaming with people.

My people.

"I built this village for our clan, a safe place for the immortal descendants of Annani to live in and thrive as a community. I didn't expect to welcome the descendants of other gods, and I sure as hell didn't expect to invite three members of a different breed of long-lived people, who we had no idea coexisted with us and humans on this planet."

"The Fates have been busy lately," Shai said.

"Indeed, they have been, and they are not done yet."

Not too long ago, they'd discovered that Annani's half-sister had survived as well. In a bizarre turn of events, Areana had ended up being mated to Navuh, the clan's archenemy who was bent on the clan's annihilation. Areana had lived in seclusion for thousands of years, locked away in Navuh's harem and unaware that Annani was alive and that her mate sought her sister's demise.

But even more bizarre than Areana being mated to Navuh was that both their sons had joined forces with the clan.

And now they were searching for Toven, another god who'd been presumed dead.

The Fates had worked behind the scenes, weaving their plans and orchestrating the seemingly random encounters that had first led Toven's granddaughter and then his daughter and son to the clan.

Their invisible fingertips were all over it.

If not for the two immortal children Toven had fathered with human mothers finding their way to the clan, they would have never learned about Toven's survival.

Shai walked over to the window and peered at the busy café below. "When we built the village, we believed that the only other immortals on the planet in addition to us were the Doomers."

Kian chuckled. "I wonder if Navuh knows that we call his order DOOM and his followers Doomers. We couldn't have come up with a more fitting name for our enemies if we tried."

Shai shrugged. "That's their acronym in English. The Brotherhood of the Devout Order of Mortdh. It doesn't work out as well in the old language."

Kian turned to look at his assistant. "Do you speak the old language?"

Shai shook his head. "I never had the chance to learn it. Maybe I could ask Edna to teach me the basics, and then I could continue on my own."

With the guy's eidetic memory, he would have an easier time than most learning the complicated language, but Shai had enough on his plate.

"When you hire an assistant, maybe you'll have time for a side project like that. Right now, you don't."

"No one wants to be the assistant's assistant. I can't find anyone for the job." Shai pushed his hands into his pockets and leaned back on his heels. "Maybe when we find more of Toven's children, one of them will turn out to be a capable administrator."

Kian chuckled. "If they are all like Orion and Geraldine, which given Toven's preference for artistic females they probably are, none will make good administrators."

It was ironic, or maybe fated, that Geraldine and Shai were truelove mates. The woman with memory issues had mated a man with an eidetic memory.

"You never know." Shai smiled. "Cassandra is artistic, but she's also good with numbers."

"True, but since she's Toven's granddaughter, she's further down the line and might have inherited a good head for numbers from her father. First, though, we need to find Toven himself. He's too smart to leave tracks for us to follow, and even if we somehow get lucky and find him, he might not want anything to do with us. If the god is so cold and indifferent that he turned away his own son, there is no reason to believe that he'll want to join forces with us."

"We will do what we can, and the rest is up to the Fates." Shai pulled his hands out of his pockets, turned toward the desk, and tucked the files under his arm. "I'll put these away and go get you your coffee. Your mood will improve after an infusion of caffeine."

"Thanks. Get me a pastry as well, please. It will tide me over until lunch."

"You've got it, boss."

When Shai left, Kian sighed, turned his chair around, and rolled it closer to the desk.

Perhaps when they found Toven and he met Annani, she would have a positive impact on him. She was the only one who had any hope of influencing the god to at least cooperate with the clan, and maybe to stay in touch with his children.

While Annani had despised Mortdh, she'd been very fond of his younger brother.

If Ahn had promised his daughter to Toven instead of Mortdh, the world would have been a different place today. Annani wouldn't have pursued Khiann in a desperate move to avoid marriage to the hateful god, and Mortdh wouldn't have murdered Khiann in retaliation for the humiliation. The gods' assembly wouldn't have sentenced Mortdh to entombment for the murder, and he wouldn't have bombed the assembly to avoid punishment, destroying the gods and altering the course of history. But engaging in a game of what-ifs was futile.

The past couldn't be changed.

Kian could only look to the future, and he hoped that Annani's upbeat personality and positive attitude would rub off on Toven. Perhaps her light could banish the darkness the god had allowed to smother his spirit. And if the Fates really wanted to do some good, Annani and Toven would be each other's second chance.

They could never be truelove mates, but they could at least have friendly companionship with benefits, which would solve the problem of replacing Alena as their mother's companion.

Kian shook his head. Once again, he was letting himself travel down the road of what-ifs, but unless those what-ifs had to do with clan security, he had no business engaging in them.

That brought to mind the next subject keeping him awake at night—the damn Kra-ell.

Discovering that two more gods had survived the bombing was a mere curiosity compared to discovering a different breed of long-lived people who, like immortals, had been living undetected among humans.

The Kra-ell were a potential threat to his clan.

The three hybrid Kra-ell they'd found so far were not much of a threat, but those who'd massacred the rest of their tribe were. If those other Kra-ell had no qualms about killing their own males so they could steal their females, they would not hesitate to do the same to his people, if and when they discovered the clan's existence. In fact, immortal females would be even more valuable to them than their own.

The Kra-ell were long-lived but not immortal, and mating with immortal females would be a new lease on life for their species. A daughter born to a hybrid Kra-ell male and an immortal female would transfer the immortality gene to her children. The Kra-ell did not have enough females, and breeding with humans was pointless for them because their longevity genes seemed to be recessive. The product of a union between a Kra-ell and a human produced a hybrid with longer life span than that of the human partner, but the children of the hybrids with humans did not inherit the Kra-ell longevity, which meant that the Kra-ell were doomed to eventually die out.

If he could avoid them detecting the clan for the next thousand years or so, the danger would be over, but Kian hadn't been as careful as he should have been.

He'd already taken a big risk by allowing two survivors of Jade's tribe into the village, and now he was admitting a third.

The rare hybrid Kra-ell female had lived in hiding, terrified of being found by the Kra-ell who'd massacred the males of her tribe. She had no one and nowhere to go, and he couldn't in good conscience turn her away, especially since Arwel had vouched for her.

The Guardian might be an empath, but that didn't make him soft-hearted. Arwel didn't vouch for Aliya out of pity but out of respect.

Perhaps the three hybrid Kra-ell arrivals were part of the Fates' grand design?

If that was the case, it was too early in the game for him to see what that design might be.

Kian just hoped that he wasn't letting a Trojan horse into the sanctuary he'd worked so hard to create for his people.

Order Dark God's Avatar today!

Join the VIP Club
To find out what's included in your free membership, flip to the last page.

The Children of the Gods Series

Reading Order

THE CHILDREN OF THE GODS ORIGINS

1: GODDESS'S CHOICE

When gods and immortals still ruled the ancient world, one young goddess risked everything for love.

2: GODDESS'S HOPE

Hungry for power and infatuated with the beautiful Areana, Navuh plots his father's demise. After all, by getting rid of the insane god he would be doing the world a favor. Except, when gods and immortals conspire against each other, humanity pays the price.

But things are not what they seem, and prophecies should not to be trusted...

THE CHILDREN OF THE GODS

DARK STRANGER

1: DARK STRANGER THE DREAM

2: DARK STRANGER REVEALED

3: DARK STRANGER IMMORTAL

DARK ENEMY

4: DARK ENEMY TAKEN

5: DARK ENEMY CAPTIVE

6: DARK ENEMY REDEEMED

Kri & Michael's Story

6.5: My Dark Amazon

Dark Warrior

7: Dark Warrior Mine

8: Dark Warrior's Promise

9: Dark Warrior's Destiny

10: Dark Warrior's Legacy

Dark Guardian

11: Dark Guardian Found

12: Dark Guardian Craved

13: Dark Guardian's Mate

Dark Angel

14: Dark Angel's Obsession

15: Dark Angel's Seduction

16: Dark Angel's Surrender

Dark Operative

17: Dark Operative: A Shadow of Death

18: Dark Operative: A Glimmer of Hope

19: Dark Operative: The Dawn of Love

Dark Survivor

20: Dark Survivor Awakened

21: Dark Survivor Echoes of Love

22: Dark Survivor Reunited

Dark Widow

23: Dark Widow's Secret

24: Dark Widow's Curse

25: Dark Widow's Blessing

Dark Dream

26: Dark Dream's Temptation

27: Dark Dream's Unraveling

28: Dark Dream's Trap

Dark Prince

29: Dark Prince's Enigma

30: Dark Prince's Dilemma

31: Dark Prince's Agenda

Dark Queen

32: Dark Queen's Quest

33: Dark Queen's Knight

34: Dark Queen's Army

Dark Spy

35: Dark Spy Conscripted

36: Dark Spy's Mission

37: Dark Spy's Resolution

Dark Overlord

38: Dark Overlord New Horizon

39: Dark Overlord's Wife

40: DARK OVERLORD'S CLAN

DARK CHOICES

41: DARK CHOICES THE QUANDARY

42: DARK CHOICES PARADIGM SHIFT

43: DARK CHOICES THE ACCORD

DARK SECRETS

44: DARK SECRETS RESURGENCE

45: DARK SECRETS UNVEILED

46: DARK SECRETS ABSOLVED

DARK HAVEN

47: DARK HAVEN ILLUSION

48: DARK HAVEN UNMASKED

49: DARK HAVEN FOUND

DARK POWER

50: DARK POWER UNTAMED

51: DARK POWER UNLEASHED

52: DARK POWER CONVERGENCE

DARK MEMORIES

53: DARK MEMORIES SUBMERGED

54: DARK MEMORIES EMERGE

55: DARK MEMORIES RESTORED

DARK HUNTER

56: Dark Hunter's Query

57: Dark Hunter's Prey

58: <u>Dark Hunter's Boon</u>

Dark God

59: Dark God's Avatar

60: Dark God's Reviviscence

Toven might have failed in his attempts to improve humanity's condition, but he isn't going to fail to improve Mia's life, making it the best it can be despite her fragile health, and he can do that not as a god, but as a man who possesses the means, the smarts, and the determination to do it.

No effort is enough to repay Mia for reviving his deadened heart and making him excited for the next day, but the flip side of his reviviscence is the fear of losing its catalyst.

Given Mia's condition, Toven doesn't dare to over excite her. His venom is a powerful aphrodisiac, euphoric, and an all-around health booster, but it's also extremely potent. It might kill her instead of making her better.

61: Dark God Destinies Converge

Destinies converge, and secrets are revealed in part three of Mia and Toven's story.

Dark Whispers

62: Dark Whispers From The Past

A brilliant scientist and programmer, William lives for his work, but when he recruits a young bioinformatician to help him decipher the gods' genetic blueprints, he find himself smitten with more than just her brain.

A Ph.d at nineteen, Kaia is considered a prodigy and expects a bright future in academia. But when William invites her to join his secret research team, she accepts for reasons that have nothing to do with her career objectives. Wiliam's promise to look into her best friend's disappearance is an offer she just can't refuse.

63: Dark Whispers From Afar

William knows that his budding relationship with the nineteen-year-old Kaia will be frowned upon, but he's unprepared for her family's vehement opposition.

Family means everything to Kaia, so when she finds herself in the impossible position of having to choose between them and William, she resorts to unconventional means to resolve the conflict.

64: Dark Whispers From Beyond

The sacrifices Kaia and her family have to make for a chance of gaining immortality might tear them apart, and success is not guaranteed.

Is the dubious promise of eternal life worth the risk of losing everything?

Dark Gambit

65: Dark Gambit The Pawn

Temporarily assigned to supervise a team of bioinformaticians, Marcel expects to spend a couple of weeks in the peaceful retreat of Safe Haven, enjoying Oregon Coast's cool weather and rugged beauty.

Things quickly turn chaotic when the retreat's director receives an email with an encoded message about a potential new threat to the clan.

While those in charge of security debate what to do next, Safe Haven's first ever paranormal retreat is about to begin, and one of the attendees is a mysterious woman who makes Marcel's heart beat faster whenever she's near.

Is the beautiful mortal his one truelove?

Or is she the harbinger of more bad news?

66: Dark Gambit The Play

To get to Safe Haven's inner circle, the Kra-ell leader sacrifices a pawn. He does not expect her to reach the final rank and promote to a queen.

67: Dark Gambit Reliance

Marcel takes a big risk by telling Sofia his greatest sin. Can he trust her to keep it a secret? Or maybe it's time to confess his crime and submit to whatever punishment Edna deems appropriate?

Three miserable centuries of living with guilt and remorse are long enough.

Once the dust settles on the Kra-ell crisis, he will gather the courage to put himself at the court's mercy.

Dark Alliance

68: Dark Alliance Kindred Souls

A daring operation half a world away devolves into a full-scale crisis that escalates rapidly, requiring the clan's full might and technological wizardry to manage and survive.

Hardened by duty and tragedy, Jade is driven by a burning desire for revenge. When Phinas saves her second-in-command, Jade's gratitude quickly becomes something more.

69: Dark Alliance Turbulent Waters

When a dangerous foe turns the tables on the clan, complicating the Kra-ell rescue operation in unforeseeable ways, Kian and his crew bet all on a brilliant misdirection.

On board the Aurora, Phinas and Jade brace for battle while enjoying a few stolen moments of passion.

Drawn to the woman he sees behind the aloof leader, Phinas realizes that what has started as a calculated political move has evolved into a deepening sense of companionship.

Jade finds reprieve in Phinas's arms, but duty and tradition make it difficult for her to accept that what she feels for him is more than just gratitude and desire.

After all, the Kra-ell don't believe in love.

70: Dark Alliance Perfect Storm

After two decades in captivity, Jade is finally free, her quest for revenge within grasp, but danger still looms large. A storm is brewing on the horizon, gathering momentum and threatening to obliterate Jade's tenuous hold on hope for a better future.

Dark Healing

71: Dark Healing Blind Justice

The sanctuary is Vanessa's life project. The monumental task of rehabilitating the traumatized victims of trafficking doesn't leave much time for personal life, let alone dating or finding her one and only.

When Kian asks her to help the Kra-ell, she's torn between her duty to the sanctuary and a group of emotionally wounded aliens who no other psychologist can treat.

She's the only immortal with the necessary training to get it done.

The Kra-ell culture and the purebloods' nearly androgynous alien looks shouldn't appeal to her, and yet, she finds one of them disturbingly attractive.

Is it the dangerous vibe he emits?

Does it speak to her on a subconscious level?

Or is it her need to put the broken pieces of him back together?

And why is he interested in her?

She cannot offer him a fight for dominance like a Kra-ell female would, but some strange and unfamiliar part of her wishes she could.

72: Dark Healing Blind Trust

Riddled with guilt over the crimes he was forced to commit, Mo-red is ready to stand trial and accept the death sentence he believes he deserves, but when the clan's alluring psychologist offers a new perspective on his past and hope for a better future, he resolves to fight for his life.

73: Dark healing Blind Curve

Kian is still reeling from the shocking revelations about the twins when a new threat manifests, eclipsing everything he's had to deal with up until now. In light of the new developments, Igor, the other Kra-ell prisoners, and the pending trial are no longer at the forefront of his mind, but the opposite is true for Vanessa. As her relationship with Mo-red solidifies, she is determined to save the male she loves, even if it means breaking him free and living on the run.

Dark Encounters

74: Dark Encounters of the Close Kind

Convinced that her family is hiding a terrible secret from her,

Gabi decides to pay them a surprise visit.

Something is very fishy about the stories her brothers have been telling her lately. Her niece, a nineteen-year-old prodigy with a Ph.D. in bioinformatics, has gotten engaged to a much older guy she met while working on some top-secret project, and if Gabi's older, overprotective brother's approval of the engagement wasn't suspicious enough, he also uprooted his family and moved to be closer to the couple.

What Gabi discovers when she gets to L.A. is wilder than anything she could have imagined. Her entire family possesses godly genes, her brothers and her niece have already turned immortal, and she could transition as soon as she finds an immortal male to induce her. Finding a suitable candidate in a village full of handsome immortals shouldn't be a problem, but Gabi's thoughts keep wandering to the gorgeous guy she met on her flight over.

Could Uriel be a lost descendant of the gods?

He certainly looks like them, but that doesn't mean that he's a good guy or that he's even immortal. He could be a descendant of a different god—a member of an enemy faction of immortals who seek to eradicate her family's adoptive clan, or what is more likely, he's just an extraordinarily good-looking human.

75: DARK ENCOUNTERS OF THE UNEXPECTED KIND

Who is Uriel?

Is he a lost descendant of the gods or just a gorgeous and charming human who has rocked Gabi's world?

76: DARK ENCOUNTERS OF THE FATED KIND

As Aru and his team embark on a perilous mission, their past and present converge in a meeting that holds the key to their fate.

Dark Voyage

77: Dark Voyage Matters of the Heart

As Annani and Syssi set out to unravel the mysteries of Syssi's visions about the gods' home world, the long-awaited wedding cruise sets sail with Aru, Gabi, and Aru's teammates on board.

While the gods find themselves surrounded by immortal clan ladies eager for their affections, they soon discover that destiny has a different plan for them.

The Children of the Gods Series Sets

Books 1-3: Dark Stranger trilogy—Includes a bonus short story: **The Fates take a Vacation**

Books 4-6: Dark Enemy Trilogy —Includes a bonus short story—**The Fates' Post-Wedding Celebration**

Books 7-10: Dark Warrior Tetralogy

Books 11-13: Dark Guardian Trilogy

Books 14-16: Dark Angel Trilogy

Books 17-19: Dark Operative Trilogy

Books 20-22: Dark Survivor Trilogy

Books 23-25: Dark Widow Trilogy

Books 26-28: Dark Dream Trilogy

Books 29-31: Dark Prince Trilogy

Books 32-34: Dark Queen Trilogy

Books 35-37: Dark Spy Trilogy

Books 38-40: Dark Overlord Trilogy

BOOKS 41-43: DARK CHOICES TRILOGY

BOOKS 44-46: DARK SECRETS TRILOGY

BOOKS 47-49: DARK HAVEN TRILOGY

BOOKS 50-52: DARK POWER TRILOGY

BOOKS 53-55: DARK MEMORIES TRILOGY

BOOKS 56-58: DARK HUNTER TRILOGY

BOOKS 59-61: DARK GOD TRILOGY

BOOKS 62-64: DARK WHISPERS TRILOGY

BOOKS 65-67: DARK GAMBIT TRILOGY

BOOKS 68-70: DARK ALLIANCE TRILOGY

BOOKS 71-73: DARK HEALING TRILOGY

MEGA SETS

INCLUDE CHARACTER LISTS

THE CHILDREN OF THE GODS: BOOKS 1-6

THE CHILDREN OF THE GODS: BOOKS 6.5-10

TRY THE SERIES ON

AUDIBLE

2 FREE audiobooks with your new Audible subscription!

PERFECT MATCH SERIES

Vampire's Consort

When Gabriel's company is ready to start beta testing, he invites his old crush to inspect its medical safety protocol.

Curious about the revolutionary technology of the *Perfect Match Virtual Fantasy-Fulfillment studios*, Brenna agrees.

Neither expects to end up partnering for its first fully immersive test run.

King's Chosen

When Lisa's nutty friends get her a gift certificate to *Perfect Match Virtual Fantasy Studios*, she has no intentions of using it. But since the only way to get a refund is if no partner can be found for her, she makes sure to request a fantasy so girly and over the top that no sane guy will pick it up.

Except, someone does.

> **Warning:** This fantasy contains a hot, domineering crown prince, sweet insta-love, steamy love scenes painted with light shades of gray, a wedding, and a HEA in both the virtual and real worlds.

> Intended for mature audience.

Captain's Conquest

Working as a Starbucks barista, Alicia fends off flirting all day long, but none of the guys are as charming and sexy as Gregg. His frequent visits are the highlight of her day, but since he's never asked her out, she assumes he's taken. Besides, between a day job and a budding music career, she has no time to start a new relationship.

That is until Gregg makes her an offer she can't refuse—a gift certificate to the virtual fantasy fulfillment service everyone is talking about. As a huge Star Trek fan, Alicia has a perfect match in mind—the captain of the Starship Enterprise.

The Thief Who Loved Me

When Marian splurges on a Perfect Match Virtual adventure as a world infamous jewel thief, she expects high-wire fun with a hot partner who she will never have to see again in real life.

A virtual encounter seems like the perfect answer to Marcus's string of dating disasters. No strings attached, no drama, and definitely no love. As a die-hard James Bond fan, he chooses as his avatar a dashing MI6 operative, and to complement his adventure, a dangerously seductive partner.

Neither expects to find their forever Perfect Match.

My Merman Prince

The beautiful architect working late on the twelfth floor of my building thinks that I'm just the maintenance guy. She's also under the impression that I'm not interested.

Nothing could be further from the truth.

I want her like I've never wanted a woman before, but I don't play where I work.

I don't need the complications.

When she tells me about living out her mermaid fantasy with a stranger in a Perfect Match virtual adventure, I decide to do everything possible to ensure that the stranger is me.

THE DRAGON KING

To save his beloved kingdom from a devastating war, the Crown Prince of Trieste makes a deal with a witch that costs him half of his humanity and dooms him to an eternity of loneliness.

Now king, he's a fearsome cobalt-winged dragon by day and a short-tempered monarch by night. Not many are brave enough to serve in the palace of the brooding and volatile ruler, but Charlotte ignores the rumors and accepts a scribe position in court.

As the young scribe reawakens Bruce's frozen heart, all that stands in the way of their happiness is the witch's bargain. Outsmarting the evil hag will take cunning and courage, and Charlotte is just the right woman for the job.

My Werewolf Romeo

The father of my star student is a big-shot screenwriter and the patron of the drama department who thinks he can dictate what production I should put on. The principal makes it very clear that I need to cooperate with the opinionated asshat or walk away from my dream job at the exclusive private high school.

It doesn't help matters that the guy is single, hot, charming, creative, and seems to like me despite my thinly-veiled hostility.

When he invites me to a custom-tailored Perfect Match virtual adventure to prove that his screenplay is perfect for my production, I accept, intending to have fun while proving that messing with the classics is a foolish idea.

I don't expect to be wowed by his werewolf adaptation of Red Riding Hood mesh-up with Romeo and Juliet, and I certainly don't expect to fall in love with the virtual fantasy's leading man.

The Channeler's Companion

A treat for fans of *The Wheel of Time*.

When Erika hires Rand to assist in her pediatric clinic, she does so despite his good looks and irresistible charm, not because of them.

He's empathic, adores children, and has the patience of a saint.

He's also all she can think about, but he's off limits.

What's a doctor to do to scratch that irresistible itch without risking workplace complications?

A shared adventure in the Perfect Match Virtual Studios seems like the solution, but instead of letting the algorithm choose a partner for her, Erika can try to influence it to select the one she wants. Awarding Rand a gift certificate to the service will get him into their database, but unless Erika can tip the odds in her favor, getting paired with him is a long shot.

Hopefully, a virtual adventure based on her and Rand's favorite series will do the trick.

Note

Dear reader,

I hope my stories have added a little joy to your day. If you have a moment to add some to mine, you can help spread the word about the Children Of The Gods series by telling your friends and penning a review. Your recommendations are the most powerful way to inspire new readers to explore the series.

Thank you,

Isabell

FOR EXCLUSIVE PEEKS AT UPCOMING RELEASES & A FREE COMPANION BOOK

Join my *VIP Club* and gain access to the VIP portal at itlucas.com
To Join, go to:
http://eepurl.com/blMTpD

INCLUDED IN YOUR FREE MEMBERSHIP:

YOUR VIP PORTAL

- Read preview chapters of upcoming releases.
- Listen to Goddess's Choice narration by Charles Lawrence
- Exclusive content offered only to my VIPs.

FREE I.T. LUCAS COMPANION INCLUDES:

- Goddess's Choice Part i
- Perfect Match: Vampire's Consort (A standalone Novella)
- Interview Q & A
- Character Charts

If you're already a subscriber, and you are not getting my emails, your provider is

SENDING THEM TO YOUR JUNK FOLDER, AND YOU ARE MISSING OUT ON **IMPORTANT UPDATES, SIDE CHARACTERS' PORTRAITS, ADDITIONAL CONTENT, AND OTHER GOODIES.** TO FIX THAT, ADD isabell@itlucas.com TO YOUR EMAIL CONTACTS OR YOUR EMAIL VIP LIST.

Check out the specials at
https://www.itlucas.com/specials

Printed in Great Britain
by Amazon